METEOR STORM

METEOR STORM

SHORT FICTION

BY

WAYNE TEFS

TURNSTONE PRESS

Turnstone Press
Artspace Building
018-100 Arthur Street
Winnipeg, MB
R3B 1H3 Canada
www.TurnstonePress.com

Turnstone Press gratefully acknowledges the assistance of the Canada Council
for the Arts, the Manitoba Arts Council, the Government of Canada through
the Book Publishing Industry Development Program, and the Government of
Manitoba through the Department of Culture, Heritage, Tourism and Sport,
Arts Branch, for our publishing activities.

Cover design: Jamis Paulson
Interior design: Sharon Caseburg

The Meteor Shower epigraph which appears on page ix has been derived from
an entry on "Wikipedia, the free encyclopedia."

Printed and bound in Canada by Friesens for Turnstone Press.

Library and Archives Canada Cataloguing in Publication

Tefs, Wayne, 1947-

       Meteor storm / Wayne Tefs.

ISBN 978-0-88801-344-6

       I. Title.

PS8589.E37M48 2009   C813'.54   C2009-904992-9

Mixed Sources
Cert no. SW-COC-001271
© 1996 FSC
FSC

For Andrew

CONTENTS

Meteor Shower (Storm): a meteor shower is the result of an interaction between a planet and a comet. Comets are like "dirty snowballs" made up of ice and rock, orbiting the Sun. Each time a comet swings by the Sun in its orbit, some of its ice or other volatile vapourizes and a certain amount of debris, or cometary fragments, may be shed. As the debris streams from the comet, it forms the comet's visible tail. The solid pieces of debris are a form of meteoroid. The meteoroids spread out along the entire orbit of the comet to form a meteoroid "stream." As the Earth orbits the Sun, its orbit sometimes takes us through a meteoroid stream and a meteor shower ensues. The meteoroids encounter Earth's atmosphere at high speed. As the meteoroids streak through the atmosphere, ram pressure causes the particles to burn and incandesce, forming meteors. When the meteoroid stream is particularly dense, we occasionally see a spectacular "meteor storm."

METEOR STORM

RED ROCK AND AFTER

L ife is a matter of patterns. You say tearful good-byes to lovers over red-checked tablecloths in pizza joints serving cheap red wine, or the foreman at the mill walks by with his eyes on the floor and you know the rumors of layoffs are true. Everything repeats itself.

Whenever my parents moved it was raining.

In May of 1964 the lawyers closed in on my father and forced him to declare bankruptcy for the second time in three years. The first had occurred in Red Rock, an iron mining town that went bust in the way of mining towns, taking Father's hardware store with it. He and Mother had worked hard there for twenty years, sinking their savings into the business. When sales of hematite plummeted in the early sixties they lost the business, the apartment block it was housed in, and their house. I was fifteen at the time. A big orange van backed across the lawn and two men in blue uniforms shifted our furniture, clothes, and appliances out of the house. Father had built that house with his own hands. He'd shovelled in the gravel for the weeping tiles and he'd hung the front door through which our stuff was being carried in a light rain. As they moved back and forth the two uniformed men ducked their heads to keep their faces dry. Mother stood in the kitchen packing the china. Bravely, she was trying not to cry.

She came from a family of market gardeners who sold vegetables to wholesalers and didn't think of themselves as business folk, as Father did. They were simple farmers who liked cabbage rolls and beer and picnics on sunny summer days. Mother's passion was flowers. We had tomatoes and lettuce and peas in a plot at the bottom of the yard, a regular vegetable garden, but around the house Mother kept her flowers in narrow, loamy beds: dahlias, peonies, begonias, sweet williams, tulips, many names I no longer remember. She came in from tending them with her face flushed from the sun and perspiration glistening on her brow, saying she felt clean and free. Mother had a youngish-looking face. She understood no better than us kids why Father was up worrying every night over glasses of whiskey.

Two more years of making payments and they would have been in the clear. But the market for hematite dried up. Father had gambled on the mine holding out and he lost. According to him the unions priced Red Rock's iron out of competition with Germany's. He was against medicare and strikes. But mostly he was against unions. He called the men who went out on wildcat strikes *gold brickers*, and worse things after he lost the hardware store in Red Rock.

The laundry he bought in Fort Frances was another thing. That's where the orange van took us in the rain in the summer of 1962. This was a pulp and paper town, a union town, too, with a sister city across the border in Minnesota and a tradition of hard-nosed success. The Fort Frances Canadians had won the Allan Cup in the early fifties. But the move turned out to be more bad luck for Father.

He was a short, wiry man with brown hair and eyes to match. He smoked a pipe. He liked owning small businesses because of the independence they gave him. A coal yard labourer during the thirties and a private during the war, he had had a bellyful of taking orders. "No one's my boss," he liked to say—and then add with a laugh, "except your mother." I remember him laughing a lot in Red Rock, and smiling over his pipe as he tamped and fiddled with the tobacco before lighting up. That was his great pleasure, smoking his pipe. ·

He liked fishing rods and guns, too, which he sold to Red Rock's miners and which he taught me how to use so I would grow up a man. He taught me to squeeze, not pull, the trigger of a rifle, and always just at the point where you started to breathe out. He taught me to walk on my heels in the woods so as not to make a sound. When I was not yet a teenager he hunted moose in the muskeg terrain around Red Rock with a handgun. He used a .38 Walther HP he'd brought back from the war as a souvenir. I had the job of blowing into the moose horn while Father positioned himself behind a tree twenty yards downwind. The sight of a thousand-pound bull moose crashing down on us through the scrub is etched on my mind forever. When it was fifty yards away Father stepped out from behind his tree, aimed straight along his extended left arm and fired one bullet into the moose's chest. I never knew him to take more than one shot. Or to think he'd done anything extraordinary. He liked moose steaks. He liked fishing on warm afternoons, too, and always predicted we'd catch our limit, though we rarely did. He was an optimist despite everything that happened to him.

Just as the laundry in Fort Frances was beginning to turn a profit, there was a disaster. The phone rang in the dark hours one night, waking us. I lay on one elbow in bed trying to catch Father's side of the conversation. I couldn't make out what he was saying but I heard the scree and scraw of trains in the yards near our house, the distant hollow thump of cars being coupled together. We lived in a rented place near the tracks with a yard too small for a vegetable garden or flowers. When Father finished talking he put the phone down and went into the bedroom where he spoke to Mother in hushed tones.

Minutes later I heard his shoes thudding across the floor to the back door, his steps echoing down the walk.

There had been a fire at the laundry. It took most of the night to put out the flames in the roof. Sirens, police cars. One fireman had collapsed from smoke inhalation when he was trapped between two upright mangles that toppled over. That wasn't the worst thing that happened, the Fire Chief said. He was a big man with soft hands and a pencil mustache. He had driven Father home from the laundry at dawn and stood in the kitchen drinking a mug of coffee which Mother had made. I lingered in the doorway, knowing something important was happening. Father sat at the table drinking whiskey. His shirt sleeves were rolled up, his eyes were wild. He looked up from time to time but he didn't focus on anything. He stared into space and then back at his drink. The Chief whispered to Mother that Father had gone off his head. He'd taken one of the fireman's axes and started hacking at the machinery in silent fury. When two policemen had tried to restrain him, he'd threatened them with the axe.

Father clenched his hands on the whiskey glass as the Chief spoke to Mother. His knuckles were white. Blood had smeared on the tabletop and then dried.

Mother said to the Chief, "You were good to bring him home." To Father she said, "Wasn't he, Tom?"

Everyone was speaking softly, like at a funeral, and I could hear the electric clock in the display panel of the stove whirring and ticking. Father raised his head. He looked at the Chief as if he hadn't realized until that moment that he was in the room. He looked back into his whiskey glass.

Mother asked, "What happened?"

The Chief said, "At first there was so much smoke it was hard to see anything. All those clothes burning, I guess." He looked at Father for confirmation, but when none came, he went on, "Then part of the roof caved in and the boys were hosing it down when Tom here grabs an axe and leaps through a flaming window."

Mother's mouth flew open. "My God. Did you try to stop him?"

"We were caught off guard. We saw him duck under the smoke and make for the front of the building where there wasn't any fire." The Chief squinted over his coffee, working to recall each detail, as if he were giving evidence in court. "He hacked down the office wall first," the Chief said, nodding at Father. "Plaster and wood chips flying through the black smoke." The Chief paused, waiting to see what Father did, and when he said nothing, went on, "It might have been funny except that Tom was so off his ... so out of control."

Mother nodded. "How'd he cut his hand?" Blood was pooling on the table from a cut on Father's wrist.

"We circled to the front of the building, the cops and me. After we shouted for him to come out, Sergeant Boyd and one of the other cops went in after him." The Chief drank some coffee. He added in a bolder voice when he saw Father was quiet, "I didn't see how he cut himself, but I saw him lift the axe toward Boyd."

Mother looked terrified.

The Chief drew a deep breath. "There was a scuffle and the cops brought him out with his arms pinned behind," he said gruffly. "That's why I brought him home. They wanted to lay charges, see."

"Charges?" Mother said, more a statement than a question.

"Obstruction of justice," the Chief said, lowering his voice again. "Assaulting an officer."

Mother looked at me, her eyes level, though her lips quivered. "Tom," she said.

Father stared at her and then at his bloody hand. He seemed to rouse himself from the trance he'd been in. "Why are you talking about me," he asked, "as if I wasn't here?" He struck his bloody hand on the table. I'd heard him say things around the house about police and firemen and I'd always thought he admired them. But his voice was filled with rage. I took a step backward.

The Chief studied his mug of coffee. "I better go," he said. He looked for a place to put the mug and settled for a space on the counter between the coffee canister and the whiskey bottle.

"You talk about justice," Father shouted. He stood suddenly, nearly tipping over the table, and said, "What the hell do the cops know about justice? With their pensions and their fat-cat wages?"

"Tom," Mother said.

He added as an afterthought, "And you firemen with your soft jobs and frigging union."

"Sit down," Mother said. "You're talking nonsense."

"I'll be going," the Chief said. "Tom, now—"

"Am I?" Father stood in the centre of the room, looking wildly from Mother to the Chief. "Nonsense. Is it now?"

"You broke the law, Tom." The Chief pulled himself to his full height. He had a pot-belly but he stood a head taller than Father. "That's all I'm saying. You attacked your property like an animal, you resisted restraint, you abused an officer of the law." The Chief drew a deep breath. His round face was red. "You attacked a man with a deadly weapon, is what I'm saying. That's wrong, and that's all there's to it." He hiked his pants up by the belt. "You're lucky to get off without charges being laid."

"Lucky?" Father came around from behind the table, pushing at his shirt sleeves. Since his days at the hardware store he'd always worn a white shirt, and this one was smudged on one shoulder with soot. "Lucky?" he asked again. His face was white and his brown eyes bugged out of their sockets.

"Tom," Mother said. "For heaven's sake, the man brought you home. He's trying to help."

"Get out of here," Father shouted. I'd never heard his voice that hard. I saw Mother flinch and realized my hands were sweaty and that I was rubbing them on my thighs.

The Chief said, "Don't you lay a hand on me." He was backing up toward the door, his big rubber boots clumping across the floor. I don't think Father knew what he was going to do until the Chief put the idea of physical violence into his head.

"I'll do anything I want to. It's my house, isn't it?"

The Chief said, "You lay one finger on me and there'll be charges. So help me God Tom, it'll be jail."

Father leapt at him then, pushing the Chief's chest with both hands. It was a gesture of impotent anger, not violence, the kind you use on the schoolyard with the class bully. You can hit a man in the face or even in the chest with your clenched fist and mean to hurt him bad. But when you shove with both hands you're only trying to push something out of your way. Father had taught me that, too, along with how you break a man's nose with one snap of your elbow. "I'll damn well do what I please," Father said. "This is my house, see. I'm still the boss here."

"Oh my God," Mother gasped. She looked wildly about the room, and then stared at me, as if realizing suddenly that I was there.

The Chief stumbled backwards into the door. There was a bloodstain in the form of a hand print on his chest. He wrenched the door open. "You'll see," he said to Father, who was standing with his face upturned to the Chief's, maybe a foot between them. "I'll bring the law down on you."

After that Father went to the window and watched the Chief climb into his fire-hall station wagon and drive away. He stood looking out into the night with one hand up to cut the glare from the glass. He was there a long time after the car was gone. He looked small to me, his bony shoulder blades protruding through his white shirt. Mother and I stood in the room listening to the stove clock. Mother had her hands folded over her stomach like she had a pain there. Maybe she was wondering how in the space of a few hours Father could have gone after one man with an axe and fought with another in his own house. Maybe she was thinking about how her life would change again as it had when we left Red Rock. I don't know what she was thinking.

I remember clearly what I was thinking because it was the first time it occurred to me, though I've thought it many times since. I realized that anyone is capable of anything. A father on the church board could be forcing his teenage daughter every night. The lady you meet in the aisle at Safeway might have killed her child and buried it in the backyard. I realized that if my father could take an axe to a man, anyone was capable of anything. I began to realize, too, that I was.

After a while Father turned away from the window and looked at us. "I don't know why I did that," he said. He sounded like a child puzzled about breaking something. His eyes shifted from one of us to the other. They were normal again.

"Let me put a bandage on that," Mother said, meaning his cut wrist. She crossed to the cupboard and took down a first-aid kit.

Father said to me, "I was way out of line there." He seemed to be waiting for me to speak. "I don't know what came over me. You'd think when a man lost his head that way he'd at least be able to say why afterward, wouldn't you?"

"Yes," I said. My voice sounded small in the room.

He looked me up and down, though I don't think he was actually thinking about me. "It just seemed to happen."

"I know."

"You do," Father said. He was calm now, not the tense silent he'd been when he'd sat at the table drinking, but ordinary calm. He looked about the room as if he were only now aware of where he was. "I wanted us to be happy here," he said. "Just happy."

"I did too," I said, thinking of the friends I'd made at school and would have to say good-bye to. I felt very weary of life.

Father must have too. He sat with his chin in one cupped palm and looked blankly at me. There were lines around his mouth, a spot of blood on one cheek, and the white welt of a scar from hand-to-hand combat during the war in Italy. His breathing was laboured and after a while he said, "I feel so hot." He touched his brow and added, "Right from my feet on up. Just hot."

Mother said, "Here." When she was done putting a bandage on father's wrist we sat around the table and drank coffee. We looked at each other, but no one had much to say. We were thinking private thoughts. I was wondering where my life would go. There had been talk of moving to the city. Father had been a realtor there before he bought the hardware store in Red Rock. Mother had always wanted to return, to be closer to her family. She must have been wondering how their life had gone into such a tailspin. There was a time not long past when they'd talked of retiring at fifty and moving to the West Coast.

Father stood up and poured himself more rye. He splashed some in a glass for Mother, and when she shook her head, he pushed it in front of me. I took a sip. It was my first taste of liquor. I felt the raw burn of alcohol down in my gut.

"I don't know what came over me," Father said. He shook his head. Some of his hair had matted to one temple with dried blood. "I just don't know."

There was a long silence and I sipped the whiskey again. It seemed smoother this time.

"I'm a reasonable man, aren't I? Most of the time?"

Mother nodded but did not answer.

He looked at me. "Yes," I said. I put the glass down carefully and pushed it away with one finger.

"Huh," he grunted. And then after a bit, "Well, that's one for the books."

I listened to his voice. It was a soft voice which rasped a little from the pipe smoke he'd inhaled. I thought of all the stories I'd heard him tell around the kitchen table in Red Rock, building to a slow climax while he tamped and fiddled with his pipe. He used wooden matches which he struck on the sole of his shoe and shook once quickly to extinguish after he'd lit up. When I was a child he'd let me blow out those matches, and I remembered sitting on his lap saying *bwow*, *bwow* whenever he lit up. I felt the urge to tell him that I loved him, but I did not. I sipped my coffee. I watched the dawn creep in at the window.

The Chief didn't lay charges, but the law came down on Father just the same. While he was planning how to start the laundry operating again, lawyers hired by the insurance company dragged him through the courts over what had happened the night of the fire. I remember him standing amidst the charred machinery with a push broom one Saturday when I was helping him tidy things up. His gaze roamed around, appraising the damage, calculating how to put things back together. I don't think his heart was in it. That day he sent me across the street to buy Pepsis and when I came back he had the classified section of the paper open on his lap. "There's a hardware for sale in Stone Creek," he said. "What do you think of that?" He told me about the town. It was close to the city, so Mother would like that. He was impressed by its clean streets and low business taxes. He'd never liked the chemical odours of Fort Frances or the effluence that blew out of the pulp mills' stacks and settled on everything in the town. He thought he could make a go of that hardware store in Stone Creek.

We drank Pepsi and swept broken plasterboard into heaps. From time to time Father lit up his pipe and gazed out the window. There were a lot of places a man in his fix would rather have been, with a family to feed and a second bankruptcy looming. He never said anything about that. He never said anything about the burdens of family life or railed about injustice the way I've heard men do since. He never said anything about what happened on the night of the fire either, though he had trouble looking me in the eye after that and he didn't lecture me any more about seeing things through to the bitter end and keeping a stiff upper lip.

He must have been preoccupied thinking of money. It looked as if the insurance payout would be tied up in the courts forever. For weeks he went off to court carrying his cardboard briefcase bulging with papers. He came back and sat at the dining-room table and sighed and claimed his lawyer was in cahoots with the insurance lawyers and the judge. His wrist had healed but he smoked more than ever and in a desperate way, as if trying to cram as much nicotine as possible into his body. He was talking about an out-of-court settlement then, and starting fresh in another town.

Mother went to work at Eaton's where she was a clerk in the accounts office. One day I dropped by to bring her the sandwich she'd forgotten on the kitchen counter. There were pockets under her eyes and she seemed to be paler by the day, but she smiled at me over her files in her brave way. She was worried about Father. "Don't hold it against him," she told me.

"No," I said.

She ran her tongue from one side of her mouth to the other. "It's easy to think when someone does something that upsets lives that they're crazy. But they're not. Not usually. It's just that they see things differently than you. At that moment. That's all. They're inside it and you're not."

I nodded. But I did not know what to say.

"If you want to blame something, blame this cruddy town." That's the closest I ever heard her come to swearing.

"It doesn't seem fair," I said. "He tries so hard."

"That's just it," she said. "Bad luck." She opened the wax paper her sandwich was wrapped in and took a bite. "It seems to follow us around. I mean it seems to follow me around." She looked out the tiny window of her office. "I remember during the Depression how your grandfather had us kids load up a wagon of watermelons one fall. That's when we had the farm in Pine Ridge. We'd tended those watermelons all summer, hoeing and watering them so they'd be round and juicy for the market, the way he insisted. He drove to the city to sell them. With what he made he'd hoped to buy flour and salt and maybe some shoes for us kids. They offered him five cents apiece. Five cents. You couldn't buy two chickens with what a pickup full of watermelons at five cents apiece would fetch. Do you think he took it?" She looked at me to see if I understood the point of her story. "He did not," she went on with a snort. "He turned the pickup around and drove out of the city without stopping. About a mile from home he backed the truck up and dumped the watermelons in the ditch." Her voice choked a little. "That's what this is, I guess," she said. "That sort of kick in the teeth."

She ate the rest of her sandwich in silence. I went out and bought two paper cups of coffee. "But don't let it get you down," she said later. "As soon as we get out of this town things will be better."

It was raining when we left Fort Frances. Father and I had been up most of the night helping the driver load our stuff onto a three-ton truck from South East Transfer. Toward dawn a light mist began to descend. Father roped down the furniture. He arranged the boxes of china Mother had packed last thing so they wouldn't be damaged. The driver pulled the overhead door down with a clang and sealed the compartment for the customs officials who had to inspect every truck crossing the border. The light drizzle misted on his face as he walked around the truck checking its tires. Father and I said good-bye to Mother and my sister, who were joining us by bus after they had cleaned the house and returned the keys to the landlord.

We followed the truck's tail lights to the edge of town, where Father stopped to fill up with gas and buy pipe tobacco. As we drove along the streets, people were turning on their lights and waking to a new day. After we'd filled up we stood beside the car breathing the morning air.

"Smell that crap from the mill?" Father asked me. "That chemical crap?" His nose twitched.

I looked toward the mill. "I won't miss that," I said.

"No," he said. He looked at me then, as if he wanted to add something. I know he'd had hopes for us in Fort Frances and I felt hollow inside because I knew he was disappointed and that he believed himself a failure, though I never thought that, and I don't think Mother did either.

When we got back into the car Father turned on the wipers. Mist hung over the highway. "I never did like this town," he said. I knew he was trying to put the time we'd spent there in a place where he could consider it good riddance and forget it. I was going to miss my friends John and Rod and playing hockey on the high school team. The wipers beat steadily against the windshield.

I felt close to him at that moment. "I hated it," I said, though I hadn't, I had made friends and had felt myself settling in. "The smells, that black crap in the air. Even the kids at school."

"That's it," he said. "I think you've hit the nail on the head."

Father speeded up as we hit the edge of town. Rain spattered the windshield, making it difficult to see the highway. At a curve there was a thump under the car. We looked at each other. Father glanced in the rear-view mirror. "I hit something," he said, a note of surprise in his voice. "A cat, I think. Its eyes flashed at the side of the road." He was a man who cared about animals. Once when I winged a woodpecker with my .22 he made me search for it in the bush and kill it to make sure it didn't suffer needlessly. He took his foot off the accelerator and hesitated for a moment, the car drifting along in silence. Then he drove on. After a while he re-lit his pipe and threw the match out the window. "The hell with it," he said. The tires of the car swished in the water gathering on the asphalt. We sat staring out the window as the highway snaked into the distance, misty, grey, and flat.

TOUGH LOVE

Connie hung up the phone and ran her index finger down the length of her nose. She had been yakking with Kathy Roper and teasing her hair with a rat-tail comb at the same time. Her cheeks were flushed. She was a tall blonde with a pretty face and a winning personality. Eaton's had sent her to Toronto on a beauty queen kind of course, which pleased her and made my mother, a blonde herself, glow with pride. Connie was in her last year of high school and was going out on dates with boys like Doug Sutton, who lived across the street, and Rich Beamish when he was home from college, where he was on a football scholarship. She was a happy girl with a bright future. Around the house she sang tunes by the Everly Brothers, but when our parents weren't home, she put Jerry Lee Lewis and Elvis Presley on the record player in her bedroom, where she danced and snapped her fingers to the beat. "Rip It Up," "Shakin' All Over."

She smiled to herself as she put the phone down and was about to say something to me when Father called out from the living room where he was reading the newspaper: "Can you not be on there so long next time, for God's sake?"

"Okay, Dad," Connie called back. But she raised her eyebrows, as if to say, *what a pill!*

"And what's this I hear about you and Bernie O'Hearn?" Father's voice echoed off the walls. By this time Connie was in the kitchen, pretending she didn't hear. After a minute of silence passed, Father called out: "I'm talking to you, don't act as if you don't hear me."

He'd been with the ground troops in Italy and when the war ended he'd worked in real estate for a few years and then bought the hardware store in Red Rock. Connie had been born while he was overseas, so the first time he saw his daughter, she was over a year old. I had come along a year later. To work every day he wore a white shirt and a tie. He read the *Winnipeg Free Press* through every night. He'd voted for John Diefenbaker, who he made fun of by shaking his jowls and saying, "My fellow Canadians," and he was a firm believer in free enterprise. It had been terrible in Italy, he gave us to understand on the rare occasions when he talked about it, usually after a glass or two of whiskey. Nothing pretty, nothing glamorous, like they showed in the movies. A lot of confusion and mayhem. In panic men had shot their own soldiers, peasants were beaten and killed, women raped, an officer had been strangled by the men in his command. Our mother told us in whispered tones that it was over there he'd punched a captain and lost his own sergeant's stripes.

I feared he might get up and go into the kitchen. Around the house he was fond of saying things like *A man is the master of his own house,* and *I'll do whatever is necessary to protect my own property.* According to Mother he had a bad temper. It was hard to disagree. I held my breath, listening for footsteps. After a while he rattled the paper and called out again: "You're getting a bit too big for your britches, girlie."

There was only silence from the kitchen and I was thankful for it.

Bernie O'Hearn had dropped out of high school a couple of years earlier and was working at Melly's Esso, where Father gassed up our 1958 Chevrolet. Tall and fine-boned, Bernie had his dark hair fixed in the style of Kookie on 77 *Sunset Strip*, and he carried a rat-tail comb that he brought out every few minutes to run through his ducktail. He drove a Mercury that was older than our car but painted bright red. On the aerial flew a raccoon's tail. He was the kind of guy who squealed his tires getting away from STOP signs, the kind of guy who mothers shook their heads at, the kind of guy who drank beer in the car right on Main Street, or out at the gravel pit with high school buddies and teenage girls. The kind, in short, who you secretly want-ed to be like—Terry Jewett and I bought combs for ourselves. The kind of flashy guy that girls couldn't help wanting to go out with on a date. Young, carefree, easy with money, good-looking.

"A high school drop-out," Father continued, raising his voice so we all heard. "There you go, enough said. Hangs out with those grease monkeys at Melly's garage, making a nuisance of themselves with their beer and loud music. The cops have their eyes on them, let me tell you."

Mother had come to stand in the doorway of the living room. "They're just boys, Ray. You were a boy too, once."

"Those *boys* drink beer out at the gravel pit, then zoom around on the roads like madmen. It wouldn't be so bad if they just killed each other—good riddance to bad rubbish in my book—but that's not what's going to happen. They're going to pile into a family and kill innocent women and children." There had been a bad car smash-up out at Dead Man's Bend the summer before. Donny Camp-bell had rolled his VW Beetle and been killed; Jim Piper and Eddy O'Hagan had escaped with their lives and many lacerations. They'd been drinking beer out at the gravel pit.

I was in the hallway now, too, standing near to Connie. She smiled at me conspiratorially. "Men cannot be innocent," Connie whispered to me, *sotto voce*. "Not in Dad's world."

"I heard that," Father said sharply. "Watch your tongue, girlie."

"Okay, Dad."

"You're getting uppity, you and your smart mouth."

"Ray, Ray," Mother said. "Enough of that tone of voice, now." She stepped in front of Connie and put one hand back like a crossing guard to keep Connie from stepping forward.

Father waved her away and went back at Connie. "You're not so all-growed-up I can't take you over my knee still, girlie. Slap a little sense into you." A cruel edge had come into his voice, a hint that he was not unfamiliar with striking the opposite sex. There had been mistreatment of women in Italy, I had gathered, and once in our basement I had overheard one of his cronies say he'd felt up the ass of another man's wife, a blonde not a lot older than Connie, and that she'd liked it as much as he did, which had made my father snort and laugh.

"Ray," Mother said, "let's have some coffee now."

Connie made a huffing sound.

"Don't put me to the test. You'll regret it."

That settled it, the threat of physical violence. It was the era of Sputnik and revolution in Cuba and Agonizing Reappraisal and the Big Bang, which, whatever it meant to scientists and the like, meant something pretty specific to Father. It had to do with the way he wielded his hand around the house. In the war common soldiers were treated brutally, I gathered from his stories, and somehow the idea of violence as a cure-all had become the way a whole generation of men thought. Might is right. In Red Rock there was a lot of fist fighting in the alley out back of the Rockton Hotel, and Father was not averse to exchanging shouted threats with other men, though I'd never seen him in a scrap, but once he had leapt out of the car in a back alley and yelled at a man in a raw voice, *fuck off*, which was the first time I'd actually heard anyone say it. When that tone came into his voice, we made ourselves scarce.

Later Mother cornered Connie in the kitchen and I heard them talking in low voices while Mother rattled the dishes. "Your father's on the warpath about that Bernie O'Hearn."

"Your husband's always on the warpath about something. Last week it was the unions and the week before the price of gas." I'd been hearing Connie speak in this tone of voice more often that year, a mixture of sass and genuine annoyance. She used it on me sometimes and it put my teeth right on edge.

"Yes, yes, but he's got a particular burr about that boy."

"And the week before that it was Doctor Gregory."

"Well, so-called *Doctor* Gregory made a mess of Tim's teeth. He's a drunk, you can smell it on him when you sit in his chair. How he keeps a dental licence ..."

"And roving hands to boot."

Mother gasped. There was a silence in which she seemed to consider saying more about the town dentist. "The point is," she went on, "the point is your father's got a temper. You know that."

"We all know that. We know that in our skin and bones."

"Your Uncle Don is always asking me about your father, how we're doing and so on. He knows he has a temper and Don is afraid for me. I can tell by the way he asks, *How are you and Ray doing together?* I know what he's really getting at." She'd spoken to me about this too, about how some men had come back from the war edgy and angry. Others drank. She'd told me that some of them slapped their wives, which I believed my father had never done.

"So I'll be careful," Connie said.

"You'd be wise to do more than that, young lady."

"Yeah, okay."

"And curb that tone of voice around your father. It's bad enough you're wearing lipstick. But talking back just puts him on edge and he takes it out on everyone else, Tim and me too. He thinks you're his little girl, he thinks you're growing up too fast."

"Yeah, okay, Mom, I get it already."

"Be sensible, not sorry."

"Yeah, okay already."

But wisdom was not high on the list of virtues of either Connie or me. That afternoon I'd shot myself in the face with a BB gun. I was tracking a giant grasshopper in our backyard, and when it sat still, I stood directly over it and fired down. I hadn't noticed it had landed on a wood plank. When the pellet missed the grasshopper, it bounced straight back at me, catching me in the cheek, not, fortunately, in the eye. But my heart played a tattoo in my chest for about an hour afterward. There would have been hell to pay for that.

After supper I saw Connie and Kathy downtown, standing on the sidewalk in front of the Rockton Hotel. I was riding my bike and came around the corner of the block, so they didn't see me. I pulled my bike over, pretending to look in the window of Fred's Hardware, where there were fishing rods on display. Kathy and Connie were standing on the sidewalk for a couple of seconds only before Bernie's red Merc pulled up to the curb. Inside were Bobby Thompson and Sandy Russell. They called out to the girls, who stepped over to the car. There was talk I could not hear and then a sudden burst of laughter. One of the guys said, "Oh, c'mon!" And then the girls were climbing into the car, which sped away in the direction of the mine road and the gravel pits. I was curious what happened out there but it was a long bike ride and I really preferred to have that adventure with Terry Jewett as company. I was worried about going out there alone. And also it would be much more fun to share such a moment with Terry. So I wheeled my bike back home, hoping for another chance on another day.

I was reading, about to doze off, when I heard Father say something to Mother in a tone that made me sit up on my bed. But I hadn't caught the words.

"Oh, Ray," she cajoled him, "it's not 11:00 yet, and that's what you told her."

"That's crap," Father said loudly. "It's 11:15."

"Ray, Ray, drink your coffee now. Go finish the paper."

"That girl is getting out of hand."

Mother's words were lost in the banging of a cupboard door.

There was a long silence. I held my breath, waiting for footsteps to come down the hall. I'd been reading a Superman comic and was twisting it in my hands. The clock in the living room ticked loudly. The Hansens' beagle, Brutus, was barking in their backyard. It was the end of summer and in the cool air sounds carried in a way that told you winter was on the way.

I heard the front door open and then bang shut and then Father's raised voice. My wristwatch said it was almost 11:30. I went to my bedroom door and opened it a crack.

"You just stop right there," Father was calling out.

Connie was almost to her bedroom door and she turned to face him. She was wearing a pink angora sweater and had put on bright red lipstick. Around the school she was known as the blonde bombshell, which was also what Marilyn Monroe and Jayne Mansfield were called, though Connie was not built the way they were: va-va-voom style. She was more on the tall, leggy side. *Vivacious* was a good word for her. Her cheeks were flushed.

"What's this I hear about you and Benny Tuesday?" Father had stood up and crossed into the hallway. He was standing at one end and Connie halfway down the passage. There was a picture on the wall of trees in a forest at fall, bright reds and yellows interspersed with shadows. I'd never paid it much attention, but on that night its colours seemed to come to life in an oddly lurid way. Father was still holding the *Free Press* in one hand.

"Nothing," Connie said. "He's just a guy Kathy and I were having a Coke with at the Park Luncheonette." Her tone wasn't brazen, but there was nothing demure in it either.

Mother was standing at the kitchen door, hands on hips. She'd had to step in between the two of them in the past year and I thought she was preparing to do the same again.

"That's not what I hear," Father said. He'd dropped the paper to the floor and come closer to her and was standing like a man ready to take a punch, or throw one, bent slightly forward. He was not a tall man but he was muscular and wiry, quick of hand and foot.

"Kathy and I were just having a Coke. With him and his brother Max."

"Indians," Father said. "Riding around in a car with a couple of Indians."

He was wearing the white shirt he put on for work in the morning and the collar was open, showing the undershirt he wore beneath it. A tuft of red hair stuck out below his Adam's apple, which was flushed bright pink and bobbing up and down.

"They're nice guys," Connie said. She looked at Mother, then back at Father.

"They're grown men and you are a girl not yet out of high school." He moved even closer to her, both hands slack at his sides. The veins stood out at the wrists and I noticed for the first time that his wrists were narrow, where my own were thick, more like my uncle Don's.

"Dad," Connie began.

"I warned you once already about riding around in cars with grown men."

"Dad, for once can you—"

"You know what they call that, don't know?"

"I know what they call men who beat their wives."

"You—what?"

"Oh, I don't know why I bother," Connie said. She shifted as if she was going to turn her back on him and go into her bedroom.

"You listen to me," he said, his voice rising. "You're nothing but a stupid little twit who knows nothing about what goes on in men's minds. Their filthy thoughts. That's what you are. A stupid little.

Putting on all this lipstick, wearing tight sweaters. And Indians! No daughter of mine—"

"Ray." Mother was standing only a few feet away, watching, her fingers kneading the material of her apron into a ball. I smelled sugar and cinnamon in the air. Though it was late in the day, she'd been baking, there was something going on at the church the next morning.

"This," father said, without even turning to look at her, "is between the girl and me." I'd seen him angry before, at me for breaking a window with a baseball and then lying about it, and at other men, and it was not a pretty sight, his face red and his hands shaking. I thought of the afternoons when we played catch in the backyard, and that did not jibe with what was happening now, and I wondered about that, how a man could be two different men on separate occasions and yet still be your father, who you put a lot of faith in.

Connie tapped her foot on the floor. She was not wearing the saddle shoes she usually wore but a shiny black shoe with an open toe, more a woman's shoe than a girl's. "They just like driving around and having a few laughs," she stated in the tone of voice that said she was the wronged party. "They're not animals."

Father snorted loudly. When he moved closer to Connie, I smelled the Fitch's Tonic water he splashed on his face after shaving, the smell of roses. "Drinking beer and taking advantage of little twits who don't know better," he said, his voice loud in the narrow hall.

"Oh, you know all about it don't you?"

"I know enough, I know enough about what you're getting up to, you little—"

"Ray, Ray," Mother interjected. She stepped forward, one tentative step. Her eyes were on him. She did not look at me or at Connie. My father was excited but she was calm, at least on the outside. Trying to figure how far this would go, probably, hoping to keep a lid on it.

"Don't Ray me. Smell this daughter of yours. You think mints can cover beer? You've got a lot to learn, girlie."

Mother made to step forward but he put out one hand and pushed her shoulder. She gasped and stumbled awkwardly back. "No," she said, a kind of wail.

"Stay out of this," he said again, the edge in his voice like iron. "You're not protecting her this time."

I had stepped into the hallway and he looked at me hard for a moment. His cowlick was standing up more than usual and his face was white, completely drained of colour. He looked a little crazy, as if he was unsure himself what he was going to do next. Mother looked at me too. Her eyes were wide. For a moment I thought she knew about the BB incident and I flushed thinking I was in trouble, but then I saw she was trying to decide if she should say something to me, order me back to my room, maybe, or make a sign of some kind. She decided not to.

Father reached out suddenly and smacked the wall with his open hand. I jumped back and so did Mother, and Connie gasped. He smiled in a wicked way, pleased that he'd asserted his authority. "You, girl, have been drinking and whoring around."

"So what?"

"I'll show you so what, I'll—"

Connie stamped her foot. "It's okay, though, for you to guzzle beer at the Legion and swill back whiskey with your precious old war buddies."

"Don't you dare." Father's eyes had narrowed and his teeth were gritted together in a snarl.

"Drunks the lot."

"You know nothing about that."

"Lying about your big war exploits and precious wounds."

"You have no idea," he spluttered. "It was life and death out there, things a man can never forget, and you—you little—"

"Ray, Ray, you're—" Mother made to step forward again but his arm shot out and that stopped her. She said, "No, Ray, this is not."

But he didn't hear her and was going on. "A little bitch out drinking with Indians, dirty red men with one thing on their minds—"

"You're prejudiced," Connie screamed. "You're, a bigot, a—"

With one hand Father grabbed Connie around the neck. "Listen to me," he said. His jaw stuck out. He had moved so close to her their faces were almost touching. "What in the world is the matter with you? Don't you understand anything?"

Connie's eyes flashed back at him.

He had his other hand raised, ready to strike. "You have to learn the hard way, don't you, girl? You won't listen but you talk back and you traipse off and make a tramp of yourself in front of the whole town and then you have to be taught the lesson you should have learned from the start if you'd listened to me in the first place." These were wild words. I'd never heard anything like them. I wondered if he realized that and it occurred to me right then why he was so furious: his whole world must have seemed like it was coming apart. He had been an officer in the army and was used to taking and giving orders, to chain of command. This defiance from his daughter shocked and bewildered him. He was the man of the house, what he said went. Or was supposed to.

He'd lifted Connie off the ground slightly, so she was standing on her toes. Her arms hung at her sides, like the arms of a rag doll.

"What is it I have to do to make you understand?" He balled his raised hand in the air.

I heard Mother gasp again and her eyes glazed over and fixed on a spot on the wall beyond my head. She looked as if she was in a trance, her mind numb, though I thought also that she might be wondering what she was doing there, as you do sometimes, a feeling like déjà vu, your mind disconnected from your body and sort of looking at your self as if you were another person. Maybe she was thinking that her world was pulling apart, that this was not the dashing fellow she'd wed during the war, or wondering how he had become a man prepared to strike his own child. That thought had flashed through my own brain.

Part of me wanted to run back into the bedroom and part wanted to step in between them. I was big for my age. I'd been thinking about the day when I'd confront him. But I did neither. I stood rooted to the floor, like my mother.

"Hit me," Connie said, her voice cracking.

"I should. Don't think I won't."

"That's what you want, so do it."

"If it would knock some sense into you, if it would wipe that grin off your stupid face. That ugly lipstick. You're not that kind of ... not a ... not a grown woman."

Connie glared back at him but she didn't flinch.

I thought then that he wasn't going to hit her, that he would stand there until something happened to make him change his mind. Half a minute went by. Connie's face was turning redder and he gulped once, his Adam's apple bobbing.

"That's enough now," Mother said. She hadn't moved but her voice had assumed an edge. Her eyes were focused now, though the blood had drained from her cheeks, too. "Enough!" she repeated loudly, almost a shout.

It brought him to a halt. He stared into Connie's face, as if waiting for her to do something, talk back or move, something he could put a stop to with physical violence, something that would teach her a lesson and satisfy his need to bring things to order. "You're out of your mind," he said finally, "you're crazy. Crazy. The whole town's talking about you. Did you know that? Tramp. Worse words than that that I won't repeat. You won't listen to reason but you challenge me in my own house, you talk back, you want me to snuff out your stupid little life over Indians and whatnot. You're a crazy and stupid little tramp. There were women like you who the men . You have no idea. I ought to kill you."

Connie looked him level in the eye. I was thinking he was the crazy one, his words hardly making sense, a man who didn't know the limits of his temper or what he might do next.

"All right," she squeaked out. "Dad." The fight had gone out of her.

"All right, Raymond," Mother said. She had her eyes on me, as if expecting I might move or say something that would break the moment. She was very calm, though her fingers continued to knead at her apron. It was then that I noticed the band in her hair, blue with yellow stars, Connie had given it to her for her birthday. It was made for a child, not a mother of two whose husband sometimes played the tyrant. I felt good about the fact she was wearing the hair band but also sorry for her then, she seemed so helpless in the face of his anger.

Father had not let go of Connie's neck, but he'd relaxed his grip and her feet were flat on the floor again. He was breathing heavily, trying to think of what he could do to her that would bring her around—choke her or hit her until she saw things the way he did and never again went against what he told her to do. His raised hand was still in the air. I knew he wasn't going to hit her. Connie did too. Maybe he was the only one who didn't know that and was trying to puzzle out how to bring his hand down without losing face.

He turned suddenly toward Mother, as if realizing he'd made a mess of things and was afraid he would ruin things completely if he acted in the way something dark inside him was urging him to. A line had been crossed. Another beckoned. His eyes were shiny and darting about quickly. Mother moved her head slightly from side to side but did not move her lips. The Hansens' beagle was barking again. Then a voice called out for it to stop.

Father turned back to Connie. "Get out," he shouted into her face. He flung her backwards and she cried out as her head cracked against the wall so it shook for a second. Her hands flew out, palms to the wall, and braced her body. She slid down the wall. Just before she hit the bottom, she pitched forward suddenly and landed on her hands and knees. A whimper escaped her lips. She'd been standing up to him like a grown-up, but in the end she was not one. She was like me, a frightened teenager who had believed for a moment that she was an adult.

"All right!" Mother shouted again, her voice tearing at something in her chest, like a cloth being rent. "Outside now, Raymond. Go. Cool off."

"You look after her," Father said to Mother. "Your daughter, your little tramp." He spat the last words out, though there was a note of desperation in them, as if he had to make what he was saying stick. Then he strode into the kitchen. In a moment I heard the cabinet below the sink open, where he kept a bottle of whiskey, and then the back door slamming shut.

Mother had gone to Connie. She was down on one knee, stooped over to take her in her arms. Connie was crying, quiet, suppressed sobs that wracked her chest. Saliva was dribbling down her chin, as if she'd been in a race and had just hit the finish line. There was a white spot on one cheek the size of a half dollar. The rest of her face was bright red.

"It's all right now," Mother said. She glanced up at me. "Water," she said.

I went into the kitchen and poured a glass and drank it down swiftly, then refilled it. Everything had happened so fast and so wildly that life seemed at that moment to be whirling out of control, like water in a rapids, swirling this way and that, giving it all a feeling of being tumbled together and maybe even pointless. I took the glass of water and brought it in for Connie. My hand shook as I passed it over. Her hand trembled as she took it. "Thanks," she said. Her voice quavered. She gulped the water back and some dribbled onto her pink sweater, leaving little dots.

Mother took the glass from her and took a sip herself and the room was so quiet I heard it going down her throat. When Connie held the glass in her hand again, her eyes came up to mine. They were blank, as if she was having trouble concentrating. I was wondering if she was already thinking that she was looking at a family she no longer belonged to the way she had only a day ago, the way I still did. She was no longer the happy-go-lucky girl who worked at the cosmetics counter at Eaton's, as she had been. Something had been torn asunder and would never knit back quite the same way. Her life as a girl was over. She would move away soon and have her own place and her own life and do what she wished in every way, even if what she did was wrong in the eyes of her father or the town. I saw all that in her eyes and maybe Mother did too. It frightened me, maybe more than it frightened Connie.

She looked at Mother, who was probably expecting her to say, *I'm leaving* or something like that, a cutting barb which would hurt Mother as badly as she'd been hurt that night. But she didn't. Instead she said, "It's okay, Mom. I'm all right now."

She looked at me again and I suddenly felt it was no longer my place to be there. I went into the kitchen and stood at the sink. Out the window there was a big bright moon and bugs were whirling around the Hansens' outdoor light, a dense cloud of them. My father was standing at the back of the yard, smoking a cigarette and drinking straight from the bottle of whiskey. He looked sad and lost and I would have liked to go out there with him but I couldn't. He was not a monster. All through the years that I was growing up he'd played catch with me before my little league games and we went fishing on Sunday afternoons. He'd taught me how to saw a board and pound nails and use a power drill. We'd shovelled gravel side by side and sat and drank Pepsi afterward and wiped our brows with red handkerchiefs. He was good around men and good with me, but did not know how to be a father to Connie. Women brought out the worst in him. He was a man of polarities, a man of his times. He'd seen things in the war that most people would never see and I hoped I never would either, things that change a person's basic personality. I would have liked to have gone out there and stood beside him in the moonlight so he was not alone, but it would have been a betrayal of Connie. I wanted to but I couldn't.

Connie and Mother were talking in low tones behind me. Maybe it was about him, never the same since the war, or about what had happened, *he loves you down deep*, or about me, *what a thing for Tim to have to see*. I did not know. You could not know unless you were there and I wasn't and it didn't much matter. They were commiserating together and Father was standing in the yard drinking whiskey and I was caught in between, but it didn't upset me, it just seemed that was the way it had to be. Loyalties were sometimes divided. Things between people were not black and white, as they were in the comics. You didn't always have to choose but you had to see that's the way things were sometimes. I realized I too was no longer the boy I'd been only a week ago.

One morning not too long after, Connie left. She waited until Father had gone to work, and then she came out of her room with a suitcase and she sat at the table and talked with Mother. From the tones of their voices I could tell Mother was pleading with her to stay. But Connie was insistent. She and Kathy had taken the bus to Fort Frances some weeks earlier and signed up for jobs as telephone operators. They had made arrangements to stay with a lady who rented rooms near the Bell telephone building. Kathy's older brother Frank was driving them, picking her up any minute. She embraced Mother at the door and then came back in and hugged me. She told me she'd left her record collection on her bed and that I was to have it. Maybe someday she'd ask me to send the Everly Brothers and the Jerry Lee Lewis on the bus to her, but the others were mine to keep. I protested, but she waved me off.

At the door she hugged me again. "You take care of yourself," she said. Her eyes were glassy and I turned away as she walked down the stairs and I felt as awful as I've felt in my life, and there have been many days for me to feel awful since. When the car door banged shut I looked up and waved. She was waving too. It was a chilly fall morning and the car's exhaust hung in the air behind it before being dispersed by the wind. The car backed out of the driveway and turned into the street. Then it was gone. I turned to go inside. Mother was standing at the living-room window, one hand raised, still waving at Connie.

About a year later she came back and visited and we all sat at the dining-room table and ate supper and laughed about cousin Marlise, who Connie had given the name "Hopeless" because she was always making a fool of herself with older men, but she never did send for the albums.

MEATHOOKS FOR HANDS

My uncle was a big man, tall and thick through the chest and with meathooks for hands, as my father said. I'd gone to work for him on his farm near Carman in the summer between grades ten and eleven, a city boy without a driver's licence. Uncle Bill showed me how to drive the little Fordson tractor, which my aunt used to putter around the farmyard and to drive out to the fields at lunchtime with sandwiches and cold water in a Mason jar. She was younger than him by a few years, a tall, rangy woman who you would not call beautiful or even pretty, but who had a spark of life that made her attractive. Bright blue eyes. Always singing while she worked.

After I'd mastered the Fordson I had a trial on the Minneapolis Moline and then Uncle Bill put me to work disking the fallow fields on the bright new red Massey. The Minnie was touchy in the steering and he thought I'd have trouble on the tight corners of the fields. I didn't, but he thought I'd do better on the Massey Harris, which I was happy to drive but frightened of too, because it was new, his prize possession.

We worked from dawn to dusk that summer, disking and harrowing his many fields. He owned more than two sections of land, almost 1500 acres. It was Red River bottom land, the best in the country for grains, *gumbo* my father called it, and in good years those fields garnered sixty bushels of wheat and more. Uncle Bill was prosperous. He drove a new Buick. My father said, "He was never bright, Bill, but he was always canny." My father told me that in school Uncle Bill struggled with reading and could hardly sign his own name. "But don't underestimate him," my father added. "There's been a few who have and they've rued the day."

He had thinning black hair and a pencil mustache. He wore size fourteen shoes, which had to be bought at a store where they were made specially to fit him. Aunt Nelly drove into the city to the store every year and then went on to the big and tall shop to buy his shirts. I was given to understand by my mother that she bought dresses and skirts on those occasions, too. She stayed in the city over a night or two with her sister, who was pretty, and they went shopping at the Hudson Bay and had lunch at the Paddlewheel Restaurant. There were glasses of white wine in the evening. Aunt Nelly had been a schoolteacher when she met my uncle, and she and her sister had travelled to Vancouver and Montreal on the train and had had a real old time, according to my mother. She had given that up to be a farmer's wife.

We worked in the fields every day. As the sun went down Uncle Bill drove out to the field I was working and picked me up and we bounced back over the fields on the Minnie, he at the wheel and me standing behind him, clutching the rim of the back of the seat, feet clinging to the transmission housing. The sun would just be going down. "Look at that," he'd say, pointing to the west where the horizon was a palette of purples and oranges. "You can't beat this country for its sunsets." He'd been to Florida and Mexico so he'd seen a few. I agreed with him, though I'd only ever lived in the Shield country and on the prairie. "Look at that," he'd say, indicating a hawk high above us in the red sky, "by gum, son, you don't see that every day in your city."

We showered behind one of the granaries, where he'd fixed a set-up with barrels that caught rain water which we hosed onto ourselves, cold water that took your breath away after a hot day in the fields. On Fridays we ate supper with Aunt Nelly and then went into town, which she didn't seem to mind. Uncle Bill liked to stop at the Wheat Sheaf for a beer or two. He bought rounds for other farmers with their hair slicked back and freshly applied aftershave. They yakked and laughed. My uncle was fond of saying "By gum," and I heard that every now and then through the general hubbub coming from the beer parlour and it was comforting to me to hear it. Whenever he and my father got together he said, "By gum, Dick," and then went on to tell my father something they both shook their heads over. My father's name was actually Tom, but he'd been fat as a kid and his brothers had called him Dick, which in German means fat. While Uncle Bill was yakking and laughing with the other farmers, I played with the pinball machines in the room adjoining the beer parlour, where technically I was not allowed, and where there was a pool table, too. I drank Cokes and wasted the pocket money he gave me for the work I was doing driving the tractor.

Usually when it was time to go I walked over to the table where the men were drinking and stood nearby. "Look at that," my uncle said to his cronies. "Six feet and he's just sixteen." He was proud of me. He and Aunt Nelly didn't have any children. They'd tried, according to my mother, and there had been miscarriages. It was a disappointment to him. He would have liked to have had a boy like me, he gave me to understand. I played hockey on my high school team and made good grades at school and was going to college to study the law, that was the plan, in any case. I was a good worker but not much at pinball.

There was one night that was different. I wasn't through playing pinball when my uncle came into the games room to fetch me. I was concentrating so I didn't see him come up behind me. In a moment I felt his hand on my shoulder. It was hot through my shirt. It covered most of my back.

"Time to go," he said.

He left his hand on my shoulder. I was just about finished being beaten again. When I was, I turned around and he took his hand away. "Let's hit the road, son," he said. It was earlier than we usually left. He had a look on his face like he knew something I didn't but I had no idea what it could be. Perhaps my father had driven over from the city. He'd done that once before and he and my uncle had sat up drinking whiskey after I'd gone to bed. I'd listened to the rumble of their voices coming through the heating register and it had made me feel comfortable.

We passed the tables of drinkers on our way to the door. One of his cronies winked at me and said, "Buy that boy a beer, Bill," but he was only kidding. The drinking age was twenty-one. My father sometimes let me have a bottle of beer at Christmas or Easter but that was it.

We drove out of town and down the highway for a few miles, then turned onto the gravel road that went to the farm. It was dark and the stars were twinkling overhead, the moon a bright disc. Uncle Bill was tapping his fingers on the steering wheel but otherwise there was silence in the car. He said to me, "You playing hockey again this fall?"

"Yes," I said.

"Defence," he said, "right?"

"Right," I said.

"But you were the scoring champ, no?"

"That was two years ago," I said. "Last year Coach decided I was a natural defenceman. Now that I've grown."

"That's right," he said. "You're big for your age. You can take care of yourself, eh? No one pushes you around."

We drove in silence for a while. He rolled down his window and spat out. He took chaw, as he called it, chewing tobacco, which came in a round flat tin he carried in his shirt pocket and tucked under his tongue in a wad.

"That's a good thing," he added. "No one else takes care of you in this here life. That's a good lesson to learn. It's you out there, and you're by yourself. You come into this world alone and you die alone. Sometimes it seems you live most of the in-between on your own, too. It's good to remember that."

He was prone to these philosophical moments. There's a lot of time for private thoughts when you're behind the wheel of a tractor for seven or eight hours and he'd come to conclusions about life on his long trips up and down the dusty fields, conclusions he liked to share with me.

After a while he said, "I wish I had a flask tonight. By gum I wish I did." He laughed in a sardonic way, his mouth twisting like I'd never seen before. "But Nelly says no."

My mother told me that Aunt Nelly disapproved of his drinking hard liquor and she'd forbidden him to come home with whiskey on his breath. A few drinks at home with my father was okay, but no flask in the car. She was afraid of him getting hurt in a car crash.

"That's a turn of events," he added. "A real twisted turn, by gosh." He laughed wickedly again. I had no idea what he meant but I had the feeling he knew something he wanted to share with me but didn't quite know how.

Several miles from the farm my uncle rolled down his window and stuck his head partway out of the car. "By gum," he said. We drove a little farther and he pulled the car over onto the side of the road and shut off the engine. "I thought so," he said. "Roll your window down, son. Listen." I heard the ticking of the motor and frogs croaking in the ditches.

"It's the geese," my uncle said. "It's early for them, that's for sure."

There were sloughs on his acreage and the geese stopped there on their flight south. He was a hunter and he liked to shoot them in the fall. I'd been out with him and had fired one of his shotguns and killed my fair share, but I didn't like the experience much. Getting up in the cold before dawn, slogging through waist-high water in waders, hunkering behind a blind, which he had constructed for the purpose, shivering and drinking steamy cups of coffee. We'd been out shooting deer, too, with my father. Deer lived in the ten-and fifteen-acre stands of bush near the sloughs that were dotted over Uncle Bill's acreage. He and my father were both good with rifles. They'd grown up on farms shooting things and wanted me to learn. I did. He owned a pump-action Winchester and it was fun to shoot. I brought down one deer, a good-sized buck and was happy it pleased them, but they were more pleased about it than me. They knew that, I guess, because we only did that the once. I'd proved myself as a man in their eyes, and maybe in my own, but it was a dubious achievement since it brought me so little joy, an inert lump of blood-spattered fur which only moments earlier had been a magnificent creature bounding through the woods.

"We'll come out one of these days," he said to me. "Shoot us a few honkers."

I nodded. I was listening to the frogs and something else chirring in the grasses, but I could not hear the geese. The slight whiff of skunk was in the air.

"We'll shoot us a few honkers," he repeated. "Have ourselves a feast."

He was expert at butchering the geese we killed. He and his dogs gathered them up from the edges of the slough and the field where they'd fallen and he cut them up efficiently, taking the breasts and the legs only. Using a large hunting knife and working quickly, he could have the breasts and legs of twenty geese in a pile in half an hour. The rest he gave to the dogs.

He said without looking at me, "You'll be able to manage that, won't you?"

"I've got a tight schedule this fall," I said. I was straining to hear the geese.

"One day out of a whole school year," he said. "What teacher complains about one day?"

"There's a lot on my plate. What with hockey and all."

"We'll see," he said. "You never know. Maybe old Dick will come out in the sloughs one last time. He's a pretty handy shot, you know."

"That's right."

"So maybe we'll get out here. All three of us. Like that time."

"You never know."

"Yeah. We'll see."

We drove to the turn at the farm and then down the road to the farm. It was not composed of so much gravel as the municipal road and when it rained, the black gumbo made it difficult to drive on; when it had rained for a few days, nearly impassable. The headlights of the Buick picked out the pines around the farmyard, a shelter belt against the winter winds. Then came the willows around the house itself. My uncle stopped the car short of the house and the garage where he parked the Buick. The headlights picked out the granaries in the distance and the machine shed closer in, where we greased the tractors and made machine repairs on days when it rained. Near to the house sat a car I'd never seen before, a Mustang. In the headlights it looked sleek and low. It was red and it seemed to be shiny and new.

"Well, well," he said. "I thought as much."

He'd shut the car off but the Mustang was still visible in the glow thrown from the yard light on the machine shed.

Uncle Bill shifted around on the seat and brought out his chewing tobacco. He spat what he had under his tongue out the window and packed a little knot which he'd scooped out of the tin between his tongue and his cheek. He spat again, this time more through his teeth, a tsst that sounded angry, like an animal spitting before it struck out.

Uncle Bill said, "You don't smoke, do you son?"

"No sir," I said. I'd never even had a lit cigarette in my mouth. Though later in college I was to enjoy the occasional toke of marijuana and smoking hash in a pipe.

"Good," he said. "You stick to that."

"I intend to."

"That's right, you do that. You don't have to prove your manlihood to no one."

We sat in silence for a minute. There were bats circling around the yard light, maybe five or six. I watched them darting in and out of the golden halo and then disappearing into the dark, only to reappear again a moment later.

"This is another turn up," Uncle Bill said, nodding in the direction of the Mustang. "It seems it's a night of turn ups."

He laughed that sardonic way again. I was wishing we could go inside where I was looking forward to finishing a book I'd been reading and where the bed was big and warm.

"What I mean," he went on, "is that it was Nelly who made me give up smoking. Bad for me, she claimed." He laughed again. "You see what I mean?"

I didn't. The innuendo was thick in the car and it was beginning to upset my stomach. I sensed that whatever was about to happen had nothing to do with me but would involve me in a way I would not want. With school and hockey and girls there was lots on my plate already and I didn't need adult stuff added on. I made to open the door and step out but just then the big light over the back door of the house went on and in a moment my aunt appeared silhouetted in the doorway. She stood there with her hands at her sides and her head cocked to one side, like she was unsure it was us in the Buick.

"Well," my uncle said, "I guess there's nothing else for it." He sighed and spat out a thin stream of tobacco juice as he banged the car door behind him. The sound echoed around the farmyard. "Come on, son," he said, "sometimes you just have to face something you don't want to."

When we got to the door my aunt put her hand out toward my uncle but he brushed it aside and strode directly into the kitchen. I followed behind them. I smelled perfume on my aunt and sensed that she was trembling. A man was sitting at the kitchen table, his hands folded in front of him, an empty coffee cup to one side. He was younger than either my uncle or aunt, but not by much. He had rusty hair and a pleasant round face that reminded me of someone on TV, Hoss Cartwright came to mind, maybe because he was big in a beefy way, a solid man. He wore a blue-and-green-checked shirt with a button-down collar and his face looked freshly shaved. His eyes, which were hazel, went from my uncle to me to my aunt and then back to my uncle.

Uncle Bill looked directly at him. "You wait right there," he said, sharp and hard.

The man nodded. His fingers stayed locked together but he waggled his hands up and down on the table top. I looked at him but he did not seem to want to make eye contact. He was breathing regular but I could sense he was nervous.

My uncle and aunt went down the hallway into the back of the house, to their bedroom, I guessed. They were talking in low tones, short gun bursts of sound, one after the other. The man at the table looked at me and then away. I was standing near the sink and I ran a glass of water. It tasted of minerals but took away the thirst that had been building in my mouth for some time. I ran a second glass and stood holding it as I looked out the window.

I heard my aunt say, "Bill, that's just ridiculous."

There was the sound of a closet door banging and then she said, "You don't realize how."

He said something like *have to see.*

"Bill," she repeated, "you don't realize how ridiculous."

By then Uncle Bill was back in the kitchen. He was carrying a pistol, it was a small thing and it was dwarfed by his meaty hand. He sat down at the table across from the man.

He glared. "She says your name is what?"

"Ryan. Ryan Wright."

"Right for who?" my uncle sneered. He had silver fillings in his front teeth and in the light from the fixture above they glinted a dull metallic grey. That made him look old and seedy, like a villainous pirate in the movies. "My wife, it seems," he added.

Ryan Wright didn't say anything. I watched the pulse in the vein of his neck.

My uncle asked, "That your car out there? That Mustang?"

"Yes," Ryan said.

"Pretty fancy car."

Ryan said, "I guess." Maybe he was thinking, as I was, not as expensive as a Buick, but he held his tongue.

"Fancy car, fancy man," my uncle said. He was holding the pistol in one hand, with the barrel pointed in Ryan's direction, but not aimed at him. The handle was inlaid with shiny wood, like the panelling on the fancier models of station wagons. "You think you're a big shot because you drive that there car?"

"No," Ryan said flatly. "I do not think that."

"A big shot," my uncle said. "A big shot in a fancy car come round to make trouble."

"No," Ryan said. "Nothing like that."

"I bet," my uncle said. He lifted the pistol up and sighted along its barrel out the window, as if preparing to take a shot. Ryan didn't flinch. His eyes never left my uncle's. My father had told me once that if a man was going to shoot another man he'd do it in the first little bit. He had been in the war in Europe and had seen all kinds of killing. Sometimes soldiers killed their own, he told me. Knife fights over women or cards. A captain who rode the men in his battalion was shot dead out on maneuvers by one of his own men when he stood up in a jeep to survey the action through binoculars. I didn't know exactly what *the first little bit* meant, so I was unsure whether it had passed. I had no idea whether Uncle Bill was going to shoot Ryan in cold blood.

He placed the pistol on the table. It was a revolver with six chambers. "Pick it up," he said to Ryan. "Pick it up and put the barrel to your temple. Pull the trigger, mister big shot. Take a chance. Spin the barrel if you like. Pull the trigger. Maybe one of the chambers is empty."

I don't know where that came from. Maybe from my father. He'd seen all kinds of things in Italy, some so bad he never did tell me. Uncle Bill had not been in the war. He did not have to go because he was a farmer and they were needed to grow wheat and raise cattle for foodstuffs for the boys overseas. It wasn't a sore point between them that he'd ducked out of service, but it was a point, the same way my uncle being a prosperous farmer and my father's business having failed was a point between them, only in Uncle Bill's favour.

Ryan studied him for a long moment. I could hear his breathing, which was even and steady. The pulse in his neck was too. He studied my uncle and then the revolver but he did not pick it up. Out the window there was a light bulb and moths were banging against it and then fluttering down, then flickering back up to bunt the fixture again.

Aunt Nelly had come to stand in the doorway. She was wearing a navy blue skirt and a white blouse with a red and white tie sewn into the button-down collar. It flattered her. She'd put on lipstick. I saw that she had porcelain white skin and with her bright blue eyes and dark hair she was prettier than I had given her credit for. She had been underselling herself in the baggy jeans and old sweaters she wore around the farm yard.

My uncle said, "Maybe you'd like me to put the gun to my head?"

"No," Ryan said, "I do not want that."

"You want my wife though. You want to take her away in your big-shot car."

Ryan said, "It isn't that. She just asked—"

"Bill," my aunt said, "enough already. You have no idea what you're ."

My uncle ignored her. He picked the revolver up and pointed it straight at Ryan's head. The two men's eyes were locked together. I could hear the ticking of the refrigerator to my side, the deep sigh that came out of my aunt.

My father once said that if you point a gun at a man, you'd better be prepared to pull the trigger. Uncle Bill didn't know that. He had his revolver aimed at Ryan Wright but he was not going to shoot him, we all knew it by then, and now he was stuck with the gun out there and he seemed foolish.

My aunt let out a long breath but she did not move. She had her eyes on me. Her lips curled almost into a smile and she lifted her fingertips to them and then away from her mouth, as if she was blowing a kiss. It was a strange thing for her to do.

"I should shoot you," Uncle Bill finally said to Ryan. "Shoot you dead."

Ryan's shallow breathing was just audible.

"I should kill you, the both of you. But what would that prove?"

No one said anything. Ryan took several more breaths. I was thirsty again but I daren't take a drink. I swallowed hard and felt a knot in my throat. Out the window the biggest moth bumped against the light fixture and weaved away into the darkness. Six or so littler moths continued to bump at the light.

Uncle Bill dropped the gun to the table slowly. "You're in love, I suppose," he said.

"No," Ryan and my aunt said almost in the same breath.

My uncle looked only at Ryan. That seemed to satisfy him in some way, because he pushed the gun a little to the side. He said, "Where'd you get that? That there ring?"

Ryan glanced down at his hand. On the middle finger was a big ring with a blue stone and something written around it in script. "Football," he said and smiled. "I played a little pro. Long time ago now."

"Huh," my uncle grunted. "They teach you that in the locker room, do they, stealing other men's wives?"

"Bill," my aunt said again, "enough." The word was without emotion. I looked at her again. There was a faint hint of perfume coming off her and her cheeks were flushed. "You're scaring—" she said, "you're scaring the boy." I knew that wasn't true and she did too, she was only saying it to switch his mind from one place to another.

Uncle Bill turned and looked at her. She nodded over toward me.

My uncle looked at me as if he'd only just realized I'd been standing there all the time. His eyes were brown and they seemed at that moment to be glazed over and weary. He dropped his gaze to the table. "All right," he said. "All right then."

Nobody moved for a minute or so. While I'd been watching the moths, I was thinking the book I'd been reading, *Mandingo*, was a lot like what had been happening in the kitchen. The violence, the whole business about women and sex, and men fighting each other to the death. But I saw now it was not. The book was steamy and over-blown with high emotions that thrilled me in a way, and yet what was happening in the kitchen was ordinary but more frightening.

"We're going, then," Aunt Nelly said. She had her purse slung over her shoulder and a suitcase which she picked up off the floor.

Ryan stood up and pushed the chair under the table and walked to the door with her.

She turned there and said, "You take this boy to the hotel. I don't trust him here with you waving guns around and such." She looked at him hard and then at me.

My uncle said, "It was never loaded. I don't keep shells in that there revolver." He smiled a crooked smile, a hateful look that made me turn away. "I just wanted Mister Wright here to have a notion of how it feels for a man to have a gun to his head."

"Still," my aunt said.

"He's okay with me," my uncle said, an edge coming suddenly into his tone. "He's like my own son, for God's sake."

My aunt looked at me and raised her eyebrows.

"It's all right," I said. "We'll be okay."

She looked at me again and then crinkled her lips in a way that told us she was giving in despite her better judgment. She had other things on her plate.

"We'll be okay," I said again. I believed that. I believed nothing in the world could make my uncle turn on me. He loved me like a son and I thought that would protect me.

My uncle's eyes followed them, and when they walked out he sat looking at the revolver.

I went to the door and watched them walk to the Mustang and climb in. The headlights came on and the car swung backwards, splashing me with light momentarily, and then it glided out of the yard. The brake lights came on once as the Mustang went past the willows, and then it was gone. There was a smell on the air like wood smoke. The night was cooling, late August. Soon Uncle Bill would be busy night and day with the harvest. I would miss that because of school.

Inside, my uncle had poured himself a glass of water and was standing at the sink drinking it. He looked at me. "I'm sorry you had to see that," he said. His voice was shaky but his hand was steady.

I shrugged and picked up my water glass and drained it in one go.

"There wasn't any manliness in that," he said. "None whatsoever."

I nodded but didn't say anything. I was thinking it didn't matter, none of it mattered. He was concerned about what I thought but I knew he'd been right when he'd said before that everyone was on their own. We had our own private thoughts and our own way of looking at things and it really didn't matter what the next person thought or did. We went our own way. In a week or so I'd be going back to school. I might never see him again. Or my aunt. Or I might see them. It wouldn't matter, any more than what somebody else did on the hockey rink or in a class would matter. In a year I'd be leaving home for college and then my parents would be behind me and they wouldn't matter after a while either. I would make my own life and go my own way.

Uncle Bill said, "It's always you and you alone in this here life. Nothing else." He raised his eyebrows. "I said that before, didn't I?"

"Yes, sir. You did."

"Don't make anything of it. Just me talking to myself, is all. It's been an odd night."

"It has."

"You want a beer?"

I shrugged. "Why not?"

"You're thirsty," he said, "I can tell. I am too."

He opened two bottles for us and we stood drinking them on opposite sides of the room. The pistol was still in the middle of the table, beside the coffee cup. It didn't seem right to sit down with the pistol there.

Uncle Bill stood at the sink looking out the window for a few minutes, sipping his beer and tapping the fingers of the other hand on the countertop. After a while he said, "It's too bad, you know, when a person can't match up what they want with what the other person wants. That's all that matters in the end. That's what makes happiness in this here life. If you don't know that already, it's a good thing to learn right now." His back was turned toward me and his shoulders were straight and square.

In the long silence that followed we tipped our bottles to our lips. Then he added, "She said life here was too limited for her. She didn't want to live in such a simple way. I think that's what she said. Maybe it was *confined*."

I nodded over the top of my beer bottle.

"You understand?" he asked. "You understand that?"

"I think so," I said.

He had half turned but his gaze was not on mine. He was still looking out the window and blinking his eyes, like a man waking up and finding himself in a strange bed. "By gum," he said. "By gum but I do not understand it."

We stood like that until we finished our beers.

SUNRISE

At 5:30, an hour before sunrise, I heard a loud bang at the back door. I was at the front door, getting the *Free Press*, and I heard Peter muttering and clumping down the hallway and calling out, "Coming, coming." I looked out across the street toward the Duttons' house to the east but there was nothing unusual going on. Behind their place I could just detect in the twilight the hump of the granite hill that stood on the far verge of Reeve Road. The tops of pine trees growing on the granite hill formed a jagged backdrop, like sawteeth. This was my favourite part of the day, predawn stillness before the rest of the world was up and about. I felt mildly irritated that it had been intruded upon.

At the back door I heard Peter speaking quietly and then the sound of several sets of feet coming across the kitchen floor and down the hallway toward the dining room. I had taken the rocker near the door and was about to open the paper when Peter came in with Alex LaJoie just behind him. Alex was wearing a pair of work pants, the kind miners put on between the pit and home, a heavy, baggy cotton, and a soiled T-shirt. He must have been working the graveyard shift and come off early because I was going on the day shift but not for another hour and more. He looked at me. I don't think he recognized me.

I was about to say something, but he shifted his eyes and took the chair at the dining-room table across from Peter. His thick black hair was mussed up and he was blinking his eyes. When he was seated he glanced around the room, his gaze lighting only for a second on one thing and then moving immediately to another, agitated and anxious.

"They're dead, then?" Peter said, half a statement, half a question. "Both of them?"

I looked up from the paper. His voice was even and steady but I heard a warning to me in it, even though his back was to me. I studied the crown of his head where the hair was thinning and marvelled at this trick of his voice and thought of our mother, who could communicate more in her tone than in the words she spoke.

Alex nodded. He placed both hands on the tabletop and then moved them off and put them between his knees, under the table. He looked at Peter, then dropped his eyes. I let the paper rest in my lap and felt the surge of blood in my temples.

Peter sat forward, elbows on the table, his fingers interlocked. "You're sure?"

"They were laying on the floor," Alex said, insistent. "They weren't moving. Just laying there." His voice, which was low, trembled, but the words were distinct. I sat forward.

"And that was it?"

"I left there. I came here."

Peter shifted back in his chair and dug his pipe out of his pants pocket. There was silence in the room, though Alex was breathing heavily. I felt my heart thumping in my chest and took several deep breaths, something our father had taught us to do when we were agitated. In a moment Peter produced a wooden match and he lit it by scraping his thumbnail along the red tip sharply. It flared and he put it to the bowl of the pipe, never removing his eyes from Alex. Smoke curled up when he inhaled and I watched it snake toward the ceiling. A door opened and closed and I heard Patti come out of the bathroom and in a moment saw her flit past the doorway and go into the kitchen. She was wearing a housecoat and slippers and seemed in a hurry.

Peter puffed his pipe. "You came right here," he said. It was a statement, not a question.

"I dropped the knife and ran," Alex said, as if that explained everything about his sudden appearance at our door in pre-dawn twilight. He'd brought his hands up on top of the table again and the fingers were splayed out, as if he were going to start up on a piano. "A butcher knife," he said. "From the kitchen. I dropped it between them and ran out the door. Maybe it's still open." He blinked, thinking about this, and his fingers clawed at the tabletop, like a cat's paws. "There was this blood, see, on them, on the floor, everywhere. Blood. I meant to kill her, I meant that, but then the old lady started screaming and I thought she'd wake the kids and I'd always hated her anyways, so I grabbed her too, I let her have it too. Jesus. She was such a bitch." He stopped, taking this in, and then added, "That was not intended."

He gazed at me, as if recognizing me suddenly. "Donny," he said. He was Elie's brother and I knew him because we played on the Mine Kings and had travelled to Winnipeg in February to a tournament. He was a light drinker and after the games when we drank beer, he sat in the corner of the room, silently nursing one bottle while Freddy and Mike regaled us with various exploits from the past. I liked him. He could take a hard pass at centre and deflect shots in front of the net. I thought of him as the strong, silent type, but like everyone else in Red Rock had heard about Becky carrying on with Eddy Cox while he worked the graveyard shift. I'd felt sorry for him and had meant to talk to Elie about it but hadn't come around to it and for a moment I felt a twinge of guilt about that, as if I were responsible in some way for what had happened, as if talking to Elie could have prevented murder and mayhem.

I nodded back at him. The situation was delicate, I had no desire to excite him with idle chatter.

"Look," Alex said. He glanced down at his T-shirt. I saw then that what I had taken to be dirt smudges were blood stains, a large one toward the centre of the shirt and several smaller ones up toward the neck. Spatters. I looked at his hands. They'd been clamped to the edge of the tabletop but when I looked, he put them into his lap again. He seemed not to know what to do with them.

Peter studied them too. "Maybe you'd like some coffee," he said.

"Coffee? No. No coffee."

"Patti's in there fixing it," Peter said. He'd laid his pipe on the table near his elbow and he half turned toward me. "Donny and I were just about to have a cup, weren't we?"

Peter was my brother and had offered me a room in the basement when I'd moved to Red Rock to work underground and play for the Mine Kings. He was older than me, a plumber by trade, and he'd always looked out for me and I had tried to repay him by helping out when he was building the house they lived in, shovelling gravel and hauling wheelbarrows of dirt for the garden out back, which was Patti's special love. She grew tomatoes, which made wonderful sandwiches in the summer.

I placed my hands on the arms of the rocker, thinking I could help by going for the coffee, but Peter's voice stopped me. "Don't—" he said quietly but firmly, "—do that."

I eased back into the chair. The palms of my hands were sweaty. It was becoming warm in the room. When my body was settled back in the chair I studied Alex again. He was breathing more steady now. A vein in one temple was throbbing and there was a sheen of sweat on his upper lip, but he was not calm.

Peter said, "You don't smoke, do you?"

"No."

"That's good. A bad habit." He cleared his throat. "But a difficult one to kick."

His elbows were on the tabletop, with his arms forming a triangle in front of him, the apex of which was his interlocked fingers. This was a favourite position of his. He assumed it when he was explaining something. He talked slowly and quietly, turning words over carefully, and there were those in Red Rock who thought he was a little slow, but he was not. He was thorough. As a boy he'd cleaned his bedroom every Saturday morning, making piles of shirts and underwear from the wash and placing them neatly into drawers. My own clothing formed a heap on my bedroom floor, through which I dug for a shirt when I got up every day. I had seen him sitting this way with Sherry, explaining how the sun rose and set, a tricky idea for a child to understand. But he knew about the rotation of the planets and the earth's axes, and at the end of his methodical explanation, Sherry seemed to comprehend. I recall that I learned a bit too.

I thought then that Peter's slow ways were the reason Alex had bolted to our place after he had knifed his wife and mother-in-law to death. Where do you go after you've done that sort of thing, blood spattered on your clothes, half mad with rage and grief? A church? A priest might help. One kind of man would need solace, another to be forgiven. Maybe another kind yet jumped into his car and drove it over a cliff. I wondered which was better. Peter and I had talked about suicide one time over a glass of whiskey. He said that taking your own life was the coward's way out but I wasn't so sure. It would be a difficult thing to hold a pistol in your mouth or steer the car into a rock face. I wasn't sure stabbing your cheating wife was cowardly either, though I believed it was something I would never do. The one thing I knew for certain was that it was not easy to put yourself into another man's shoes and say what you might do in the abstract, so to speak. You had to actually live through his experience to say that with conviction.

I noticed my shadow was visible on the floor. The bay window, which faced east, was behind me and the faint outline of my form was on the hardwood.

Peter said, "You have the two kids, right?"

Alex looked up. "Guy," he said softly, "who's four, and little Michelle."

"Right."

"Oh, God." Alex blew out his cheeks and ran one hand back through his hair. "The kids. I forgot about them."

His shifted in the chair and it seemed he might leap up and bolt out the door, but Peter said sharply, "And they were—"

"They were sleeping," Alex said. "Their room is down the hall. God, that door was open."

Peter nodded and sucked on his pipe. One foot was tapping the floor. I had the feeling he was getting ready to ask another question but didn't know quite how to frame it.

At the mention of the children, Patti appeared in the doorway. She was holding her housecoat closed with one hand and had the other on the door frame. Peter was facing her and he tipped his head slightly, a signal to keep silent. "Here's Patti," he said, "she's going to bring in the coffee now." He tipped his head again toward the kitchen. Patti stepped back but remained framed in the doorway. She was peering at us hard and I realized she didn't have her glasses.

Peter said, "You were saying about the children."

"Michelle and Guy," Patti said. Her voice was as sharp as a bicycle bell in the room and it startled all three of us.

Alex turned sharply toward her, as if she'd jerked a string attached to the back of his head, his eyes wild. Peter drew in a breath. I felt the hairs on the back of my neck stand up. Patti took a half step backward, mouth open.

"What about them?" Alex's voice rose sharply.

"I was just—" Patti had raised her free hand to her forehead, as if she meant to push back a lock of hair.

"What about them?"

"Nothing. I just—"

"They're all right," Alex shouted, "the kids are all right. Didn't you hear me, woman?" He stood suddenly, knocking over his chair. Peter's pipe rolled off the table onto the hardwood floor. Alex's throat was red and his Adam's apple bobbed above the neckline of the T-shirt. He took a step toward Patti. "What are you saying?" he shouted.

"Alex," Patti said.

"What are you saying?" Alex blinked his eyes.

"Peter," Patti said. "For God's sake." Her eyes had bugged out and there was a shrillness to her voice, something I had never heard before. She was frightened that she had provoked violence that might turn on her the way it had turned on Becky and Mrs Malmot. Patti was not used to that, the ways of men, and it scared her.

"Patti's getting the coffee now," Peter said. There was a tremor in his voice. "From the kitchen, Patti. Now."

Alex was glaring at her. He raised one hand and pointed his finger at her. It was smeared with blood, from the nail down to the wrist, where it had dried into the shape of a jagged knife blade. "I said they're sleeping," Alex shouted. "Did you think I meant sleeping with God? Did you think I'd murder my own kids?"

"Peter," Patti said again, almost a whimper. Backing up, she was bumping her shoulder on the door frame.

"My God," Alex screamed, "my God, Patti."

I felt my face heating up.

"Easy now," Peter said. He had not moved from his sitting position. But I was standing, the *Free Press* dangling from one hand. I dropped it onto the chair. I sensed that the calm that Peter had been maintaining in the room was about to break. I had no idea what would happen but I knew I had to be prepared. I did a mental calculation of the steps across to Patti and what might be necessary once I got there. I had seen men scrap in the alley behind the Rockland

Hotel and once Jimmy Salvatore had taken a shovel to Bobby MacKenzie in the pit and Big Ned Johnson had had to step in between them and had taken four stitches to the skull for his trouble. Later he had told me you never try to grab a man's head, you always go for his ribs and squeeze hard until he faints out of breath. He'd been in the paratroopers and I thought he must know. He'd told me too that you always had to go at your man as hard as you could, get him down and don't let up until you saw that he was beat. I was thinking about that, getting up the resolve to act on it.

"What do you take me for?" Alex shouted. He moved forward and banged one hand on the wall nearest to him, a few feet from Patti's face. The plaque on it rattled against the plasterboard. It looked like it might fall off and Patti studied it hard. Her face was ashen. I was thinking that she was wishing herself far away, which was what I had been thinking only a moment before, warm under the covers at Elie's place.

"They're my kids," Alex wailed, "my babies. Patti! How could you think?"

Patti had thrown both hands up. She was pretty, a slender brunette, but her face was puffy at that moment, and red.

"Patti!" It was a wail, the kind of cry an animal makes when cornered. Peter stood up then and stepped around the end of the table, placing himself between Alex and Patti. "Go fetch that coffee," he said to her sharply, a tone I'd never heard between them before.

She was wide-eyed and still clutching the neck of her housecoat tightly in one hand, but she stepped back toward the kitchen and in a moment I heard her being sick over the sink.

It was a Friday and on Fridays at the end of day-shift we got in our cars and drove to the Rockland and drank beer before moving on to the Rainy Lake for steak dinner or pickerel and fries. That's when the wives and girlfriends joined us, and I always felt a little surge in my chest when Elie came through the door, her dark hair swaying on her shoulders and a bright smile on her lips. That seemed a long way away and I felt again a twinge of irritation and resentment toward

Alex. I realized how foolish it was, given what was happening, but I felt it and there's no getting around it.

Alex was standing in the centre of the room with both hands over his eyes, as if trying to block out a bad sight. It was all coming clear to him then, the horrible road he would have to go down. Police, a trial, jail. The thought of a trial unnerved me. What if we were accused of being accomplices? At the very least there would be cops and reporters crawling over the town, besmirching Red Rock's reputation. It was not uncommon to hear mining towns referred to as hellholes and for miners to be depicted as brutes and fools. There would be photographers and radio crews with microphones, a real circus, but all of it bad, the kind of stuff that drives wedges between neighbours and leads to hard feelings.

"Patti," Alex said in a quiet, pleading voice, craning his head toward the kitchen, where the sounds of her being sick had not ended. "Patti, please." He was trembling and though the wildness had gone out of him, he was as agitated as a cornered animal, and there was no way of knowing what he might do next.

Peter stepped toward him, one hand out, as if he were about to take his wrist.

"I'll run for it," Alex said suddenly, his voice high and bright. He looked around, his eyes darting here and there and settling on me for a second. They were dark eyes, almost black in early dawn light, and sunk back in the sockets and rolling about crazily. "There's gas in the car," he went on, turning toward Peter, "and you can cross the border into the States at the Fort. It's just an hour away."

"That's a bad idea," Peter said. He wanted to say more and he had his mouth open but the words would not come. But the look in his eye told me he knew more than he was saying.

"Cross the border and keep driving south until I hit Chicago or somewhere. St Louis."

"They'd catch up to you," Peter said. He had put his hand on Alex's forearm.

Alex shook it off and went on as if he hadn't heard him. "I gotta go now," he said firmly, glancing around as if he might be forgetting something, "gotta go now. There's gas in the Chevy and you cross the border and they can't bring you back. It's against the law, you're out of their, out of their—"

The word *reach* was on my lips.

"No," Peter said. "They'll catch up to you and it will look bad for you then, really bad."

"They can't bring you back. You hire a lawyer and he, and they—"

"You'd be fleeing the scene." Peter put his hand out again and rested it on Alex's arm.

Patti reappeared at the door. She looked at Peter and nodded her head. He nodded back and she stared at me hard, her eyes sliding back toward the kitchen. Her lips moved but I could not make out the words, only that she was trying to tell me something other than to keep quiet.

Alex was insistent, his voice rising as he spoke. "There was that banker in Toronto. He went to New York and they couldn't bring him back." His eyes flashed from Peter to me and back to Peter, a look of satisfaction on his face. We'd all read the headlines in the newspapers and had followed the business on the radio. Alex's voice was filled with satisfaction. "They could not make him. He was out of their jurisdiction. He was free."

"That was about money," Peter said. "And this is not about money, this is about …" He paused, not wanting to go on. He was waiting for Alex to do or say something he could contradict, rather than continue his train of thought. He could not utter the word.

"The rich always get away." I hadn't meant to speak and was as surprised as anyone in the room to realize I had. I gulped then and swallowed and studied the picture on the wall over the couch, a winter scene with bare trees and a path in the snow.

"They won't get me," Alex continued, his voice rising. Maybe he hadn't even heard me. "They won't take me alive." He was twisting, trying to shake free of Peter's grip.

"This is crazy talk," Peter said. "You're both talking foolishness." He looked over his shoulder at me. There was a question in his face but I couldn't read it. He didn't know what to do but he couldn't let Alex go, that much was clear. He wanted me to say or do something but I couldn't guess what and I've never been good at thinking on my feet.

"Let me go!"

Alex tugged his arm violently and tried to pull away from Peter but Peter would not let go. They tugged and pulled this way and that. In a moment their faces were red from exertion. Peter was taller and heavier but Alex was filled with fury and desperation and that made it an even struggle. They were both breathing hard. I felt the impulse to intervene but that seemed a bad idea. They were struggling to a stalemate and that was better than either getting the upper hand. I'd seen that in back alley scraps where men clutched each other's shoulders, lurching sideways, and breathed heavily into each other's faces until they both stepped back and that was a better solution than the times one got the other down and kicked at him until someone had to step in between them. They had both been grunting hard but Alex suddenly went still and said in a strained voice, "You called the cops, didn't you?"

Either the effort of speaking or the meaning of what he'd just realized seemed to take the fight out of him. He sighed heavily and staggered backwards. Peter kept his hands on his shoulders and duck-walked him until he was propped against the wall. Their eyes were fixed on each other. Peter said, "We had to." He let go of Alex's shoulders and kept his gaze fixed to his face but his lips were curled down in a puzzled grimace. He believed in standing behind friends and doing the right thing and was not a man to turn against another man lightly. I felt at that moment how much better a man he was than me, but I didn't resent it, I was proud to be his brother.

"And the cops are on the way?" Alex's voice cracked.

"Duncan will be here any moment."

Alex slid down the wall, landing on the floor with a thump. He moaned and shook his head once, like he was trying to clear it. His legs stuck out straight in front of him. "She was a bitch," he said with finality. "Becky." He was looking at his boots, which he hadn't taken off on the way home from the mine. Like everything in Red Rock, they were stained deep rust from iron, though they were not muddy. It had been a dry spring. "She was," he went on, "she was a little bitch. You know that. Everybody does. I knew about her and Eddy Cox for a long time and I thought it would go away, I thought it would just stop and we could go back to how it was before but that didn't happen and I knew people all over town were talking and the guys in the pit laughing behind my back, but I would look into her eyes and I could hardly believe it was true. She was doing all that behind my back and I loved her. Do you see that? Donny?"

I was surprised he addressed me and for a moment I thought I hadn't heard right, but he was looking directly into my eyes. I realized it was because of me that he had come to the house. We were teammates and I was his sister's guy. It wasn't Peter's thoughtfulness he'd come for but the fellow-feeling that he sensed between us in the hockey locker room. He seemed to want something from me. It was impossible to say what.

What I could say is that I felt that in speaking I'd betrayed Peter somehow, sided with Alex against him, and that was not what I'd intended, but I saw that loyalties could suddenly shift between people in ways they'd never expected, and that such abrupt shifts might alter everything between them, whatever they'd intended. It was as if my whole world shifted the tiniest bit in that moment, not spectacularly but importantly, and I told myself this was something I'd have to be wary of in the future.

Peter cleared his throat.

Alex coughed into his hand.

I wanted to say something but didn't know how to begin. I wanted to tell him there was a way out but all I could think was I was glad I was not him and that when the day ended I could be with my girl Elie and not wherever he would find himself.

Alex dropped his head. His dark hair fell forward into his face. "We married too young," he said. "She did." There was silence in the room. Saliva had formed at the corner of Alex's mouth, making him look like a rabid dog. I felt my heart thumping in my chest and looked at Patti and thought about her fear when dialling the numbers to the police station. The phone was in the kitchen near the back door and sometimes when Elie and I were talking I dragged the long cord out to the back step and closed the door for privacy. Alex wiped one hand over his mouth and then was talking in a quiet voice, more to himself than to us, it was clear, going over the ground, trying to understand what had happened to him. "She was pregnant right out of school and never had a chance to be a little wild. It caught up to her. Us. I tried to see it that way, what went on with Eddy Cox, I tried to forgive her, I'm a Catholic, you know, we both are, but there was her mother picking away at us, picking away at me, all the time, picking, such a stupid old woman." He looked up. "If it hadn't been for her," he said. "If that old woman just hadn't."

Sherry had come in from her bedroom, rubbing sleep from her eyes. She was wearing the pajamas I had given her, blue with brown bunnies. "Caesar was barking," she said. He was the neighbour's dog and he sometimes started up just at dawn.

"Come with me," Patti said, taking her hand. And she led her into the kitchen

"Caesar woke me up," Sherry was saying. "What's going on, Mommy?"

Patti said something I could not make out. I was thinking of Alex's children, asleep in their beds with two bloody bodies and a knife lying in another room. I prayed they would not wake up and stumble onto that scene. Maybe a neighbor had gone over to the house, maybe the police had sent someone to fetch them. Maybe Elie. She would be frightened but she was their aunt and she took them swimming and out for picnics and she would be a comfort to them. Maybe she would have to care for them now. I pictured her with them and had a nice feeling. She would know what to do. She was strong and she was steady. We hadn't talked about marriage but it came to me then that it was not a bad idea. I would tell her that, tell her soon.

The sound of a car pulling up outside was immediately followed by a door slamming and the clump of boots on the front step. I turned. Cal Duncan did not bother knocking. He came straight through the door, one hand on the top of his holster. His eyes flashed this way and that and he was surprised to see us standing quietly in a circle, Alex on his feet too.

"Easy now," Peter said, stepping forward. "He's calm, he's just—"

Duncan had a round fleshy face and was built like a bull and he pushed past him and shoved Alex roughly toward the wall and then grabbed him by the hands and whipped out a pair of handcuffs and clicked them over his wrists. "Right," he said loudly.

"For God's sake," Peter said. "The man is not a threat, you don't."

Duncan wheeled on him. "You're out of it. You've interfered enough already. Consider yourself lucky I don't." His face was aflame as he shouted and I saw Peter take in a sharp breath and felt myself do so too. Duncan jerked at Alex's wrists and began pulling him toward the door. The heat of his body seemed to fill the room. "This one," he said, shifting positions and shoving Alex in front of him roughly, "this one is for the slammer now. The chair, if it was just me."

"For God's sake," Peter said again. He had followed Duncan toward the door and his voice rose with each word. His fists were clenched at his sides.

"Don't come in the way of the law here," Duncan shouted. "Don't obstruct justice."

"For God's sake," Peter said. "It's my house, can you at least ."
He sounded at the end of his rope and I knew the feeling. My knees
were rubbery and I reached out to the rocker to steady myself.

At the door Duncan turned toward him, beady eyes ablaze.
"Who do you think you are?" he shouted. "This man is a fugitive and
you've been harbouring him. A murderer. What are you playing at
here, a plumber and a miner? You're lucky I'm not taking you in as
well." His face was red and when he finished speaking the vein that
ran down to his neck from his jaw leapt with each heartbeat.

"Get out," Peter said quietly.

"You're a meddler," Duncan said. "Don't think I haven't taken
note of that."

"And you're a disgrace to that uniform." I had heard Peter say
this before. Duncan had been thrown out of the army and was a bully
in his opinion and should never have been hired by the town to enforce the peace. Peter was generally calm, but once his temper was
up, it got the better of him and he was not easy to stop. I held my
breath. The two of them stared at each other and for a moment it
seemed they might take things one step further but it was only a
stare-down, the moment passed and there was a tense silence in the
room, the sound of heavy breathing and the throb of anger. Neither
man blinked.

Alex cleared his throat loudly. There was a glaze in his eyes but
he had recovered himself and his voice was quiet. "You're not to
blame," he said to Peter. "You did the right thing."

I wondered if he would ever be able to say that of himself . Maybe there would be times when he thought about his children that he
would be able to say, At least I spared them the stabbing, the deaths.
Whatever. It was a terrible thing that he had done and a terrible
place that he was going to. I wondered if I would ever see him again.
I wondered if his motherless children would. And it occurred to me
that everything in their lives had changed and they had had nothing to do with it. Not one thing. They were powerless to stop what

had happened and powerless to change what was going to happen to them. But children are strong, much stronger than we acknowledge, and they would go on and make lives despite what had happened. Maybe even be happy and have children of their own.

I studied Alex and tried to fix what he looked like at that moment and what I thought of him so that I would be able to answer those questions when the time came. In a courtroom, say. He was not an evil man, but he had done an awful thing. There would be many who could never forgive him. Could he forgive himself? It seemed to me too that most of what had happened to him was the kind of bad luck that can fall on anyone, like an auto accident or getting cancer, but that what made the difference between him and a man like Peter was how he dealt with the bad luck, which was in a person's character, and I hoped that I would have the character to face up to troubles when they came my way, which they were sure to do. Mostly I just wanted to draw deep breaths and read the paper for a while and let my mind rest and my heartbeat drop to where it wasn't burning my throat. I wanted to be with Elie and to forget the bad things and move on into a life that was uncluttered by troubles. Free of troubles and running on smooth as a train at night.

Alex wrenched sideways at the door and fixed us with his eyes and said again, "You did the right thing."

Duncan huffed and tugged them both through the doorway and out to the cruiser car. When it had pulled away, Patti came to stand beside Peter. Sherry was holding her hand and Peter put his arm out and pulled Patti into his shoulder. "What a creep," she said. Peter grunted. After a moment she added, "Those poor kids." We were looking out the window at the house across the street. The sun was just beginning to come over the granite hill, spreading a deep orange into the sky above and purples down the horizon.

WEDDINGS ARE A SMILE

At least I once thought so.

My cousin Miriam's occurred in the fall, late August. My father had driven our family to a little town near the US border and we had booked into the motel on the outskirts. The wedding had been in the Lutheran church and the sun had shone on the smiling couple as they came down the steps after the ceremony while friends and relatives tossed confetti at them. Afterwards a guy my father had introduced me to on the church steps earlier named Ricco came up to me. His girl was in the wedding party, one of three bridesmaids wearing pink dresses and sporting pink bows in their hair. Leona, he told me, one of the other bridesmaids, was without a date for the night. Would I like to be her date? His own girl, Cindy, thought the four of us could kind of hang out together at the reception and whatnot. They were all older than me by a couple of years but I didn't hesitate. I was up for a little partying.

Leona was thin with russet red hair and bright green eyes. Back at Uncle Len's house we sat beside each other on the sofa after the bridesmaids had taken off their shoes and rubbed their feet. Leona's hair smelled of hairspray and she was wearing a perfume that reminded me of lilies. Uncle Len looked dazed when he came into the living room carrying four beers, which he offered around, even though we were all under age. Leona took one and, after she'd had a big swig, passed it to me. There was kibitzing and smart remarks for a while among the wedding party and then Leona poked me in the ribs and said, "C'mon with me to the can, I want to show you something."

We bumped our way past knees and outstretched feet into the bathroom. Leona closed the door behind us. "God," she said looking down at her dress, "what a monkey suit! The things women aren't made to do." She lifted her skirt and fumbled around underneath and pulled off her underpants. "Christ," she said, hopping from one foot to the other, "what a relief." She tossed them into the tub. "That's for later," she added with a laugh. She threw her arms around my neck and started kissing me, big wet kisses with her tongue in my mouth. When she paused for a breath, she said, "I want to lay you later and I don't want those things in the way, Charlie. Charlie," she repeated, "right?" Before I could answer, she started kissing me again, her fingers clutching the hair on the back of my neck and her crotch rubbing hard against mine. Grunting and moaning.

Just then there was a knock on the door and Aunt Tilly came in without waiting for a response. "Oh, ho," she said, raising her eyebrows. "Ex-cuse me." She laughed and grabbed a handful of Kleenex and retreated, chuckling softly.

"You didn't see nothing," Leona called after her. "Remember that."

Aunt Tilly laughed all the way down the hallway.

I was blushing. I felt hot all over. "I guess we better get back to the rest."

Leona pushed herself hard up against me again. I smelled

hairspray and turned my face away. "Just a taste, Charlie," she said. "The main meal's later."

At the Union Hall the bride and groom were at the head table. Only the best man and the maid of honour got to sit with them, along with the two sets of parents and the pastor, who said grace and blessed the couple. My father gave the toast to the bride. When she stood up to respond, Miriam smoothed the front of her white dress with both hands. The slope of her enlarged belly was noticeable. Leona poked me in the ribs. "Shit," she whispered into my ear. "Miriam was always an idiot. Sorry," she added right away, "forgot. Your cousin."

"No big deal. We're not that close."

Leona wrinkled her nose. "That's a relief."

"She looks happy," I said.

"What a fool."

I didn't know whether she meant Miriam or me. I watched my cousin closely. She was smiling and nodding at everyone's jokes and interruptions but Leona was right, behind the smiles were eyes with resignation in them, tired eyes, shoulders that sagged when she sat down heavily beside her new husband and listened to his speech about what a lucky man he was. Leona grunted at the things he said and blew out her breath when he was done.

"What a pile of crap," she whispered.

I studied the groom. He was short and had thinning blond hair. He did the books at all three service stations in town and was studying at nights to earn an accountant's certificate. My father said he'd made a down payment on a bungalow in town and was talking about building a cottage at Finger Lake.

"It's over," Leona was saying. "Bloody hell, another one down."

I looked at her and raised my eyebrows.

"Miriam," she said, "Christ, Charlie, try to keep up."

I gazed at Miriam and wondered what it would be like to be

having a baby. It would be good in one way—new life, a little creature to care for and mould. But scary, too. All that responsibility. A future in your hands. Not to mention the way it changed your life. No more late nights. But up all night. I looked at Leona. "You mean ..."

"I mean down on the floors with a·wash rag and fixing bacon and eggs the way his mother did and doing laundry day and night and getting red hands and a big ass and ... I mean marriage."

"Wow," I said, "you really think—"

"You think she's happy? Kiddo, how old are you anyways?"

The beers I'd had at Uncle Len's had gone to my head. I looked into Leona's green eyes. They were blazing. She leaned in closer to me to whisper. I could smell the faint odour of beer on her breath. "Listen," she said. "Listen, Charlie. You're a man, you have no idea. There's no getting out for her. It's the house and the mortgage and the car payments and the parent-teacher crap and up the stump again and nothing to look forward to but fat old age. Zippo. She's not even twenty, for Christ's sake. And that blockhead she's gone and married ..."

Her voice had risen. My mother looked over from their table and shook her head.

"Christ," Leona whispered to me. "Sorry."

Is that what Miriam thought? She played the flute and had been on the volleyball team that had travelled to Vancouver. We'd been in school together. Up to that point things had seemed straightforward to me. Life is all about possibility. You want something, it's there for the taking. My older sister had made a trip to Winnipeg that had been organized for pretty girls who were interested in becoming stewardesses. My pal John and I were talking about flying to Amsterdam on Icelandic Air and then backpacking around Europe after we graduated and before we went to college. I was aware that life might present bottlenecks that could frustrate and anger you, but I was pretty certain that it wouldn't happen to me. My younger sister often said that I got away with stuff she could never dream of doing. A cousin on the West Coast had a son who had Down's syndrome, one of my uncles had had his foot cut off in a farm accident, a guy on the hockey team had been blinded in one eye by an errant shot. These were folks who had been sailing along, eyes on a bright future, sunny prospects, but then something fell on top of them out of nowhere and tangled them up in these disasters and tragedies, a kind of web they couldn't shake free of. *Up the stump*, Leona had said. Miriam's future was plotted out for her, and it was not a happy scenario for her. Or for Leona, it seemed.

When the toasting and tinking of wine glasses and eating and drinking wine and toasting and tinking of cups and laughing were over, the tables were pushed to the edges of the Union Hall floor and the band set up on the stage up front. They started with "Tennessee Waltz" and "Que Sera, Sera," but soon were doing Elvis and Fats Domino. Leona dragged me onto the floor. She was a bundle of energy and she danced a wild jive, whipping us both around. The skirts of her dress flew up, her hair flew into her eyes. "Jailhouse Rock." When "Whole Lotta Shakin' Goin' On" came on, Leona threw both arms in the air and danced away from me, then came rushing back, pounding her feet on the hardwood floor so they made a loud thumping sound. Heads around the hall turned our way and mothers tut-tutted. She looked around. "The hell," she called out to me over the music. "The hell with them, Charlie!" I was sweating trying to keep up to her. I stepped over to the table where I'd put down my bottle of beer and hung my jacket on the back of a chair. I caught my father's eye. He was sitting at a nearby table with two of his old friends and they were smiling and laughing at me. The band switched to "Love Me Tender." I wasn't much of a waltzer. I had won the scoring championship the year previous in the NorthWest hockey league but my skill was all in my hands. My father said, *You could stick handle out of a phone booth, Charlie.* But on the dance floor my feet seemed out of touch with my brain. That didn't matter to Leona. She hugged me close, her small breasts pressing against my chest. She hummed along to the music, eyes closed, hands locked behind my neck. The heat of her small body was on mine. I was becoming uncomfortable in the crotch area. She looked up at me and laughed. "Later, big boy," she whispered and laughed again. But she didn't stop rubbing her crotch into mine.

We went outside. Ricco needed a smoke and the fresh air was welcome. Cindy and Leona went to the Ladies' and Ricco and I stood on the steps of the hall. Up above, the moon was bright. The breeze felt chill on my damp shirt. "It's going okay?" Ricco asked. "With Leona?"

"Yeah," I said. "She's a nice girl."

"She's a wildcat," he said. "I'd take a run at her myself if it weren't for I got my own gal." Ricco had thick dark hair in the ducktail style, lots of Brylcreem, and he had a habit of smoothing the section over his ears back with both hands.

"She's got a boyfriend," I said, "she tells me."

"Had," Ricco said, blowing smoke out of his nose. "Had, before he dumped her and took off to Regina. Or was it Calgary? Can't remember. She's kind of sore about it."

"So, no boyfriend?"

"Far as I know. She's one hot little number, though. A little crazy in the head, but on the rebound, if you catch my drift."

"I don't want to make no trouble."

"Don't worry about that. I'd say she's looking to make a point right now."

"Huh," I said. The sound of geese flying overhead distracted us for a moment.

Ricco studied me through narrowed eyes. "You know how women can be. Getting back at one guy by going with another." He blew smoke into the air, then laughed and shook his wrist out of his shirt cuff and said, "Just about time for us to take a little drive."

When the girls came back out we went to Ricco's car, a new red Ford, and Leona and I got in the back seat. Cindy sat right up against Ricco's shoulder up front and fiddled with the radio. Static, waves of music that filled the car's interior and then suddenly dropped off, leaving a shrill silence. Leona slid across the seat to me and put her hand on my thigh. It jerked when she squeezed my knee. "You're nervous," she said. "That's cute."

Cindy looked into the back seat. "You kids okay back there?"

Leona said, "Never better."

"Good," Cindy said. "We want you to be friends. Charlie?"

"We're doing okay."

"We're gonna be good friends, young Charlie and me," Leona said, chuckling. "Don't you worry about us."

Cindy laughed. "That's good then. You kids just do that."

We drove through town and out to the gravel pit. Leona hummed along to the music and stroked the inside of my leg. At times she sang softly to herself: *Leona's gonna get lay-yed.* And then she laughed softly and poked me in the ribs. The car headlights splashed on the walls of the gravel pit and then into the recess at the bottom. There were two other cars parked there, windows steamed up. Ricco stopped the car and put his arm around Cindy and moments later they were locked together.

"C'mere," said Leona, and she put her hands on my cheeks and began to kiss me. In a moment one of her hands went to the back of my head and the fingers of the other were stroking my chest. "Rub my tits," she whispered. Up front there was shuffling on the seat and repositioning of bodies and then I heard Cindy call, "Oh!" and I could see the hump of Ricco's back going up and down. Leona lay back and pulled me on top of her and hoisted up her skirt. Her fingers were on my belt buckle. "First," she whispered, "you have to put on this. Then fuck me, Charlie, fuck me, fuck me hard."

On the drive back to town Ricco opened a bottle of beer with his teeth and then passed it around. My mouth was dry. My heart thumped in my chest and my brain was cloudy from drink.

Cindy shook out her hair and sighed. "You kids okay back there?"

"Never better," Leona said. She took a swig of beer and passed the bottle to me and I took a swallow and passed it back up front.

Ricco said, "I like weddings. You, Charlie?"

"They're a smile."

"That's right," Ricco said. "A smile."

We came to the town and streetlights shone into the car and I saw that Leona had a smile on her face. When she realized I was looking at her, she turned in my direction and winked at me. Cindy turned up the radio. It was Jimmy Rogers singing "Honeycomb."

Ricco laughed and said, "I like bridesmaids. They're horny." He'd lit up a cigarette and blew smoke toward Cindy's face. "Right, bridesmaid?"

"Shuddup," she said. She punched him in the shoulder.

"Your turn next," Ricco sang out. "Your turn's a-coming, baby." He puffed a ring of smoke at her.

Cindy shoved his shoulder with both hands and the car swerved across the centre line but Ricco brought it back under control before it hit the far curb. "Easy girl," he said.

Cindy laughed. "It's good to see you a little bothered." She put both hands in his hair and ruffled it up and laughed. "Bothered but not hot."

"Hey," Ricco said. His voice had an edge of anger in it.

"Oh, Ricco's upset," Cindy cooed. "Well, well."

"That's enough now," he said, smoothing his hair back into place with his free hand. Cindy made to help him but he pushed her hand away.

"Don't be upset," Cindy cooed. "C'mon now, what's young Charlie here going to think—you getting testy and all?"

"All right," Ricco said, "I'm all right now. It's just my hair. You know?"

After a bit they both laughed.

We got out of the car in the parking lot at the Union Hall. Leona and Cindy straightened their dresses and Ricco chucked his cigarette away and smoothed his ducktail. He and Cindy headed into the hall but Leona took me by the hand and led me in the direction of the bridge that ran over the river in the centre of town. We strolled over there holding hands and stopped halfway across and rested our elbows on the railing and looked down at the water. A night bird was calling softly. Ripples of waves slapped against the river bank. I gave Leona's hand a squeeze. It was a small hand with thin but warm fingers. She squeezed back.

"That wasn't much," she said.

"No. Sorry."

"It wasn't you." She snorted, then laughed softly. "That was my first time."

"Me too."

She squeezed my fingers lightly. "Next time," she said, "we'll both do better. Coach will be proud."

We both laughed then. We watched the water dancing below in the moonlight. She had a flask in her hand. I don't know where it came from or where it was while we were in the car. It was the smallest flask I'd ever seen, smaller than a mickey bottle but bigger than the bottles my father brought back from planes. Halfway in between. She opened it and took a swallow, then passed it to me. It was whiskey and its sharp burn took away my breath.

After we'd sucked in the night air for a moment, she said, "Poor Miriam."

"Her big day, I heard her say. She and—"

"Jesus. Her life is over and she knows it. Big day! Hardly. But I understand why you might think it. It's because we're good at that, we girls, smiling on the outside while we're busting up in here." She thumped her chest.

I didn't say anything. I watched the moon on the water.

"That's not happening to me," she said finally. "Up the stump. It doesn't have to happen. See? You can get fixed up with a coil, you can make the guy wear a safe. You can't let yourself get caught, is the point."

"I guess." I exhaled and thought about the amount of booze I'd consumed. Too much.

She squeezed my hand hard. "You think a girl shouldn't say things like that? You think I'm a kook? Ricco does. Looney Leona. Only good for one thing."

"No. You're nice. I like you, you're—"

"Christ, Charlie. You're not much good at that, you know? Lying."

"But—"

"Look, Charlie, you don't have to be kind to everyone, but you have to get better at being untruthful. Otherwise this shitty world is gonna eat you alive."

I gazed up at the sky. It was clear. Bright stars, a big shimmering moon. Hockey season was coming. On the air was the smell of wood smoke.

Leona sighed. "What I'm saying is girls can have fun too, but they have to be careful. We have to look out for ourselves. You guys sure aren't. Look at the blockhead Miriam's gone and hitched herself up to. Jesus. Didn't even use a safe, didn't think to ..."

"But sometimes there's the heat of passion."

"Piss on that. *Passion*. How old are you anyways?"

She held the flask up to the moon but brought it back down without taking a drink. We drummed our fingers on the railing. The night was beginning to be chilly, I could almost detect ghosts of breath when I exhaled.

Cars went by behind us. Occasionally headlights splashed on the far bank of the river where there was a low building with a tall stack. I listened to Leona's breathing and felt my pulse hammering in my temples. It was all that booze.

"We all end up like that," she said after a while. "You know?"

I grunted. I wasn't sure what she meant.

"Up the stump. Two or three kids hanging onto the hem of our dress. Cooking eight thousand meals a year for a man who doesn't know the difference between pork and chicken and wouldn't care if he did. Fall Fair. Women's Auxiliary. Church bloody suppers." She shivered dramatically and added, "What a pile of crap."

I grunted again. The whiskey had made my head muzzy. I thought there was a contradiction between what she was saying and what she'd said earlier but I couldn't figure it out right then. Across town a church bell rang out 1:00. The sound reverberated on the still night air.

"Not me," she said, "I won't let that happen to me." She tipped the flask up and took a small sip. "I'll get an abortion, I'll get two, three. Whatever. The one thing I know for sure, I'm not getting tied down."

"I thought you were a Catholic."

"Shit on that. We're talking about something serious here." She snorted. "The Pope. Christ almighty." Her voice cracked and she gulped audibly.

I sensed that she was shaking and when I glanced over saw tears coursing down her cheeks. I put my arm around her shoulder. I thought that she would shove me away but she buried her head against my chest. The faint smell of lilies was coming off her throat. "I don't know what I'm going to do," she whispered harshly, "I don't know what's to become of me."

"You'll be okay," I said.

"Charlie," she said, "you're a nice guy. You are. But you don't get it."

"I guess not."

"No." She sighed. "But I don't blame you."

I took the flask out of her hand. It was almost empty. I tipped it back. There wasn't much but it burnt all the way down. She was right, I didn't get it. The way she'd come on to me, the way she'd come apart. Her anger, the way she'd turned on me. She didn't mean it, I knew that. It wasn't me. She was still trembling and I heard her sob, "The hell with it, the hell with the whole damn works. Weddings, marriage, men. The hell with it."

I put the little flask in my jacket pocket and took several deep breaths. I wondered what I was doing there on a chill fall night with a strange girl I'd only just met. After a few minutes she stopped trembling and pulled away from me and placed both hands on the railing again, elbows locked, arms straight out, jaw thrust forward. For a moment I thought she might jump but I realized that wasn't it at all. She was steeling herself. I was glad of it. From the direction of the Union Hall a car horn tooted, then another.

"We should get going," she said, "they'll be cutting the wedding cake soon."

WALLEYES

When we'd checked into the Mooswa Cabins I'd noticed Gloria's bright green eyes and the twitch in her one hand, which I had put down to her being tightly wound. But she had an open smile and had joked with us as we signed in for the cabin and the boat. Her husband Horton, a quiet, balding man, had hung back and let her do all the business as if he were a security guard rather than the owner.

Later, as I was tearing open a bag of charcoal briquettes, Gloria, who I now recognized was thin and short, came out of the empty cabin next to ours and made her way directly across to me. The light was draining out of the sky and she was carrying a flashlight in one hand, though it was not switched on.

"How did it go, then?" she asked me.

"Slow," I said. I'd turned away from her to begin dumping the briquettes into the bowl of the barbeque. "Not really the right time of day."

"You'll be eating steaks then tonight." She laughed very lightly, a lilt to her voice. Her ash blonde hair was twisted up at the back of her head in a red elastic. She was wearing a tight long-sleeved top in a shade Maureen called sage. The angle of her jaw lent her a strength of character I was coming to appreciate in women.

"And pickerel tomorrow," I said laughing.

"You'll do better in the morning," she said. "They're biting then."

I chuckled. "I don't know how early this lot will be up."

She laughed. "We got heavy drinkers in the cabin?" Her voice was bright and she looked up at me with her green eyes and I thought a man could do a lot worse. She was in her mid-thirties and had a spark of life about her that was easy to like. In the falling light her features were softened and there was a sweetness in her voice and I understood what a man might see in her.

"More like heavy talkers," I said, "than heavy drinkers. College boys."

"They were having a lot of fun down by the pier earlier. By the sounds of it."

"Catching frogs. They have the idea frogs will bring on the pickerel tomorrow."

"A jig with a hunk of bacon works just as good. Maybe better."

"I think they liked the idea of catching frogs. Rolling up their pants and splashing around in the water. Behaving like kids."

"Forget about your fancy rigs and whatnots. The simple pickerel jig is the ticket here."

"The thing is, they're dead keen on the frogs."

"You'll see. I know the fish in this lake."

We watched a raven that had fluttered down from the spruces and was pecking in the dirt. It was about half the size of a turkey and had a wicked look in its eye.

To break the silence I said, "It's wonderful up here. Quiet, empty. We saw a bobcat at the south end of the lake."

Gloria made a sound, like *humph*, and scraped her toe on the ground between us. She was wearing black workboots that laced above the ankle and gave her a military appearance. "You a college boy too?"

"No." I'd dumped the briquettes into the bowl and was pushing them around with a stick, levelling them out before I sprayed the lighter fluid on. I was flattered she thought I looked the college type. But I was a friend of a friend, along because I knew the area. It was Shield country north of Fort Frances, a place called Sioux Narrows, where there were fishing lodges and cottages on the lake and places like the Mooswa, cabins for rent. I'd met Reg Smith at the mill in the Fort where I worked on the floor when he was down from the city with some paperwork and we had talked about fishing in the area and then he'd contacted me when he and his buddies planned to come and check out the Narrows. "No, I'm not a college boy," I repeated, "I'm more the grunt in the group. Know how to light the barbeque and start the outboard engines."

"Well," she said, "the guys in number 6 are into whiskey."

I looked over that way and cocked my head toward the sounds of rough laughter. "Trouble, you think?"

"Trouble's the name of the game around here. Last week we had a couple going at it in a boat tied up at the dock."

I raised my eyebrows, picturing this.

"Not what you're thinking. Pulling each other's hair, slapping faces. Screaming." She laughed and said ruefully, "Might have been better if it was sex."

"Takes all kinds," I said.

She laughed again, snorted, really. "Had to go down there and step between them." She stuck her chin out and her lips tightened in a stern grimace. She was not a beauty but I thought she had what my father called sand.

"Well," she repeated. "Let me know if the guys in 6 keep you up."

"No worries," a voice behind me said. It was Kevin, who had come off the deck of the cabin, and he came up to us with two beers and held one out to me. I was spraying the fluid on the coals but I took the bottle from him and had a quick sip.

"Can I get you one?" he asked, tipping his bottle toward Gloria.

"Not my drink," she said, maybe sharper than she'd intended. Then she added, "Horton likes it and on hot summer days when me and him have been working hard, I'll take one. But usually g-and-t does it for me."

"Same as my old mom," Kevin said brightly. "How about that? Preferably with a slice of lime."

"Mine drinks white wine," I said, "mixed with ginger ale. Ooh, now that's a concoction for you. Mothers, eh?"

"Mine died when I was fifteen," Gloria said. "Car crash. I don't think she drank at all. But the guy behind the wheel of the other car, well...."

In the ensuing silence I let out a breath and pretended to be busy with the briquettes.

"I'm sorry to hear that," Kevin said finally.

"Long time ago," Gloria said, waving one hand. "Ages past." She paused. "But thanks."

There was another silence and then I said, "You been doin' this a long time?" I made a gesture with my arm, taking in the cabins and the lake.

"Ten years next month," she said. "Huh. Horton wants me to throw a party. He gets the craziest notions in his head, that man."

I poked about in the briquettes with the end of the stick. Kevin chugged back some beer and then held the bottle up to see how much was left. He was a tall redhead who spoke with a slight lisp, which was almost not discernible because he had an accent that I couldn't quite place, sort of Irish but gentler. He was a soft man with a quiet voice. Out in the boat earlier he'd hummed as he was reeling in his line, tunes that Frank Sinatra had done, in a quiet unaffected way. He was so tall that he seemed to be looking down at the world, a position I thought might be interesting. I was average height myself and I knew there were advantages to that but I had always envied tall men.

"They're from Chicago," Gloria said, nodding her head toward number 6. "And they behave like Americans, if you know what I mean."

"Ugly Americans," Kevin said laughing. He tipped his beer at me. Like the others, he was from Winnipeg and didn't have much time for guys from south of the border.

"How so?" I'd brought a match to the coals, and flames suddenly sprung up, causing me to step backward quickly, almost bumping into Gloria who made a little *arghh* sound.

"You know," Kevin said, "city cowboys. Braggarts with bad attitude."

I stepped back to the barbeque and watched the flames jumping from one coal to another. When I was satisfied that the fire had taken, I turned to Gloria and said, "Nearly made a steak out of myself there." I was thinking that she'd seen a lot of big talkers and bums in her day and that she wasn't so much maligning everyone from south of the border as the bullshitter types that come up and swagger around like they own the place. I'd seen that on the streets of the Fort and was not too taken with it myself. I'd met Albertans like that too.

Gloria cleared her throat and toed the grass at her feet. She might have thought she'd said too much and she left a silence and then said tersely, "I'll leave you to it, then. Your steaks and whatnot."

"Right," I said. Allen and Reg had come out onto the deck of the cabin and were arranging chairs to look out toward the lake and take in a view of the cabin where the office was located.

"No need to rush away," Kevin said chuckling. "Always nice to talk to a pretty lady." He glanced at me and raised his red eyebrows humorously.

Gloria's jaw tightened and her chin jutted forward and I thought she might say something sharp back at him, but the look passed quickly. But it was enough to tell me Gloria was not a person to be toyed with. She was quick to the mark and it would be a good thing to keep a distance from her, attractive as she was.

Reg and Allen were sitting and talking quietly but passionately about a book they'd both been reading, something about a tin drum, their animated voices coming down from the deck. The chairs were Adirondack , painted teal blue. The cabins were each painted a different colour, red, orange, yellow. Ours was green.

Allen, a short man with glasses and a hook nose, called out to me, "Those steaks are ready to be burnt now." He'd been inside with salt and pepper and a sauce he'd concocted himself, an old family recipe. He seemed to be the leader of the group, a man with a ready smile who smoked and fidgeted in the car on the drive from the Fort. He was intense. Even exhaling cigarette smoke, he blew it out in quick, short bursts. On the lake he'd reeled his line in fast and I'd had to tell him to take it easy.

"It'll be a while," I said. I looked at the sky. It was pitch black above, with bright stars already clear near the western horizon and high up to the north. I took a deep breath. The air had the freshness of spring and smelled of grass. But a sharp bite, too, which brought something out in the pickerel. It was late May, a good time to fish at the Narrows, and I knew we would have good luck in the morning. I turned back to the deck. Kevin had climbed up to join the others. They were laughing about the frog business earlier. One of them had sat down in the lake and filled his pants with swamp water and leaves and sticks, and they all found that very amusing. "Twenty minutes," I called up to them, "before them coals are ready."

"That's good then," a voice said behind me. I turned, startled, and beer sloshed out of the bottle's neck and onto my hand. "Scared you, huh," the voice said. It belonged to a man who'd come up in the dark from the direction of cabin 6. When he stepped into the light thrown by the flames of the barbeque I saw he was thickset, with bulky arms and legs. He was wearing the kind of boots construction workers wear, sandy-coloured with laces that ran up past the ankle. A ball cap was jammed on his head and with the lumberjack shirt he was wearing, he appeared not to have a neck at all. He pushed past me and clumped up the steps onto the deck. "What you boys drinking?" he asked. "You clowns gonna offer a thirsty man a beer?"

Allen said, "You betcha." He jumped up from his chair and stepped inside, letting the screen door bang shut behind him.

"Billy," the man said. He put his big hand on the chair Allen had vacated and twisted it around so it faced the others directly and then plunked himself down. "Yep," he said, "thirsty." His face was pock-marked and there was a scar over one eye.

I checked that the coals were going strong and stepped across toward the deck.

Billy had his legs stretched out in front of him. "You boys catch anything today?"

"Not one thing," Reg said. "Not one bite."

"Didn't think so. Damn fool time to go out for walleyes."

Allen came out of the cabin carrying a beer and looked surprised that his chair was taken, but he passed the bottle over to Billy. "Cheers," he said.

"Cheers?" Billy said. "You boys limeys or something?" He tipped the beer back and took half of it down in one swallow. I watched his Adam's apple bob. His throat was red and so were his hands, big thick hands like hams. Sitting, it was clear he had a big gut too, it bulged over the belt at his waist, a thick black belt with a heavy buckle. Billy sniffed. "Never met a limey wasn't a cunt."

Nobody said anything. I was standing at the foot of the steps with a boot poised on the bottom one and my free hand resting on the railing. It smelled of cedar and I took in a couple of deep breaths and held the scent in for a moment. I watched to see if a ghost came out of my mouth when I exhaled but none did. The night would be cool but not cold and the fish would be eager at dawn. That spring was lovely, with crisp, clear nights and light winds from the south, which promised a good summer, long slow evenings with mist rising off the lakes and nights clear as bells. Reg coughed and Allen reached for a chair that was on the far side of the door and pulled it over closer to the group. He was on Billy's right. You could have put another chair between them. I was thinking I could do that when Billy said, "You know them there pissy fish we call snakes up here?"

Reg said, "I've heard that term." He turned to face Billy and the light reflected off his glasses, sending little knife probes of light off his face. "Snakes is what—"

"Snakes is them cunt jackfish they got up here instead of walleyes. A man comes up here to fish walleyes and he hooks into these cunt jacks, you know? Sickening. We take them by the tail and whack them against the side of the boat. Whack. Real hard. Knocks the brains out of the bastards. Knocks the shit out, too, you see what I mean." Billy sat back and grunted and took a swallow of beer. He blinked and put his free hand up to the scar over his eye. "Snakes." He made his disgust obvious by curling up his lip.

Reg said, "I've heard the term."

"You kill them snakes like that?" Billy looked straight at Reg and grinned. "You knock the shit out them cunts when you hook into them?"

"No," Reg said. "We just throw—"

"No," Billy said, "no, I suppose you don't have the jam for it."

Kevin said, "We hope to catch pickerel."

"Pickerel?" Billy said. "Them's walleyes you're talking about. You boys *are* limeys, now, ain't you?"

"Up here we call them pickerel," Kevin said, his voice rising slightly. He leaned forward in his chair and rested his hands on the rests. He had Celtic skin, peaches and cream with lots of freckles. His arms and legs were big boned, though, like certain Celts too. He'd told me on the drive up that he played rugby in a league in the city and that he liked the bashing around.

"That so. That so, Red." Billy laughed. "I bet the little broads

86

back home go for that red hair. Or is it not skirt you're interested in. Maybe you're more the bum-fucking type, big Red?"

"The name's Kevin." When he said this he sat back in his chair and took as big a mouthful of beer as Billy had done earlier. They eyed each other for a moment. Billy was older than him, in his mid-thirties, older than anyone in our group, and there was a hardness around his mouth. The guys from the city were in their mid-twenties and I was a year or two younger. Billy's eyes narrowed and there was a curl to his lip, which seemed it might be a permanent feature. I figured he'd brought on a few scraps in his time.

He tapped his beer bottle on the arm of his chair. "Is it now? I knew a Kevin once. A weasel. Come to think of it, he was a limey, a limey who ran a drugstore. What line you boys in? You don't look like druggists." He laughed loudly and smacked his free hand on one knee.

"We're students," Allen said. Reg shot him a look but he went on. "Kevin's in law and Reg and me are grad students." He ran his fingers round the collar of his shirt, which was a checkered print in blue and green. Like Reg and Kevin he was wearing jeans, freshly washed and with a crease. They were all clean-shaven, as was Billy. I had a two-day growth of beard, which Maureen had told me was sexy, though it scratched her tummy.

"A lawyer," Billy said. "I had some dealings with a lawyer once over a divorce. Nasty little prick stole half my money. And my pick-up." The edge in his voice told me he was a man who did things on the spur of the moment, mostly nasty. I'd seen it before.

I was beginning to feel my scalp prickle and I reached up and scratched behind my ear. The movement caught Billy's eye. He stared down at me. His eyes were washed-out grey and they narrowed to concentrate on me. He had figured the others out but was uncertain how I fit in. I was wearing work pants and a soiled sweatshirt and my face was tanned dark brown from being out of doors a lot.

"I'm doing commercial," Kevin was saying, "commercial law. No divorces and such."

"Lawyer's a lawyer," Billy said. "Weasly little shysters. You're not a Jew, are you? Them Jew lawyers gotta be the worst. Cunts the lot." He banged his fist on the armrest of his chair. "That Jew lawyer was here, I'd rip his face off." He had not put down the empty bottle, which was in his other hand. The knuckles had turned white, and if the bottle had been a tin can, it would have crumpled under his grip. There was a scar running across the back of his wrist and it was bright red under the tension of his fist.

Reg shifted in his chair. It was true that he and Allen were grad students doing degrees in English and history. They were bookish and wore glasses but Reg worked summers in a logging camp with a chainsaw and Allen had played on the football team in his undergrad years, he told me. They were short, wiry men, who when they took off their shirts out in the boat on the lake were muscular and fit. With a little work I could have turned both of them into boxers, as I myself had done in high school. I wondered if either of them had ever thrown a punch in anger and decided it was unlikely.

"You know, boys," I said, "we can put them steaks on now." I tipped my head toward the barbeque. Reg nodded at me. A look of relief passed across his face.

"I got a thirst on," Billy said. "You got a problem with that, boy?" He burped loudly. I remembered that Gloria had said that over in number 6 they were hitting the whiskey hard and I saw now that Billy was more drunk that I'd first thought. Drunk and belligerent. There are some men who go quiet when they drink and others who become maudlin, but Billy belonged in the group that got angry and then looked around for something to punch. Or someone. I thought he had been eyeing me up, but it was Kevin he had in mind now. Kevin was a head taller than Billy and outweighed him by a few pounds but I doubted he had ever had to use his fists. A guy like Billy could see that too, and it was the main reason he'd singled him out rather than me. There's nothing some men like more than knocking a man bigger than them onto his knees.

"The thirst has come off us." I drained the beer out of the bottle so it would be empty and could be used in a certain way. But the truth was I trusted my fists. I'd been in a few prize fights in the Fort and across the border in the Falls and had come out okay, though there was a little scar in my lower lip that stung whenever I drank anything stronger than beer.

Billy was gauging our voices. He'd heard anger in Kevin's and had expected the same from me, but I'd learned that an even tone was like holding your cards close to the chest in a poker game, it gave an advantage.

"I know you from somewheres," Billy said, looking down at me. His voice rose sharply. "I know that ugly mug."

"Not unless you spend time at the κ Club in the Fort," I said.

"Huh," Billy said. "I seen you somewheres but just can't remember right now. I just gotta get a fix on your mug. You work as a border guard?" He pointed one finger at me. It was thick and had been broken at the top knuckle so it was slightly bent. "You're a border guard. I've got you now, mister secretive."

I was a little surprised and my face must have shown it. My older brother, who didn't look anything like me, was a customs officer. He was short and pudgy with blond hair where my hair was coarse and black, and I was, if anything, a little thin.

"Border guards," Billy said. "Bastards the lot." He spat on the deck. I looked at him closely then. His washed-out eyes reminded me of a nasty guy who'd head-butted me in the ring, an evil southerner I'd taken pleasure in putting on the canvas.

"Those coals will be red hot now," Reg said, glancing down towards the barbeque.

"Steaks," Allen said brightly. "Good idea." He started to lift himself out of his chair.

"Hold on there, bub," Billy said. "Grab me another of them

beers, college boy." He held his bottle up to the bulb over the door and studied its contents. "Lite," he said, "that's kind of pussy beer, ain't it?"

"Like your crap," Kevin said.

"What's that you say, Red?"

"Your American beer. Watery crap."

Billy lurched forward in his seat. "You're starting to piss me off, you know, Red."

Kevin said, "The feeling's mutual."

"You the big man here? The tough guy?"

"Who's asking? Which ugly American?"

"So you are the tough guy."

"Tough enough."

Billy stood suddenly. He shifted the bottle so he was gripping its neck and he smashed it on the chair. Glass flew up and Kevin raised his hand to cover his face. A shard landed near my foot. Kevin stood. He rubbed his hands on his thighs.

"Hey, now," Allen said. He took a half step forward. "That's enough."

"What's enough?" Billy raised his hand toward him, jabbing one finger at his chest.

"Enough of you—you and your mouth."

"Oh, you gonna shut it for me?" He jabbed his finger again.

Allen stepped backward.

Billy snorted. "No." He turned and took each of us in. "So which pussy is it then?"

"You fuck off now," I said. I hadn't been planning to say that but once the words were out I found I'd taken the last step up onto the deck.

"Yeah," Billy said, "I thought so. Mister secretive is mister tough guy." The curl in his lip broadened into a grin of satisfaction. He was going to get what he'd really come for.

I squared myself to him and shifted my feet for maximum balance.

Billy said, "C'mon, mister secretive border guard cunt. C'mon on, then."

We were at eye level. My coach had told me once that there were three important times in every stand-off, the time to listen, the time to talk, and the time to start throwing them. He had told me to watch the other man's hands for the cues. People looked into each other's eyes, he told me, but it was the hands that gave away what a man was going to do. When they were open at his sides, you listened; if he closed them into fists, you talked back; when they started to move, so did you. The time for talking had passed.

Billy waved the shattered beer bottle in my face. "You got the jam, pussy?"

I was still holding my empty bottle in one hand and I could have smashed it off at the neck and matched him one for one, but I trusted my hands more, so I chucked it down onto the grass near the bar-beque where it made a *thunk*. I dropped my chin and raised my fists above my belt into the ready position and said to myself, Okay now, go in fast and don't come out until one of you is down.

A voice behind us shouted, "Hey, buddy, you got the wrong cabin or something?" It was Gloria, who came out of the shadows from the side of the cabin. Billy's mouth dropped open, like a kid caught stealing cookies, and he took a step backward, stumbling over one of the legs of the chair he'd been sitting in. "C'mon, now," Gloria said, "these boys have been good enough to share their beer but they've got steaks to cook." She'd come up the steps fast and was beside me on the deck and I felt the heat of her tense body. But she had eyes only for Billy. She was focused on his face and her shoulders were bent slightly forward, as if she meant to reach out and seize his wrist. The twitch had gone out of her wrist and even though she had stopped short of Billy, the rigidity in her hands and arms made it seem that she was still moving. Billy had regained his balance. He was about to say something but she cut him off. "Put that bottle down, now," she commanded, shifting sideways and taking it out of his hand before he knew that she had done it. "And come on, now, your buddies got a poker game going and they need you in there." She put her hand on his wrist and gave him a gentle tug as she started down the steps. He resisted for a half second, but then followed her, his boots clumping on the cedar. He staggered on the bottom step but he continued on and in a moment they had faded into the shadows.

I stared into the darkness and could just make out their forms. She was walking ahead of him at first and then to the side, and finally she broke off and made her way toward her own place while he went toward number 6. The lights were on at her cabin, which also served as an office, and I could make out the form of Horton standing in the doorway. One hand was resting on a waist-high object and at first I took it to be a broom, but then I saw it did not have a brush end. He was standing quite still, holding a rifle, like a guard on duty

Behind me Reg said, "Well, Jesus." He took a long swallow of beer.

I heard the crackling of cellophane and knew Allen was fumbling with a cigarette pack and in a moment he lit up and blew smoke noisily and said, "Anyone for a beer?" He was trying to laugh it off.

Kevin was behind me, breathing heavily.

I took a couple of deep breaths. The air was still warmish and there was a scent on it now of swamp water and something musty too, a pleasant smell, like moss. The tops of the pines near the cabin were swaying in the breeze. Overhead the sky was dotted with bright stars. I looked for the Big Dipper and the North Star. Frogs were croaking in the shallow waters down by the pier where the boats were tied up for the night. My heart was still thumping. I drew more breath in through my nose and felt Kevin standing beside me at the railing. "Thanks," he said quietly.

I nodded but did not turn to look at him. I was wondering what it took for a hundred-and-some-pound woman to walk across the space between her cabin and ours and put herself between men prepared to do violence to each other. I had witnessed scraps on the floor at the mill and it was not a pretty sight and I had known better than to come between the men punching at each other. Gloria must have known that Billy would not outright strike her, the way he had been preparing to hit Kevin or me, but she had no way of knowing that he wouldn't push her and knock her down, maybe so she fell down the steps of the deck. She'd risked being seriously hurt. People died falling over living-room couches and down the stairs to the basement. Some men take a certain pleasure out of hitting women and there's no way of knowing which they are. Billy could have been one of those. She'd had to put that out of mind when she started across the grass to our cabin. It was the kind of simple courage that can be confused with blindness and I felt a warmth in my chest for her then and hoped that I would have that sort of sand if the time came when I needed to. It would be good, too, to have a man like Horton standing not too far away with a weapon in his hand. At first I'd thought he was too weak for her, that he should have been the one to put things in order when they got out of hand. But I realized I was wrong about that, that they had their own established pattern. With drunken fishermen it was better for her to be front line and for him to be back-up. I was thinking that and about how quickly the violence on the deck had escalated and then diminished at the arrival of Gloria, chin thrust forward, voice firm and challenging. One of us could be lying on the deck seriously hurt, but instead we were getting ready to cook steaks and Billy was sitting down to poker and whiskey. In an hour we'd be laughing about what had happened and in a month maybe have forgotten it entirely. Life was a poser sometimes. The heat of rage went up and down as fast as the flames had leapt into my face when I'd lit the barbeque coals.

Reg and Allen had moved down the steps onto the grass near the barbeque. Allen had a package of meat in his hands and Reg held four open bottles of beer. "Nice night," he said.

"Bright," Allen said. "We should have a good day tomorrow."

"Smell that cedar," Reg said.

"Listen to them frogs."

"There will be good fishing," Kevin said, "tomorrow." He tapped his fingers on the railing between us. Allen and Reg turned and looked up at us. Their faces were little splashes of moon on water.

"You betcha," Allen said, laughing. "Maybe hook us into some of them there watcha call, walleyes."

METEOR SHOWER

Tony was meticulous about machinery and told me that you should always put a tool back exactly where you found it, so you'd know where to put a hand to it the next time. He told me that after I had not done it and he'd flown into a fit. He had a temper, but mostly he was fun to be around, a manly man, and I think my mother Doreen liked to see the two of us together.

In the fall of the year that I was graduating high school Doreen was seeing Tony off and on. She worked as a waitress at the Headingley Hotel and that's where she had met him—he drove a bulldozer for a construction company, seasonal work. He was the last hire and so the first laid off in September. He was from the north country but his family had moved into the city when he and his brother Nathan were in their twenties. This was about the time my father was electrocuted up a hydro pole, working for Manitoba Hydro. He made some kind of mistake connecting wires and in an instant was dead. I was ten at the time and what I remember about the funeral was how many people showed up at the church in sweatpants and baseball jackets. Our family rarely saw the inside of church, but Doreen had standards: you went to weddings and funerals in good clothes, out of respect for what was happening.

Tony had a room on the edge of the city but he spent a lot of time at my mother's house, a little place just outside of Headingley with a double garage and a gravel driveway. She would go to his room in the city sometimes and call home to let me know where she was and how long she'd be gone, and I had the feeling she felt guilty but didn't know what to do about it. I didn't mind. To me it seemed that's how things worked, she had her own life to lead. I had my own girlfriend and she came over sometimes and that was just part of life too.

Tony drove a motorcycle, a Triumph Bonneville that he repaired himself. He was often in the garage late into the night, tinkering with this or that. He showed me how to adjust a carburetor, twisting the set-screws until the mixture of oxygen and gas was just right. It was a finicky business. But it felt good when you had the engine running smoothly. He showed me how to grind valves with a hand drill. Metal parts littered the work bench in Doreen's garage, oily rags and tools with stained handles. I liked him. He whistled while he worked and he often had an open beer on the workbench and he invited me to share it and to look over his shoulder at whatever he was doing. Up north he had spent a lot of his youth shooting things—ducks, geese, deer, moose—and he liked to do that and often was up early in the morning to drive out to some place with a rifle. He always asked me to come along. I came to be a good shot but I didn't like killing things the way he did. His brother Nathan didn't either. He still asked me to come along, but after a while we both knew I'd decline and he'd go out on his own.

When he wasn't out hunting that fall, he hung around the house, and that bothered me. I'd grown up used to a lot of space and time to myself, and someone else rattling around in the house put me on edge. Tony too. For a week or so it was okay between us, but after several more had passed he became irritable and accused me of being a surly teenager, which I probably was. We'd snarl at each other and he'd leave in a huff, banging the door behind him. I'd hear the bike cough to life and see swirls of gravel and dust behind it as he left the yard. I wasn't sure where he went on those days, but it was probably a bar. It didn't much matter. He was out of the house and I had it to myself. It was the one thing Doreen gave me: space and time.

In late October Tony was in a foul mood about being laid off. He spent a lot of hours in the garage and at night he and Doreen went out places, dancing, or visiting friends. He was edgy because he was out of work and Doreen was edgy because he was edgy. I thought maybe they'd call it quits, the way she had with other guys, and it was not a prospect that displeased me. The house seemed to be getting smaller and smaller, the flare-ups and silences more frequent and intense. I fought with my girlfriend sometimes and was mean to friends at school. We were reaching the boiling point when Tony got a call from his mother one night. It was late, I was asleep when the phone rang.

Doreen came into my bedroom sometime later. "Jimmy," she whispered, "Jimmy, are you awake?" I could tell by her voice that something serious had happened. It wasn't Tony out on his motorcycle—something Doreen never tired of fearing—he was standing behind her in the hallway. I could just see his head of dark hair over hers. "It's Nathan," she said when she saw that I was awake. "Nathan has killed—Nathan has committed suicide." She started to shake then and I knew she was trying not to break down.

I remember sitting up in bed. I remember Doreen holding me while she cried and also that Tony came into the room and placed a hand on her shoulder. His fingers knitted on her nightdress like a cat's paws as the tears ran down her cheeks and he hugged her awkwardly from behind and said, "Doreen, Doreen." I was in a daze from sleeping deeply and from being awakened suddenly to such shocking news. It was the first time since my father was killed that a person in my acquaintance had died: and he really didn't count either, seeing how young I was at the time. I hope that doesn't make me sound callous. I loved my father, but I didn't remember him all that well, only that I missed him once he was gone.

Doreen's crying was like the snuffling of a child. After a moment Tony stepped away from her and moved the football off the chair in my bedroom and put it on the dresser. But then he decided not to sit there and came and sat on the end of the bed. He ran his hands back through his hair and blew out his cheeks. "I shouldn't never have given up smoking," he said. After a bit he began to tremble and I realized that he cared for his brother, and I wished that I had a brother I could feel about that way.

Nathan's death wasn't entirely unexpected. He had been depressive since before he left high school. He could not hold a job. He moved out of his parents' house and lived in a halfway house with others like him who spent time in and out of hospitals and took a bunch of pills and were generally so miserable to those around them that no one wanted much to do with them. He looked like Tony: stocky, muscular, with a head of dark hair and eyes that flashed with anger over the least slight. They didn't get along and rarely saw each other, but they were brothers, and on the night he killed himself, Tony was as upset as I ever was to see him, or any man.

After the funeral service we went to their parents' place, which was on a scrubby plot of land past the town of St Francis. They lived in a big mobile home, a double they called it, with several bedrooms and a kitchen and a spacious living and dining area. The mother, Edna, greeted us at the door and offered us a beer. She was chain smoking, her fingers stained yellow from tobacco. The rooms were thick with smoke, like at the bar, and Doreen waved her hand in front of her face when she sat down on the sofa beside me and took a sip of her drink. The father was a small man with red hair. His name was Eric. He sat on the opposite end of the sofa with a glass of whiskey in his hand, looking like a bird that might take flight at any time. There were sliced meats and cheeses and rye bread on the table and we ate, and Eric and Edna talked about every imaginable subject except Nathan. There were only a few friends present and soon it was only us and I could tell Doreen and Tony were restless. The sun had set an hour or so earlier and the sky outside was darkening. I had been excited earlier, at the cemetery, but felt dull in the heart and wishing I was home in bed, reading and listening to the radio.

Doreen tapped her watch and glanced at Tony, then me, mouthing the word school.

"We gotta go," Tony said. He was standing at a side table examining a photo of Nathan with the family taken when the boys were in their teens. It was in colour. Tony was wearing a Toronto Maple Leafs sweater and Nathan a Canadiens. "Jimmy here's got homework," he said.

"Right," Eric said. "We don't want the boy growing up ignorant like the rest of us." He smiled at me and tipped his glass in my direction.

"Right you are," Doreen said, standing.

"So soon?" Edna said. "You haven't seen your father in months, Tony, and then it's up and go before we've hardly had a word. Before—"

"Edna," Eric said sharply, "you've had plenty of words, plenty."

But Edna was intent on what she had to say. She shot him a mean look and said, "If not for your father's sake, then Nathan's."

Tony sighed. He was pulling on his jacket.

Edna screwed up her face. Smoking had put black lines under her eyes, and creasing her skin in a scowl made her very unattractive. "Your brother loved you. Even if you didn't love him. You know that, don't you?"

"Maw," Tony said. He placed one hand over his stomach.

"He looked up to you and wanted to be like you. When you were boys he—"

"He hated me," Tony said, his voice rising. "That time I went to his apartment, he told me to piss off and die. He was not my loving little brother, he was a monster, he treated you and Dad like crap. And me—he told me he never wanted to see me again." Tony was trembling, worrying his thumbs against his other fingers. He was red in the face.

"But you," Edna went on, as if she hadn't heard a word he'd said, "on the day we bury your baby brother, you can't make tracks away from us fast enough."

"Edna," Eric, said, "for heaven's sake now, woman."

"Maw, you're upsetting me."

"I'm upsetting you!" Edna stubbed a cigarette in an overflowing ashtray. She started to cough, a deep smoker's cough that threatened to leave her without wind. Her face turned beet red. She waved one hand in the air and coughed and gasped. It was something Eric was used to. He didn't stir, hardly glanced at her as she recovered her breath and put one hand over her chest, gasping and clawing the air with her other hand. Tony stared at Doreen. He looked helpless.

Doreen passed Edna her bottle of beer and Edna pulled at it for a minute and then seemed recovered.

Eric said, "You go now, son. We'll be all right." He stood and put his hand on Tony's wrist and gave it a squeeze. "She's just upset," he added. "We're all upset. I am, she is, and you are. Maybe Doreen here and Timmy too."

There was a long silence. I could tell Doreen was struggling not to correct Eric about my name and it was clear that Tony was hoping she wouldn't do that. He took his father's hand and held it in his. Eric had green eyes and they bugged out slightly. His mouth crinkled down as if he was going to weep but he took several deep breaths and did not. It was a point of honour with him, I guessed, and I admired him for it. He patted Tony on the shoulder.

Edna seemed hurt that we were leaving and when Doreen wasn't looking gave her a sharp stare that made me feel protective of my mother, a feeling I didn't have often. I stood too and put my unfinished beer on a side table.

"Well," Eric said, "so, then we'll ..."

Edna brightened suddenly. "Before you go," she said, standing, "I've got something for you, Tony." She went into a back room. While she was out, Tony looked at Doreen, who was shaking her head and muttering to herself. A tabby cat had been sitting under the table and glancing in the direction of the food. It came out and leaped onto a chair and licked the edge of the plate with the cold meats, but then seemed uninterested and jumped back down on the floor and went under the table again.

By that time Edna had returned. She was carrying a rifle. "This here was Nathan's," she said before anyone could react. She was carrying it in the way an honor guard does, to arms, and she shifted it and thrust it toward Tony.

"Maw," he said, backing away, hands up like a cop halting traffic. His voice cracked. I'd seen him angry and upset with Doreen or me about this and that but never with the look in his eye he had right then. He seemed frightened almost, and close to tears. I wondered if maybe he thought he was responsible for Nathan sticking his head in that oven.

"Take it," Edna insisted. "You were the one always liked guns."

"I can't," Tony said. He'd placed one hand over his stomach and was shaking his head.

"You can," Edna said. "You will."

"Oh God," Doreen moaned. She stamped one foot on the floor. "will you for—"

"Maw," Tony said, "you don't know what—"

"He wanted you to have it," Edna said sharply. "He said I should give it to you." It was clear to me that she was lying, and I guessed that Tony knew that and maybe Doreen did too. Edna had fixed the idea in her mind, though, and there was no changing it, you could tell that too.

"It's a .22," she said.

"I know what it is," Tony said.

"You father bought one for each of you when you were boys. Christmas."

"I know that too, Maw." Tony's voice was growing increasingly irritable.

"Take the damn thing!" Doreen was almost screaming. "Will you just?"

"And he wanted you to have his, see, his last request kind of thing."

"For God's sake, Maw," Tony said in a rage. "He didn't even leave a note."

I didn't know whether to laugh or cry. Edna was so clearly lying and so insistent that she was absurd, and Tony looked so forlorn and panicky he might have bolted out the door. Maybe he was afraid that bad luck came with the rifle, maybe he thought it was terrible to take it when his mother was so obviously trying to guilt him into it. I don't know what he thought but there has never been another time in my life when I've seen someone so uncomfortable with a gift.

"Take it, son," Eric said sharply. "Just get the damn thing out of here."

Tony sighed. He reached out with both hands and took the rifle from his mother.

"Good, now," she said, a note of triumph in her voice, "you see." When we were at the door she added, "You mind now, that thing may be loaded."

Tony sighed. "It'll be all right," he said with finality in his voice.

Outside the air was cold. On the drive out we'd heard on the radio that it was snowing up north and the moon overhead was so bright it was blue. Doreen shivered against the cold. I had on a sport jacket and my neck was open to the wind and it was the cold wind that comes down from the north and freezes the water in the rivers and lakes.

Doreen owned an old Datsun with rust spots but she asked Tony, "You wanna drive?"

"No," he said. "I've got the bad gut." He moaned slightly when he spoke.

Doreen slammed her door when she got in the car. When she frowned, the lines of her face hardened and she was not attractive at all. She sighed aloud and said, "Jesus, now. Jesus."

Tony threw the rifle into the back seat beside me. "What was all that?"

"Just leave it," Doreen said.

"I should be the one all riled up."

"Shut it," Doreen said sharply.

"All right, all right." Tony sighed and settled into his seat.

"Let's get the hell out of here," Doreen said.

There was silence in the car, which was all right with me. I thought about the fact that I'd be leaving school in a few months and expected to live like an adult. Maybe I'd move into the city and have a room somewhere. I thought I'd go to college but I had no money and neither did Doreen, so it seemed I'd be working for some time before that. Which was okay with me. I'd had my fill of school. I thought, too, about what my mother would do after I'd left. I did not think she would marry or even live with Tony. She'd said as much. She had talked about taking a course and improving her life. Paralegal maybe. She had her own plans and that was all right by me. I wondered if Tony would move on and what would happen to him. He seemed to have the look in his eye some days of a man who wasn't sure where he was going, only that it was not where he'd set out to get to, and I felt sorry for him in a way, but not too much.

My thoughts turned to hockey. The tryouts for the Braves had been held and I had made the team, had in fact been named the team captain. My coach said the New York Rangers were sending a scout to sign me to a card and there was every likelihood I could play in the pros, if I set my heart and mind to it. I didn't think I could do that. It seemed to me that there was a lot of yelling at players and pushing them around by the managers and coaches, things I didn't like in my own coach. And I probably wasn't good enough to make it to the Rangers, so I'd be putting up with all that and playing in the minor leagues. I thought college was a better prospect. I'd always liked reading and watching the news on TV. Maybe I'd become a teacher or journalist.

We came to St Francis. There's a wide opening at a curve in the highway there, where the Assiniboine River is visible, and the moon was dancing on the water and it looked pretty. The geese had come down from the north by then and most had passed through, but a few stragglers were still left and some were in the field between the highway and the river. Tony looked over at them. He shifted on the car seat. "Christ I'm glad to be out of there," he said.

"You are? You?" Doreen said. "Your mother. Jesus."

"She's a piece of work alright."

"Amen to that."

"Family," Tony said and shook his head. He glanced into the back seat. "You okay?" he asked.

"Fine," I said. Though the truth was I had a knot in my stomach and was wishing away the miles.

Tony was still looking at me. "You did great there," he said. And then he added with emphasis, "*Timmy*." And he laughed a quiet laugh and so did Doreen. I did too and my gut felt a little less tight.

"I'm all right," I said, "Timmy's okay." We all three laughed. I had rolled the window down a crack and was happy to be breathing fresh air. I don't know how Eric lived with all that smoke. People become used to each other's habits, I put it down to. It drove me crazy when Tony sniffed and snorted when we sat and watched TV. I don't think I could ever have adjusted to that. And Doreen hated it when I clipped my toenails in any place other than the bathroom. But she had no idea how annoying it was when she whistled along to her Abba tape in her squeaky off-tune way.

After a while Tony said, "My guts are in a knot."

"I don't want to hear it," Doreen said. She was intent on the road, her mouth set hard. She liked driving and she liked to drive fast. In the city she zipped between lanes, dodging past buses and taking the curb lane where cars were parked, cutting people off as she whipped along. She played Iggy Pop on the stereo and thumped her palms on the steering wheel to the beat. Often she had a cup of black coffee in one hand. I'd only just got my licence and the way she maneuvered took my breath away. Dangerous, I thought, but I did not say it.

We came to the junction of the highway and the Trans Canada and Doreen slipped into the feeder lane. A car was coming along the Trans Canada but she cut into the lane in front of it. I suppose she thought she had a lot of room but the Camaro was moving fast and the driver lay on his horn when he came up behind and then took the outside lane, slowing to drive right beside us, horn still blaring. Two men were inside and they glared at us and gave Doreen the finger. She gave them the finger back. The other driver hit the horn again. We drove like that for some time, the two guys staring into our car. Then the Camaro scooted ahead and we thought we were done with that but the car went directly in front of the Datsun and the driver intentionally slowed, hitting the brake, and Doreen had to hit the brakes too. We were all three thrown forward. "Jesus," Doreen cried out.

"What the hell," Tony snapped, putting one hand on the dash.
Doreen snapped back: "What?"

"You're driving crazy."

"He's driving crazy," Doreen said.

"My guts are already in a knot and then you go drive like a crazy person," Tony said in a tone that made Doreen look at him and frown. "You always drive crazy," he went on.

"Back off," Doreen said and wheeled past the Camaro in the open lane, the little engine of the Datsun working hard and the car shuddering. We were at the place just before the gravel road toward Lido Plage. The speedometer shot up further. The men in the Camaro glared at us as we rushed past. They were guys in their mid-thirties wearing T-shirts and ball caps. They had scraggly hair and black brush mustaches. "Fuckin' assholes," Doreen yelled, glaring at them. When the Datsun passed them I looked back. The driver had sped up and his headlights were not far from the back of our car.

Tony had his feet braced against the firewall and one hand on the dashboard. "Will you cool it," he shouted, "for the love of Christ!"

Doreen said, "Who's behind the wheel here, who's driving this here car?" She slowed a little to make the turn onto the gravel road, tires squealing. The Camaro followed behind, its headlights momentarily splashing into my back-turned face. I had a bad feeling about what was going to happen.

When we were on the gravel, Tony asked, "They behind us? Jimmy?"

"Yes," I said.

"Shit." He turned in his seat to look out the rear window. "Now look what you've gone and done."

Doreen glared at him and then into the rear-view mirror. I could see the jut of her jaw and the way she was biting down on her lower lip. "Me?" she said. "Oh, isn't that just typical."

At a straight stretch the Camaro shot up beside us and then a little ahead and then cut in front, braking hard, so Doreen had to brake too, and the cars fishtailed around on the gravel, the Camaro on the left and ahead as both slowed and swerved about. Doreen sawed at the wheel and kept the Datsun on the road, but gravel pinged on the undercarriage and the suspension made grinding noises. The Camaro sped up ahead again and cut in sharply. "Fucking hell," Tony shouted. Both cars fishtailed crazily again. I could see the man closer to us and he was yelling and trying to hang onto the dashboard of the Camaro. Then the cars came to a juddering stop, making horrid metal sounds and scattering gravel. I was sweating and Doreen was breathing hard and Tony was saying, "Shit shit shit" in a high-pitched voice filled with rage. The guy on the passenger side leapt out of the Camaro and was yelling at Doreen as he came toward the Datsun. There was some distance between the cars and he was crossing it slowly, jabbing his finger at Doreen and yelling, "Stupid fuck! Stupid cunt!" You could hear him clearly, and he was out of control.

"Drive!" Tony shouted. He looked down the road, illuminated by the headlights, a straight stretch with a long curve at the far end.

Doreen's hands were locked on the wheel. The knuckles were white and her arms were shaking, from wrist to elbow.

"Drive away," Tony said. "Drive on. Now!" He pointed straight ahead. The Camaro was half in the ditch and the Datsun had a clear path in front of it.

"Mom," I shouted. The guy was closing in on the Datsun. He was going to do something violent, like smash his fist through a window, that much was clear by the set of his shoulders. He had a crazed look in his eye, which appeared worse because we were sitting looking up at him. I thought my mother might die right there. I thought I might.

"Drive!" Tony shouted again.

"I can't," Doreen said weakly. She threw her head back and howled. But her hands would not move. Her window was down and the sounds of the man's boots crunching on gravel came closer.

That's when it became apparent the guy had something in his hand, a thick stick or a club.

"Christ almighty!" Tony shouted. It was a wail. He could see what was coming, as could I. Maybe Doreen could too.

The man raised the club and smashed it against the roof of the car. Doreen screamed. He pulled the club back again and peered down into the car. It was not clear what he meant to do next. He might have been content with what he'd done, but it looked like he was going smash the windshield. Doreen was howling, a screeching sound that made the hairs on my head stand up. My eyes were locked on the man and the club. It was wrapped in black tape, a cop's nightstick kind of thing. I wanted to leap out of the car and pummel him in the face, beat him until he couldn't move. I was that angry. He was about to kill my mother. The rage I felt registered as the surging of blood in my head and I wondered if this is what animals feel just before they're killed.

I didn't see that Tony had grabbed the .22 out of the back seat. "Roll your window down!" he screamed at me. "Now!"

I did. Almost immediately there was the loud report of the rifle, louder than I ever could have thought, as the impact of the charge reverberated in the little car. Doreen screamed. The man with the club dropped it and grabbed his left shoulder, which was bleeding visibly. His face was contorted. He looked surprised at what had happened. He staggered backward, then fell to his knees on the gravel. He made an odd sound when he hit the road, *humph*. The other man, the driver, was out of the car and making his way toward him, not quite running but moving fast. He threw off his ball cap and it fluttered behind him into the ditch.

"Drive!" Tony shouted at Doreen. "For Christ's sake!"

The shock waves from the rifle shot had brought her back to her senses. She stamped on the accelerator and the Datsun leapt forward, spraying gravel behind. I caught a glimpse of the two men through the rear window. They were both standing then, fast diminishing shadows, one of them holding his hand to his injured shoulder, the other staring at our car as it sped away.

It was only a short distance to the road that led to my mother's little house. My heart was beating wildly in my chest. Doreen was fuming the whole way, letting us know, if there was any doubt, that she was furious with Tony. There was no use in pointing out that she had brought the business on. When we drove up to the house, she sat without moving, her arms locked over the steering wheel and her head down. "Get that thing out of here," she said.

Tony had the butt of the rifle stuck between his feet with the barrel pointed up, almost touching the roof. He climbed out and so did I. The wind was up then and cold on the face. We didn't say anything but started walking away from the car and house. The property sat near the river, slanting steeply at the bank, but we'd both been down there many times and knew our way even in the dark. We stumbled a bit but were okay. An owl hooted in the trees and we both started and looked about and then laughed. Tony was carrying the rifle and when we came to the riverbank he took the end of the barrel in both hands and twirled himself about, like a man throwing the hammer at the Olympics. He made a half spin and released the rifle, which sailed out over the river, spinning like a helicopter blade, then fell into the water with a loud *plop*.

"That's that then," Tony said, wiping his hands together. I knew he meant more than the rifle and I felt sorry for him. He always had good intentions and this was another example. He had meant to stand up for my mother, but in her eyes it had gone horribly wrong. We stood and looked at the river. A log floated by. On the far side something twinkled in the moonlight, a piece of aluminum or glass. I studied it for a while, wondering who had left such a thing there. I wondered if I'd see Tony again after that night and concluded it was unlikely and I felt badly for him again, but I was not much bothered by the prospect of him being gone from our lives. Other men had come into Doreen's life and gone. He was not the first. He was thinking something like that, too, I gathered.

"I had high hopes," Tony said, "for me and your mother." He had his hands thrust in his pockets then, shoulders slumped forward. "Not that I thought we'd get married or anything," he went on.

My nose was cold and I rubbed it with my hand.

"I guess I'll light out now," he said. "I've always fancied Albuquerque, New Mexico." He laughed. "Want to know why?"

"Why?" I said. I was curious. I realized it might be the last time I'd ever speak to Tony.

"I like the name. Sounds good when you say it. Albuquerque, New Mexico." Tony laughed again. "Imagine that, travelling thousands of miles because you like the name of a place."

"It's a good reason," I said, "as good as most."

"I guess. Or maybe California. I hear there's a construction boom on. I think I could like California. You don't have to wear a helmet there on your bike."

I was thinking how it was that a person's life could turn on one small act, like firing a gun. Life was strange. Tony and Doreen had seemed solid, as solid as most couples, and that had ended in one moment. Our hopes and dreams were fragile, I realized. You went along thinking your life would continue as it had been, planning and projecting into the future, and then one thing happened and it all tumbled apart, as fast as pulling the bottom card out of the house of cards.

Tony cleared his throat. "Your mother's pretty and a fine woman," he said quietly, "but her ideas and mine about life are not always the same."

I didn't know what to say to that, so I said nothing. I felt the cold creeping in around my ankles and shuffled from one foot to the other.

"I like it here, though," he went on. "I'll miss it."

"It's quiet," I said. My heart was still thumping hard in my chest. It would be hours before I calmed down enough to sleep and that was a shame, but I could read a book or watch TV.

"Yes," he said. "Peaceful. A man needs that sometimes." He'd taken his hands out of his pockets and was rubbing his chin and staring out across the river.

I had the feeling he wanted to say more, or have me say something, but my mind was blank. My ears were still ringing from the rifle concussion and I was numb in a different way too, void in the heart. I was turning over the picture of Tony holding the rifle butt against his shoulder for a moment after he'd squeezed the trigger. The look on his face could only be called grim. Doreen's mouth was open and her hands by then were in her hair, tearing at it. She looked wild and he looked crazy and I felt at that moment as if everything I'd known and thought had suddenly disintegrated, like I was about to die. It was an awful feeling and I hope never to experience it again.

Tony coughed and I was back on the riverbank with him, feeling hollow inside. It had been a terrible day. I imagined I would not sleep well and felt a twinge of sadness about that. On the way back to the house we didn't speak and when we came up to the stoop, Tony turned toward his motorbike. He was rubbing his gut with his palm, slow little circles just above the belt. "You're how old now?" He peered at me in the moonlight, as if fixing my face in his mind.

"Seventeen."

"I thought I knew what held life together then. Do you?"

"No."

"Now it just seems so. I don't know. So arbitrary."

"Big, it seems to me. Overwhelming."

"Yes. Not something you choose but something that chooses you."

We stood silently for a few moments. I thought maybe he was waiting for me to say something but it was one of those times when I could not find the words.

"Good night," I said as he walked away.

"Good bye, Jimmy," he said. "And good luck to you."

I watched him walk toward his bike. When he got there, he turned and added, "Look after your mother now." He was not a fool, I thought right then and I wanted to tell him that, but I didn't, because I did not have the words to say it.

"I will," I said. I felt alone then, which was not unusual and not a bad thing, though I was coming to wonder about that.

"Good," he said. "That's all right then."

He sat on his bike a moment before firing up the engine, a breeze raising the hair on his head. He was not a bad man but he had done an unforgivable thing, at least in the eyes of my mother, and he knew it and didn't know how to undo it. I wondered what I would do in his shoes. Does anyone ever think they're a bad person? It's difficult enough to admit you've made a mistake—I'm wrong, I screwed up. Much easier to do what we all do, find excuses for the crappy things we've done—the lies, the betrayal. Justification. We don't even do it consciously most of the time. We're blind to our faults, to our base desires and motives, and we want to believe we're good, we're decent, we only did that rotten thing because we were provoked, betrayed, done wrong. He started it! There are blind spots in the way we see others, in the way we see ourselves, and they are as dangerous as the visual blind spots that cause us to turn the car into the lane next over and smash up our lives and someone else's.

Later that night my mother came into the room where I was watching TV and said, "Come and look at the sky." She was wearing her housecoat and she looked pretty again, a girlish grin on her face, the hardness of her features softened by moonlight and the time that had passed since we'd come home.

We stepped out onto the stoop and she pointed at the sky. There was a meteor shower, tiny dots of light falling like fireworks, bright, and then diminishing to nothing. I followed one or two down their arc but it was impossible to tell just when they flared out.

"That's something," she said, "isn't it?"

"It is," I said. And it was. It was the first time I'd seen a meteor shower and I've never seen one again as bright, or that lasted so long.

"There's beauty in some prairie nights."

"Magic."

"I love it out here," she said. "So did your father."

We stared at the sky and breathed in the cold air and that was good for both of us, cleansing to the spirit. After a while she said, "You don't mind me mentioning him, do you, your father?"

"No."

"He was so much better than—than that one. Stronger. Where it matters. In the heart."

I nodded. The meteor shower was starting to run down.

"He was a kind man, a good man. I see something of him in you." She had never said this before and I found it strange that she'd chosen this moment to mention it.

"I suppose I'll get that big nose one day soon," I said, laughing a little. "The old Baumer schnozz."

My mother laughed too, a little tinkle of sound. There was a silence. "I'm going to go to Vancouver," she said, "to go to college. They tell me it's nice there." It was the first I'd heard of this and I turned and looked at her. "Don't worry, next summer," she added, smiling, "after you graduate. That's okay with you?"

"It is."

"I'm still a young woman," she said, chuckling. "Well, young enough."

I nodded. I had noticed the way men looked at her at the Headingley Hotel. "Tony says that you're pretty and that you're a fine woman."

She snorted in a way that told me she found that amusing—and more, that she knew things that I didn't yet understand about men and women. She pulled the collar of her housecoat close around her neck. The wind was cold and her legs were bare. "You can come too," she added.

"I might," I said, though I think we both knew I would not.

"I have to get away from here," she said. "Men driving pickup trucks and waving guns in the air." She paused, waiting for me to say something. "Oh, Jimmy," she continued, "I just feel so, so—you know—like I'm at the end of things."

"I know," I said. "Me too."

"I need something to happen in my life, something good, something that doesn't involve motorcycles and shooting."

I nodded. There was an intensity to her voice that told me I did not need to say anything. She was saying what she had been wanting to say for a long time and it didn't require an answer, only my silent presence.

"You won't hold it against me when I leave?"

"No, I will not. You have your life to lead. It's yours and nobody else's."

"There," she said. "That's exactly what your father would have said. Poor Ernie."

At the mention of his name, I felt a lump in my throat and could not speak.

We stood and watched the meteor shower for a few more minutes. It was running down and we were cold and we went inside. She may have said something else but I do not remember, only that we stood at the far ends of the hallway as we went to our bedrooms and looked at each other and grinned.

COLLATERAL DAMAGE

My friendship with Gil Dufault was based on him driving us around in his hand-me-down Chevy pickup and me paying for gas. Most of the time he had only one hand on the wheel, the truck bouncing and swaying on the gravel roads that ran off the main highway near Riding Mountain Park. He needed to use one hand to talk, waving and gesticulating in rhythm to his words. The only time he wasn't doing that was when he shifted gears, jerking the lever on the steering column. And cursing. There was something wrong with the transmission. It clunked going from first to second and sometimes went into neutral and wouldn't move until the truck was brought to a complete stop.

Gil had driven up beside me on the street just past 10:00 on a Saturday evening and tooted the horn. I'd been drinking beer with Greg and Mikey. I hadn't been expecting Gil. That's the way he was. "Hey," he yelled when I looked over at the pickup. Its engine was chuffing and blue smoke belched out of the exhaust. "Henri has some little piece up at the tent. He says we can have her if we want."

Henri was Gil's older brother, the one who'd given him the pick-up truck. He was maybe thirty and his hair was long and greasy but he always wore a fresh shirt. In high school he'd beat up one of the teachers and he'd done time for stabbing a guy outside the Parkland Hotel who'd claimed Henri owed him five dollars. It wasn't a long sentence but he came back with a busted nose and the chain-smoker's cough. After that he'd worked in the oil fields in Alberta but had come back to the Park when their mother had died about a year earlier. He'd been married to a woman there but she had stayed on in the trailer park in Alberta, which was okay with Henri, who never seemed to have trouble turning up women, though that bothered Gil and led him to say mean things about Henri at times.

"That's typical," I said.

"You mean the broad?" Gil chewed on a toothpick most of the time, a habit he claimed kept him from smoking like Henri, two packs a day, and he shifted it around from one side of his mouth to the other.

"I mean the sloppy seconds part."

"Piss off." Gil gunned the engine and had the pickup rolling before I had the door on the passenger's side closed. I had to swing it full out and then bang it shut.

"Not my favourite person, let's say. Your brother."

"There you go again. Always complaining," Gil said. "She's there, we'll fuck her."

"Yeah, that'll be fun. Some squaw or some such." It came out meaner than I'd intended, the beer talking, the buzz in my skull.

"Like we can choose, jokers like us, like we can afford to be fussy." The truck hit a pothole and Gil had to put both hands on the wheel to keep it from going into the ditch. We were on the road into the campground where Henri had pitched a tent.

"Jesus, man," I said. "Steady on. Keep 'er on the road."

"I'm driving here, fuck. I'm driving."

"I want to live to be legal," I said, "so ease off, eh." We were seventeen, Gil older than me by a few months, and we had to ask Henri to buy us beer and mickeys of rye whiskey, which was Gil's favourite. I was still in school, on summer break between grades eleven and twelve, but Gil had decided that he wasn't going back. He'd failed just about everything. He was heading to Alberta to work as a roughneck and make big money. I had no idea what I would do with my life but college seemed a possibility. I did okay at maths and physics and had a vague notion that engineering might be up my alley.

Gil looked over at me and grinned. "You dumping crap on my brother? You talk that way, I give you a smack," he said. He waved his fist in my face and laughed. "Big smack."

"Big talk," I said. "Big talk from a small man." I was over six feet, almost a head taller than Gil, a scrawny kid who hadn't filled out but was a scrapper. I pushed the Coke bottles and t-shirts on the seat between us toward Gil and kicked the newspapers at my feet with my cowboy boots until they had a place to settle flat against the firewall.

"We'll see who's the small man," Gil said, "when we lay hold of that little broad. Come to think of it, I'm gonna fuck her whoever she is."

"Maybe that's not what Henri has in mind."

"He doesn't give a shit."

"I wouldn't want to mess with his woman."

"No. He'd fuck you up like that teacher, right. He doesn't care. He's been in the can and he doesn't give a shit. I know. He shot at me once. Lucky thing the gun was old and misfired; I'd been dead, fuck." Gil was wearing a denim jacket with HELL'S ANGELS written across the back, the letters faded and scrubbed out. The cuffs at his wrists were ratty and threads hung from them and from the collar, which he had turned up.

I blinked my eyes to clear my head. "I ain't getting beat up over a woman."

"Maybe it'll be her who beats you up. She'll be wanting it so bad."

I grunted and then laughed.

"Nice white boy like you, all scrubbed and polished and fancying himself at college." Gil laughed. "Give me that thing," she'll say, "give me that white-boy meat." He was pointing between my legs and gawking there and the truck hit the curb and pitched toward the ditch, but he caught the wheel and brought it back onto the road and then we were both laughing and soon we could see the top of Henri's tent nestled in under the trees.

Her name was Tina, she told us. She was a scrawny little thing with frizzy blonde hair and a freckly complexion. She came out of the tent to meet us and had a mickey bottle of whiskey in one hand. "I hate this," she said, indicating the bottle, "but he left it for youse." She was wearing an army jacket, khaki, and jeans, and a green T-shirt. "I hope you're not drunk already."

"We been drinking," Gil said, "but we're not drunk."

"Not outright," I said, laughing. I blinked again. A hangover was setting in.

Tina stood looking at us. She held the mickey bottle out to Gil and he took it. She had her other hand in her jacket pocket, balled into a fist. The one that had been holding the whiskey had a ring on the middle finger, a cheap ring with a big blue stone. Her fingers were small and red, the nails bitten back.

"Let's go inside," I said.

Tina waited until I led the way and then she followed after, putting one hand on my arm as we ducked through the tent flap.

There was a half box of beer in one corner of the tent and sleeping bags and blankets piled roughly in another. Two empty beer bottles. A pair of soiled jeans thrown carelessly on the floor, a newspaper opened to the comic section. The inside of the tent smelled of oil mixed with onions and some other odour, sweat maybe, or the smell of sex.

We sat down in the middle of the tent. Gil kicked one of the empty beer bottles into a corner. He unscrewed the cap from the mickey and took a swig and then passed it to me. It tasted sharp after the beer I'd been drinking. My nose tickled and I scratched it. When Gil offered the bottle to Tina, she waved it away. Her bottom teeth were tiny and crooked and she seemed to have a perpetual pout. "I was drunk all day yesterday," she told us. "That's how I ended up with Henri. We were in the Parkland drinking beers."

She was younger than I'd thought at first, about our age, maybe a year older, a girl really, but she had a look of experience about her, a way of looking at you and sizing you up. It was a little unnerving. She was thin and couldn't have weighed more than a hundred pounds.

"Rick doesn't like the Parkland," Gil said. "Too pricey for Rick. The draft gives Rick a sore gut." He seemed to be angry about some-thing. The next swig of whiskey he took was a long one and he held the mickey up to the little light seeping into the tent and studied the contents sloshing around in the bottom and put the cap back on without offering it around. It didn't matter, I'd had enough to drink, I'd been mildly drunk for more than a day and felt a serious hangover edging into my skull.

"I like rum and Coke," Tina said.

"I like it too," I said. I was feeling good. There was a lilt in my voice. I smiled at Tina, what I wished was a hopeful smile.

"It's sweet and it gives me a headache the next day but it's better than that stuff." She shivered, nodding at the bottle in Gil's hand. "Too strong. I feel like puking."

"It's a strong drink," I said. "An acquired taste."

Gil snorted. "Listen to you." His lip curled down and he looked away when Tina turned towards him. "*Acquired*," he sneered.

"You're an odd pair," she said.

"We're brothers," Gil said, "brothers in blood." And he snorted again. He fumbled in the pocket of his jacket and brought out a toothpick and started chewing on it. He had dark eyes which were hooded, and bushy eyebrows, so even ordinarily he looked menacing. He'd told me that he and Henri had gone after each other with knives one time. I didn't believe it for a moment.

"You don't look like brothers," Tina said.

"What do we look like?" Gil asked.

"You look angry," she said to him. "And Rick—Rick?—Rick looks tired."

"I'm not," I said.

Tina tapped the hand with the ring on one knee. "What's your story, then?"

"He's the son of an entrepreneur," Gil said. "Fancy word, eh? Learned it from Rick here. He's the son of a man who lost a business and went bankrupt but did not give up on life. It's an important lesson—even if shit happens, you don't give up. Right, Rick? His mother does sewing and shit at Eaton's. That's the story. Rick's family. Dreams that died. Now Rick's got his own dreams." Gil sat back and smiled at me, a mean smile. Everything he said was true and it's what I thought but when it came out of his mouth it sounded small and petty and I did not want to look at Tina so I pretended to pick at a scab on my wrist.

"Tired," Tina repeated. "Are you tired, big man wearing cowboy boots?"

"It's my eyes," I said finally, looking into hers , "I always look sleepy even when I'm bright-eyed and bushy-tailed, even when I'm all gung-ho." I laughed and leaned back on my elbows a little, stretching my legs out and crossing them at the ankles. The cowboy boots were tan-coloured with a cross-stitch in the toes.

Tina studied them for a moment and then looked at me and smiled. "And are you gung-ho now, cowboy Rick?"

"In a way, yes."

"He's gung-ho for your ass," Gil said. He'd unscrewed the cap of the bottle again and drained off what was left. "He wants to fuck you."

"See," Tina said, "angry. What makes you so angry?"

Gil threw the empty bottle into a corner of the tent. "What does it matter to you?" he snarled at Tina, pointing one finger into her face. "What the fuck does it matter to you?"

I said, "Maybe we should open one of them beers."

"Shit," Gil said. "Warm beer. Might as well drink piss."

We sat in silence for a while. I wanted to ask Tina where she came from and what she did but I knew as soon as I opened my mouth Gil would say something snarky and cruel. Maybe Tina knew that too. She sat between us, the three of us forming a triangle in the centre of the tent, and she twiddled her fingers together and looked at her shoes. They were thin, light shoes with almost no heel, I'd heard someone British call them *plimsolls*. Tina's were silver-coloured but soiled at the toes and badly scuffed up. They reminded me of ballet slippers, but they weren't that either. After a few minutes Gil said, "We should have music in here. I'm going to turn on the radio in the truck."

After he said that he didn't get up to go but Tina thought he was going to and she moved toward me, putting out the hand with the ring to touch my knee. Gil stared at it hard. I glanced from her to him. Tina was stroking my leg but not looking at either of us. "Fuck," Gil said. "Fuck the both of you." He stood up suddenly and you could tell by the way he did it that he was drunk, drunker than he appeared. He threw open the tent flap and ducked out. "I hope you fucking die," he snarled. "The both of youse." The sound his shoes made outside indicated he was staggering. In a minute there was the loud bang of a door closing and then the truck's engine turned over and the tires scattered gravel as it spun out of the camping space.

She was thin and small and when I lay on top of her she made fists of both hands and beat them on my back. "Plank me," she whispered in my ear. And then, "Oh, God, plank me!"

It was over fast and I threw the condom away and we lay on our backs and looked at the roof of the tent. It was dark now, the thin light of the moon barely making anything visible in the tent. "You want a beer?" I asked.

"No," she said. Her mouth had tasted of whiskey and when we were kissing I'd felt the sharp points of her small teeth against my tongue. Her ribs had hardly any flesh on them, she was that thin.

"Where are you from?" I asked.

"Everywhere," she said, "and nowhere." She laughed. "My old man's army, we've lived in every goddamn hole in the country. Every piss-ass little town you can name from Nova Scotia to the West Coast."

"Shilo?" It was the closest military base. The German army sent recruits there and on weekends sometimes they came in a bus to Clear Lake on leave, wandering the streets of town in light blue uniforms and eating ice cream.

Tina cleared her throat. "My old man's a captain now. Big fucking deal."

"There's a name for kids like you," I said, "but I can't remember it."

"Army brats," she said. "Base bastards. There's others. My mother had enough of it last year and she split and lives in Brandon now and wants me to be the little lady. Private school kind of thing." She snorted. "Where was she back when?"

"Are there guns around your house?"

"The only time we ever saw a gun was when he threatened to blow his head off."

There was a silence before I said, "But he didn't pull the trigger." It was a stupid thing to say but Tina had left a silence that seemed to require me to speak.

"Get real." Tina laughed aloud and it was almost pretty. "He'd found out my old lady was having it off with some other guy at the base and he came home and stood right in front of us in the dining room and pulled out his gun. I was maybe twelve. *Is this what you want?* He put the barrel in his mouth. Big war hero. The tough guy. Threatened to blow his brains all over the room. Not hers, mind you, not the other guy's, which I might have respected, but his own. Some war hero."

"You're being pretty hard on him. Sometimes a person is just pushed to the edge."

Tina turned and looked at me and smiled. I could just make out her teeth in the darkness, little points of white. "You're a softy. A big dumb softy." She laughed again and this time it was pretty. "I like that," she said after a minute. "I like you." She reached over and took my hand and squeezed it. "I'm glad it was you."

"Me too." I squeezed back. I thought of the way we'd thrashed around on the tent floor. It had been good but not as good as it should have been.

"What's with your friend, though?"

"He's had a rough time of it."

"He's angry. He scares me. Henri, now, he's gentle, you can see it in the eyes. He's gentle with a woman. But this other one. Scary. Scare-y." Tina squeezed my fingers again and leaned over and rested her head on my shoulder. Her breath smelled of beer. It was her body giving off that musky odour, the smell of sex.

"He grew up without parents. Basically. His mother ran off with some guy who worked for the railroad and his father died in a car crash when Gil was ten or something. Twelve. He lived with his grandmother. Day-old bread, Kraft dinner, baloney sandwiches at school. All pretty dismal. He has these dreams where he wakes up shouting."

"Me too."

"I dream that my father has run off with another woman and

left us alone. Which is weird because nothing remotely like that ever happened."

"Abandonment." Tina sighed. I felt her pulse on my wrist. "It's a crappy world."

"It is indeed." I closed my eyes and listened to Tina's breathing and thought, So this is what it's like to be a man and woman lying together. Small talk, a warm body touching yours, hearing the other person breathe. Wondering what they were thinking but not really caring.

Tina acted like she didn't care for Gil but they were a lot alike, more like each other than either was like me. They'd had crap dumped on them and were angry and resentful. I had too, but not as much, my luck seemed both bad and good. That was the difference. I thought that was true but I also thought that people make their own luck, that getting by in life was a matter of taking up the cards you were dealt and making the best of it. I believed that then, that you coped with the crap that came your way and that that was the measure of a person, how you stood up to things that just happened to you.

We lay thinking our own thoughts and then the sound of the pickup grinding up the hill and over the gravel broke the silence. "Shit," I said. I lifted onto one elbow.

"He'll have been drinking," Tina said. "He's the type."

I stood up quickly and was out of the tent before the door of the pickup slammed shut behind Gil's form. I stumbled about a little, head-rush. It was dark in the campground, the moon just above the trees shedding only a faint light onto the road behind the truck.

"I want to fuck her," Gil said. He had another mickey bottle and it glinted when he raised it to his mouth.

"No," I said, "that's not on."

"Oh, that's how it is, is it? You have her but then she's precious once you've been in there and no one else gets a shot." He tipped the mickey bottle up and drained the contents and flung the bottle into the bushes.

"It's not like that." I stepped toward the pickup, keeping myself between him and the tent flap.

"Fuck you."

"Gil."

"I never liked you, you know. You think you're better than everyone else. Go to fucking college already but don't throw it up in everyone's face all the time. Fuck."

"C'mon," I said, "we'll have a beer. We'll have several beers."

"Fuck off." He moved forward suddenly, staggered actually, and I thought he would fall and I let down my guard.

If it hadn't been as dark as it was under the trees I would have seen the punch coming, but it caught me unawares. Still, instinct caused me to duck and the blow only caught me on the ear. I hadn't realized Gil wore a big ring on his right hand but I felt it almost embed itself in my flesh and scrape along the cartilage of the top. I hit out at him and struck his shoulder and then we had each other by the arms, swaying this way and that. I tried to push Gil back toward the pickup and at the same time he kicked out at my legs and we both went down awkwardly. His head struck the wheel well of the back tire and I pitched forward, striking my shoulder on the ground. A flash of pain raced from my elbow through my eyes and into the top of my skull. Stars danced in my eyes, there was a sudden ringing in both ears. When I righted myself I saw that Gil was crumpled against the wheel, his head twisted at an angle, blood running down his neck from a gash in the back of his skull. He's dead, I thought, I killed him. I crawled across toward him and listened for breathing and put my hand under his nose but felt nothing. I'd killed him.

I rolled away and pushed my back up against the side of the pickup. My heart pounded in my chest and my arms shook. I thought of driving down to the RCMP station and turning myself in; I thought of throwing Gil's body into the back of the pickup and driving out to

Moth Lake and leaving it there and hitchhiking back; I thought of driving there and pitching the body into the reeds along the edge of the lake and driving back and then high-tailing it out of town. The moon was shining down through the trees and touching the toes of my boots. Everything looked unearthly, the trees, my outstretched legs, the shadowy outline of the tent. I closed my eyes and felt the darkness wash over me.

The sound of Gil's breath, harsh and gasping, woke me up. The moon had moved higher and was in my lap. I looked over at Gil. He was breathing in rasping, metallic snores, hands and feet twitching as if he was far off in a dream. I envied him for a moment. I watched drool come out of his mouth, silvery in the moonlight, strings of drool that dribbled down his chin and onto his jacket. There might have been blood mixed in, I could not tell.

I stood up and steadied myself by holding onto the ledge of the truck box. He was not dead. That's good, I thought, I'm not a killer, I'm not doing time. I went back to the tent and ducked inside and came out with a blanket and placed it over his legs and tucked it behind his shoulders. Gil's neck and head were still twisted at an awkward angle and I was tempted to straighten him but thought that would wake him and I didn't want that.

I went back to the tent. Tina was curled up like a child and snoring rudely. One hand was under her chin. The other jerked and twitched. She was dreaming, too, a long way away, and I stood and watched her for a moment and then dragged a couple of sleeping bags over us and snuggled up against her, soup-spoon style. She moaned and said incomprehensible words. I wondered what it would be like to do hard time for murder and was glad that I did not have to find out. Broken noses and chain smoking were not in my future.

The sound of the pickup coughing to life woke me. Thin light was coming through the tent fabric. Birds were twittering in the bushes. The pickup's tires rolled across the gravel and then it spluttered away, the sound of the engine diminishing slowly. I was lying on my back and Tina's head was tucked into my shoulder. She was breathing easily, short small gasps. My mouth was dry. It tasted of burnt oak, the taste of whiskey. I lay and watched the sun lighten the tent's fabric and thought about nothing. It was surprising after all that had happened. My mind was blank, thoughts and images popped into it and then faded and I could not have said what they were. It was like I was suspended, an astronaut of the mind, somewhere far away, floating, and it was not a bad feeling at all, pleasant actually, a place that was comforting for its blankness.

After a while Tina woke up. "What time is it?" she asked.

I looked at my watch. "Almost 6:30."

"Shit, I gotta go," she said, rising on one elbow. "Shit."

We stood and straightened our clothes a little. There were creases in Tina's jeans and her face had marks from where her cheek had lain against the hard ground. Her eyes were big and wet. She looked at the condom lying near the tent door but neither of us said anything. She ran her fingers through her hair and gave her head a shake. Outside we started down the road toward town. It was over a mile by the asphalt road but a path cut through the woods that took you downtown much quicker. We went that way, walking single file through the singing birds and dew-spattered grass. Tina was ahead and I watched her curly hair bounce with her steps and studied her skinny shoulders and it occurred to me that sometimes when you get what you want it turns out not to be such a good thing. Reality does not match up to desire. Sometimes it does, but a lot of the time it doesn't, and whether a life goes on and makes sense to a person or doesn't depends on how many times it works out against how many times it doesn't. Mostly you think things will always work out but growing up means realizing that it doesn't and accepting that, or not accepting it and turning into someone you hadn't set out to be, frustrated and angry, defeated by life. I wondered if Tina felt that way. There were signs of it in Gil, as if he felt tragic even to his own self.

The path descended sharply toward the town site. First you saw the roofs of the hotels and cabins up toward the camp ground, then the blue, red, and white sign at the Esso station, then the roads and sidewalks that criss-crossed the centre of town. When we came to the sidewalk I took Tina's hand. Her shoes scuffed the concrete as she walked, every step, scuff scuff scuff. She squeezed my fingers. "He raped me," she said. There was a silence. "My father."

"You don't have to tell me," I said. Larry the paper boy was doing his route on a bicycle and we waved at each other. Tina had her eyes down to the sidewalk. I heard a few small sobs and saw tears run down her nose and onto the concrete, leaving little dots about the size of dimes. She took her hand out of mine and wrapped it through my elbow. We came to the intersection and turned toward Main Street, where the restaurants were located.

Tina released my arm and looked up at me. Her eyes were green. There was a little scar in her lower lip. "I'm collateral damage," she said.

I grunted.

"He told me about it. My father. You get blown up accidentally."

I thought of TV images, the Vietnam war, children burning from napalm. "Incidentally."

"Yeah. A side effect. Not intended."

We came to the intersection at Main Street. The sun was coming over the pine trees in front of Dance Land. Clear Lake was a beautiful place. Green and quiet. The water in the lake was clear and cold. Birds sang in the bushes. Locals waved and called out to each other. The Chamber of Commerce had hung potted flower plants from the lamp posts. It was the kind of place that made you forget about how ugly life could be. "I'll buy you breakfast," I said.

"No," she said. "I'll puke."

"You'll feel better. A little toast with butter."

"No. I have to get back to Brandon. My mother will be going up and down the walls. I was supposed to be home by midnight. She'll rip my face off."

When we walked past the trash can in front of the movie theatre, Tina took her hand out of her jacket pocket and threw a balled-up piece of paper into it. "There," she said.

I glanced that way. It seemed to be an envelope.

"An application to a dance school in the States," she said. "A fancy private school. My parents wanted me to go. To continue my dance." She laughed and it was not a happy sound. "Well, fuck them." Then she did something that surprised me. She made a little curtsey and went up on her toes and did a few quick steps in front of me and pirouetted. She was a different person at that moment, focused and intent. Her body was at her command. It was lovely. She came back toward me smiling. "That could have been me," she said. "But fuck them."

She had talent, that much was clear. She had talent and she was throwing it away and that was very sad, as sad as Gil's not having anything at all and wanting to, but there was strength in Tina, too, the courage to say no to what others wanted for her and the determination to see it out. I admired her, I thought that was a good way to live. Too many people based what they did on what others wanted them to do, or on what they thought others wanted them to do, and after a while they didn't know who they were and what they wanted. Sometimes it was important to say no. Otherwise you were living someone else's dream. "Parents," I said finally. "Fuck them."

We were on the other side of the street from the Lake Lodge but I saw Mikey and Greg sitting at a restaurant table looking out the window onto the sidewalk. I felt Tina's hand locked onto my elbow again, her fingers gripping my flesh. "How will you get home?"

"I'll hitch."

"Jesus," I said. "This time of day?"

"There's always a man who will pick me up."

We passed the bowling alley and the roller rink. Tina took her hand away from my arm. Her shoes scuffed with every step she took. I thought, This woman would drive me crazy, can't she lift her feet when she walks? And then I felt shitty about that and I reached out and touched her arm gently. "Goodbye," she said. We had stopped walking.

"I'll go with you. Wait 'til you catch a ride."

She unbuttoned the two top buttons of her jacket and put her hands on the hem of her shirt and straightened it under the jacket. "No," she said, "then I won't get a ride." She walked away. After a few steps she stopped and turned around and came back to me. "You're a good man, Rick," she said to me. "It is Rick, isn't it?"

"Yes." I did not feel like a good guy, I felt like a bastard. I'd used Tina, who was after all just another person trying to get by, and now it felt to me as if I was chucking her away, like trash, and that's no way to treat anyone. "You're wrong about that," I said flatly.

"You're a nice man, Rick. You'll make some girl happy some day." Her eyes looked up at me and I felt the whole of my insides slide away.

"It's in my eyes?" I said, laughing.

"You're half asleep," she said. "That's good in a man. Takes the edge off aggression. You know? Men. You're all so angry."

"If you say."

This time she did not pause as she walked away. The road rose slightly as it climbed to the exit of the park. Near the top she turned and faced back toward me. She raised one hand to about shoulder height and waved, the tiniest wave, like the Queen going past. I'd once heard someone say that life comes down to how much you're prepared to change, and I'd believed that was wise, but now I was not sure. Maybe it was more a matter of what you were prepared to lose. I took a tissue out of my back pocket and blew my nose. I had hurt Tina. I had wanted something from her and I had taken it and I had not cared much what she felt as long as I got it. I wondered if I was becoming a man who brought pain to everyone they claimed to love. I thought then that they were a group apart, those who hurt others in pursuit of their own desires.

In a minute a car came by and she stuck out her thumb, but it drove past, and the next one did too, but then a pickup came along and just past where she was standing the brake lights came on and the passenger's door flew open and she ran toward it and hopped in and in a moment the brake lights went off again.

The sky was beginning to be filled with light. Streaky grey clouds were on the horizon to the east but the west and north were clear and blue. A mongrel came out from behind the Pizza Place and crossed the road and trotted into the bush behind the bowling alley. I was thinking about what Tina had said. It was true. I was half asleep, I seemed to understand the importance of things only after they'd passed. I wondered if it was an important fault, if all women saw it.

I walked down to the Wigwam and Greg and Mikey were in there, at a table up front and I sat down beside them.

"Hoo-hoo," Greg said, "a little poon tang, eh?" He lifted his ball cap in salute. "Good man, Rick. Rick's buying today."

Mikey laughed. "A little of the old wham-bam-thank-you-ma'am." He made a gesture with his arm, pumping his raised fist toward his chest.

The waitress was serving the next table and she looked over at us and shook her head. Her name was Brenda. I'd danced with her at Dance Land on Saturday nights and walked her back to the Wigwam when the band shut down. We stood and kissed at the bottom of the steps that led upstairs where there were rooms the waitresses slept in. She couldn't invite me up there. We kissed but that was mostly it. One time we rubbed our crotches together and I came in my pants and we both laughed.

Mikey jerked his thumb toward the back of the room and rolled his eyes that way. I stood and walked to the last booth before the washrooms. There was Gil in the far corner of the booth, hunched over a cup of coffee. "Fuck you," he said, not even looking up. "Fuck everybody."

I slid onto the wooden bench and propped my elbows on the tabletop. The gash at the back of Gil's head had not been cleaned up. The hair was matted and streaks of dried blood ran from his ear into his throat. The collar of the jacket was soaked through and looked stiff and hard with dried blood and bits of gravel.

Brenda came up and I said, "Two times two eggs over easy, bacon, white toast." Gil raised his hand from the coffee cup and waved away the order. "Go on," I said to Brenda. "Bring the two plates." When she'd walked off I called out, "And coffee." I touched my hand to the ear where Gil had punched me and flinched and reminded myself to have a look at it in the bathroom mirror later.

"It was nothing," I said. "Nothing happened."

"Fuck you."

Out the window the sun was coming between the trees onto the green lawn and black birds were hopping about and pecking and then flying up into the trees and then others fluttered down and pecked in the dirt around the flowerbeds. I wondered where Tina was, maybe still on the road, maybe safe at her mother's house in Brandon. I glanced at my watch. 7:30. I hoped she was okay. I hoped her life turned out okay but I had my doubts. I sighed and tried not to think about that.

Gil shifted around on the seat and took a sip of coffee and then raised his eyes to mine but neither of us said anything. Someone had started up the jukebox in front, a song popular all that summer, "Silence is Golden." I smiled to myself. I looked into Gil's dark eyes and saw the same thing I'd seen in Tina's, emptiness, and I knew that that there would be better days ahead for me but right then the world was a grey and lonely place.

BORDERLINE

Hal strode across from the bar toward us and slapped a package of cigarettes on the table. His eyes went from Rodney to me and then back to Rodney. He weaved a little. We'd been drinking since noon, first at the Rain Lake and then at this bar in the Falls since we'd tracked down Rodney. "There," Hal said, sitting down. "Your smokes." There was an edge to his voice.

Rodney reached for the cigarettes with one hand and for his beer glass with the other. He had big hands with chipped nails that had black dirt under them. When he had the beer and cigarettes in his hands he looked at them, as if he couldn't decide which to act on. He was drunk. His eyes had trouble focusing and his speech was slurred.

"Smokes," he mumbled. He looked at me. "You wan'?"

"No," I said, "I don't."

"Weed, maybe," Hal said, laughing. "Johnny likes the occasional toke." He had a mustache and he stroked it with the back of one finger.

"That right," Rodney said. He busied himself with the cellophane wrapping.

"God's own truth," Hal said. He winked at me and chuckled.

Hal and I worked at the paper mill, me on the floor attending to the giant rollers, oiling and keeping an eye out that the machinery was functioning smoothly, a dog's job, but okay with me because I was just out of high school and not certain I wanted to hang around Fort Frances or light out for the city. Hal was my foreman. We played on the Fort Canadians hockey team where he was a steady defenceman and I his unpredictable partner. At the mill we'd been eating lunches together for months and sat beside each other to dress for games. I'd visited his house a couple of times. He had been married and had a kid and we talked about that and how he wanted to live on his scrub brush farm near Emo once he had enough money put away. He told me about Marvin and I told him about how Carrie and I were fighting, and we groused about coaches and the mill owners, and it was okay, the kind of things men do together when they're making their way in the world.

At the bar there was a guy sitting on a stool and leaning heavily over the counter as if he was about to pass out. A country song was playing through the speakers overhead. The guy leaning over the bar raised himself up and looked in our direction. He ran his hand through a dark head of thick hair and he shook his head, as if to clear it.

There were booths along the wall opposite the bar. At one of them sat a man and woman in their forties. They were wearing team jackets, yellow and black, and they had on baseball caps. The woman was mouthing the words of the country song and her husband tapping the rhythm on the tabletop. At the next booth down was a burly guy with a scraggly blond beard wearing a black leather jacket. He'd been playing pool when we came into the bar but he was sitting alone now, smoking a cigar and drinking whiskey with a beer chaser.

"Shoulda done like you," Rodney said to Hal. "Shoulda got outta here ages ago. Stinkin' hole, stinkin' America." He waved his arm around, indicating the bar but meaning something larger. "America," he said again with a snort.

I looked around: at the Schlitz signs, the Marlboro logo over the bar. It was America. I was a little surprised to be there and shook my head to recover my bearings. In the Rain River at 5:30 Hal had suddenly looked at his watch and said, "Shit, I have to get Marv from the landlady's and then see Rod gets on that bus. I promised Aunt Judy." We were there to see he made it to boot camp. Rodney's number had been picked in the draft lottery and he was due at the bus pick-up at midnight. It was make it to that bus, Hal had told me, or another stint in the slammer.

Hal said, "It won't be so bad, Rod." He glanced at his watch.

"Fuck that," Rodney said. "Like you would know."

"Like you would," Hal snapped back.

They were brothers. It was past 10:00 and we'd been sitting in the bar since after supper, burgers at a joint down the street. It had not been a good day for Rodney. He'd had to take his pickup truck back to the dealership and then dispose of his dog. Tomorrow was not looking like it would be much of a day for him either. Arriving at boot camp with a hangover big as Lake Superior.

Rodney said, "I shoulda done like you, big bro, I shoulda fucked off to Canada."

Hal said, "Too late for that now. Drink up." There were eight or ten draft on the table, and two bottles of Budweiser. I blinked, bringing them into focus.

"But I never thought that far ahead," Rodney was saying. "I shoulda been thinking, see, like you, you had it all figured, bro, you got all the luck ..."

Rodney took a sip from his glass and stared past Hal's shoulder. He was facing the bar and he suddenly shot up his free hand and shouted at the guy with the mustache, "Hey, buddy!"

The Hungarian peered toward us. He shook his head and said

something to the bartender. The bartender was wiping glasses and he said something back and then flipped his towel over his shoulder and turned away. The Hungarian stared down at the bar.

Rodney looked at the guy wearing leather in the booth. "Hey," he shouted.

The guy in leather blew smoke toward the ceiling and eyed us. The jacket had the name of a motorbike club written on it and a logo, intertwined serpents maybe.

"All right," Hal said. He put his hand on Rodney's arm. "Cool it."

"Jus' wanna offer them guys a beer," Rodney muttered. "Jus' being frenly."

"Okay," Hal said, "let's not get ourselves into something here."

The bar was a shimmery kind of green, I noticed. Objects were going in and out of focus. I was drunk too, which had been not a bad feeling a while ago but now not so much. I lifted my glass and looked at it and then drained the last of the beer. The draft tasted thin compared to the stuff we were used to at home. Over the bar and between the rows of bottles of hard liquor there was a flashing neon sign that said PABST, and beside it an old-fashioned clock in a wooden frame. One of the clock's hands was bent. It was pointing downwards toward the 6 and I struggled to figure out exactly what time it was.

Rodney was fumbling with the cigarette pack. When he had one out and lit he said, "Can't a fella be frenly any more? You gonna take that away from him too?"

Hal muttered something.

"You gonna steal that from me too?"

"I'm not taking anything away," Hal said. He scratched his chin where there was a big pimple. At the Rain River he'd said, "C'mon, Johnny, keep me company over in the Excited States, I'll buy." I should have said *no*, I should have gone over to Carrie's and made it up, but I was sore at her and it had seemed a good idea at the time. I liked Marvin and I liked yakking with Hal, he reminded me of my father, only he listened to rock music and didn't tell the same war stories over and over.

I studied the clock at the bar, twisting my head to line the bent arm up with the numbers. Marvin was out spending the money Hal had given him after we'd had supper at the burger joint. What was the kid doing there? What was I doing there, listening to Hal and Rodney go at each other, picking away at old wounds? I wondered about that. The situation had just evolved, and now we were seeing it through. That's what I told myself. Drink up, I told myself, Hal's paying.

"You're a taker," Rodney said, pointing his cigarette at Hal. "And I'm always gettin' taken."

"Whatever was taken from you, bro, you took away from yourself. Lost, more like."

"Oh, here it comes, the lecture." Rodney turned to me, pointing the cigarette in my face, smoke tickling my nose. "You ready for it? Listen good here Johnny. We're gonna hear the gospel according to Hal."

"Shove it along, Rod," Hal said. "Johnny has no interest in—"

"My big brother. The Man. The big operator got his own place, a two-bit farm in the bush, you really wanna know, Johnny."

Hal shook his head in disgust and took a sip of beer. He did not look at me.

"He doesn't even know what to say," Rodney said. "How to answer me." He looked at me and I thought he was a fool, a man who didn't know what to value in another person. Rodney went *huh* and turned his eyes from me.

I sat back. Another glass of draft was in my hand and I tipped it to my mouth. The country song had changed to something with female voices. I waited until Rodney took a drag on his cigarette and then I leaned in toward Hal. "You ever notice how the country chicks are lookers but the rock singers kind of tire biters?"

Hal said, "I hear you there." He was drinking Budweiser from the bottle because of his bad gut and poured from the bottle to a glass, letting the foam build up right to the mouth.

"I'da been okay," Rodney said, "if you hadn't leff me behind. Things coulda worked out for me. Steady job at the mill. 'Stead of this here. Boot camp and shit." He blew out smoke.

"No one left anybody behind. One of us had to go with Auntie Joan and one with Judy. It was that simple. It was me to Canada because I was sixteen. You were too young."

"You coulda brung me later."

"Good Lord, Rod, this is ancient history, man."

"You was all I had," Rodney sniffed. "You coulda."

"You could have moved up later. Auntie Joan offered, remember? She had the spare bed in the basement. But there was that girl, remember, that girl you just had to be with, the love of your life?"

"Yeah, that girl. That was stupid." Rodney sighed "But good times then."

"Right. Good times then, not so good now. You made your own bed, Rod."

"So did you, Hal, so did you, big bro."

"I know it," Hal said. They were referring to Marvin's mother, who had run out on him with another guy and gone to the city and never bothered with the boy since. "I know it," Hal repeated, touching his gut, a reflex from the ulcer he'd developed since he'd been left with Marvin and the mortgage and all that.

Rodney said, "Wha'd we do with Chester?"

"We took care of it," Hal said.

"We take him to the vet?"

"We took care of it. Drink your beer, little bro."

"My fren, my old fren Chester." Rodney blew smoke out of his nose. "He's at the vet. We took him to the vet and he's fine now. Yup."

It was a good thing Rodney didn't remember. Hal had said the vet would be best, a quiet needle, but Rod had insisted we drive out into the country with the dog and the .303. We found a quiet gravel road that led into the hills. Hal had jumped out and taken Marvin with him back to the highway on the pretext of having spotted a bobcat at the turnoff. Rodney had stumbled from the car. He'd been drinking from a whiskey bottle and he wrestled the .303 out of the back seat where Chester and I had been keeping him company on the drive. The dog was getting on. Hal couldn't take him back across the border because he had no papers, and didn't want him anyway, and Rodney couldn't stand the idea of giving him to a stranger. He meant to do the honourable thing, take Chester to a quiet place and see it through with him. But when he raised the .303 his arm was not steady and he hesitated and the dog turned suddenly so he ended up shooting him in the belly. Chester yowled and thrashed sideways and Rodney had to take a second shot and then a third. By the time it was over Chester had crawled into the ditch bleeding from the guts and Rodney had sweat running down his red face and was breathing like a man about to die himself. He coughed and threw the .303 into the grass and bent over and vomited beside what had been the only creature that loved him the past years.

"Only fren I ever had," Rodney said. "A fuckin' dog."

"We're here," Hal said. "Me and Johnny."

"That's right. My frens Hal and Johnny." Rodney dug around in his pocket and pulled out his wallet. He opened it and slapped all the bills on the table. "I'm paying," he said. "Rodney is buying on this last night of his freedom, fuckin' eh."

"Put your money away," Hal said.

"What I got need for money?" Rodney smacked one hand down on top of the bills and stared at Hal, then me. "Where I'm going, the US Army pays. Uncle Sam. By God, they better pay."

"All right," Hal said. He looked toward the door and then at his watch. He was thinking of Marvin, who had gone off down the street looking for a candy and magazine store when we had gone into the bar. He was ten, a scrawny kid with dirty blond hair and pimples on his nose.

"I'm paying," Rodney muttered. "Don't tell me my money's no good here, Hal."

A man in a business suit had come in and joined the Hungarian at the bar. He ordered a drink and gazed warily around the room and, satisfied with what he saw, turned back to his drink.

"I could come up to Canada with you guys," Rodney said brightly, as if the idea had only then occurred to him.

"Impossible," Hal said. "They'd stop you at the border."

"Fuck that," Rodney said. "You could smuggle me."

"No," Hal said. "They got a special guard checking for guys like you."

"They smuggle people all the time, refugees and Mexicans and negroes and like that."

"Good Christ, man. You don't know what you're talking about."

"Worth a try."

"And what then? You could never come back, you'd be a criminal. In both countries."

"You just gonna abandon me, then, your little brother?"

"Rod, for Christ's sake. I got the kid with me, there's Johnny here. You want to see everybody thrown into jail? Think, man."

Jail gave us all pause. Rodney had done time for passing bad cheques and Hal had been given an order from a judge after he'd raised a ruckus at his in-laws. I'd spent a night cooling off after a barroom scrap that I couldn't recall even when I looked in the mirror at the scar over one eye.

"You'd do it for Johnny," Rodney finally mumbled. He looked at me, then at Hal. The cigarette dangled from his lower lip and ash dropped onto the table. "But me, your own flesh and blood, no." He'd balled one hand into a fist.

Hal said, "Drink up." He glanced at his watch. I gazed at the busted clock. Almost 11:00.

Rodney said, "I could swim. It's only a hundred yards or so across the river."

"For Christ sake, Rod. You'd never make it. There's a current, the water is freezing."

"I'd make it. I'm the swimmer, right? It's the Rainy River, it's nothing. It's a creek."

"It's a stupid idea. You'd drown."

"You wanna get rid 'a me—is that it?"

"Even if you made it, then what?"

"Fuck off and die—is that it? The useless little brother. Like that time in Duluth?"

Hal had placed his hands on the edge of the table, as if intending to stand up. I slid my chair back slowly. I had no idea what might happen but was bracing myself. The room was a lighter tinge of green than before. I was having a little trouble focusing. The couple at the booth were staring in our direction. Their ball caps were soiled at the brim, I saw now, and they both had the same kind of beak nose, hawk noses, I thought, and I laughed aloud. The voices of Hal and Rodney had risen without me noticing and the music seemed louder too. The bartender stood near the Hungarian with both hands resting on the countertop, peering over at us. The biker had disappeared.

Just then the swinging door into the bar squeaked on its hinges and Hal looked that way at Marvin, who was standing with one hand raised up to his eyes, peering into the dim and smoky room. "Hey, buddy," Hal called out. He half stood and waved. Marvin was beginning to back up toward the exit. Hal stood suddenly. "Silly little bugger," he muttered. He started across the room, waving one hand but Marvin was not looking any more. I noticed the biker was back at his booth, digging through his wallet. Standing, he was bigger than I'd thought, a barrel-chested type with a big gut and skinny legs, like the guy who'd hit me blind-side the night I spent in jail. I followed Hal as he made his way across the bar. Marvin had stepped back through the swinging doors but Hal reached him soon after and in a moment they both reappeared, crossing toward the table. I was standing, it seemed. The room began to revolve before my eyes: the couple in the booth hung at a crazy angle in the air, and Hal and Marvin were located somewhere up near the ceiling. In a moment the room tilted the other way. I said aloud, "Bugger," but I took another drink from the bottle in my hand and cleared my throat.

"Where's Rod?" Hal called out to me.

I turned. His chair was empty.

"Shit," Hal said coming up to the table, "I leave you alone with him for one minute." He studied the table and then said, "Crap. Smokes are gone. Money too." He banged his fist on the table.

Marvin had come up beside me. "Hey," I said.

"Hey," he said. He had a comic book in one hand and there was toffee on his lips. In the car earlier he'd asked me about the dog and I'd put him off by asking him about the boots he was wearing, black cowboy boots with a diamond pattern stitched into the toe.

"Shit," Hal was saying. He pulled a wad of bills out of his pocket and put a twenty on the table, glancing toward the bartender and pointing at the money. Hal looked at his watch. 11:10.

We hustled out of the bar and onto the street. The air was fresh and cool and hit my face in a rush. Overhead the moon shone down brightly. The frost was coming. I puffed my breath into the air, looking for ghosts, but there were none. Beside me Marvin did the same. His face was pale in the moonlight and his eyes bugged out. Hal pointed down a side street in the direction we'd arrived from. We started running. I had Marvin's hand in mine and we trailed behind Hal, who was picking up speed with each stride. The jostling of my knees was not good for what I was feeling in my guts, but Hal had decided we were in a hurry, so I kept on running. Beside and behind me Marvin was gasping and panting, trying to keep up.

Hal disappeared around a bend where the road turned to gravel and fell off toward the river. I heard him calling out to Rodney and then a voice answering back. Shouts, curses. I slowed our pace to a walk. The sky had lowered and the view toward the river was filled with impenetrable deep-blue shadows. What a pity, I thought, that there wasn't a soft bed right in the alley. It was a perfect spot for a long, hard sleep, a perfect spot to lie down and forget Rodney and Carrie and Hal's bad gut, a quiet place under a dark sky where a man could just close his eyes and feel the oblivion of sleep coming down.

Marvin scuffed his feet as we walked along. "What happened to Chester?" he asked.

"We took him into the country," I said. "There was a man there, see."

"Did he die?"

"He's okay now."

Our feet scuffed in the gravel. Marvin was breathing hard and I was having to work hard to keep objects in focus.

"There were shots," Marvin said. His hand was hot in mine and he squirmed it free. "Did you shoot him? Did Uncle Rodney shoot him with the gun?" He looked up at me, lips clenched together.

There are times when you don't know what to say. You don't want to tell a kid an awful truth but just as much you don't want to lie to him. They're smarter than we think. If they figure out you've lied to them, they won't trust you the next time and pretty soon what you've got is silence where there should be something else, give and take, trust. I turned all that over and reached down and took Marvin's hand again. We stopped in the road and I dropped down on one knee and looked him in the eye and said, "Yes, Rodney thought it was for the best. He shot him. Chester was old and he didn't want him to suffer the indignity of the vet pumping him full of drugs."

"I thought so," Marvin said. His lower lip trembled.

"It was for the best. Sometimes you do things that look bad but they're better than the other thing you might do. You understand?"

"I think so." There was a glaze to his eyes, but he squeezed my hand in his and swallowed hard.

"Good," I said. I stood up, paused for a second to clear the head-rush pounding in my temples, and then we continued walking toward the river bank.

Marvin said, "I liked Chester."

"So did I," I said. Though the truth was I was having a hard time thinking good thoughts about anything right then. There was a buzzing in my skull and I was tangled up in things I had no stomach for, other people's problems, and I wanted to be stretched out anywhere with my head down and a blanket over top. I'd had about enough of Hal and Rodney. We tripped along in the gravel, following the sound of voices down to the river.

When we came up to them Hal and Rodney were locked in a grip, each holding the other's shirt at the shoulders, material bunched in their hands, bodies swaying back and forth in a crazy, intense, sidestepping dance. They were panting. Hal was taller and bigger through the chest and he was slowly getting the better of Rodney, who was trying to kick Hal's legs and teetering but also visibly weakening. The cuffs of his pants were wet to the knee. Algae and weeds stuck to his shoes. After a minute or so Hal said between gritted teeth, "All right, now. Enough."

"All right," snarled Rodney.

Hal released his grip and so did Rodney but Hal kept his eyes fixed to those of his brother. His hands were up. He was ready to defend himself or grab out again. "Come back to the car, now," Hal said. "We're running out of time." There were beads of water on his mustache and they glinted in the moonlight.

Rodney grunted but we started up the slope, away from the river.

We trooped back to the car, Rodney first, his shoes squishing with water. Marvin and I were behind and Hal brought up the rear. The alley we were in was cluttered with garbage and a stray dog was nosing around one of the trash cans. A few streets over a siren was wailing. The moon was partly obscured by cloud now and I felt cold and wondered if Marvin did too. I heard him sniffing every now and then. I was hoping the cold air would clear my head.

At the car Hal put Marvin in the front seat and took the driver's seat for himself. I climbed in behind Hal and Rodney took the other back seat. He'd lit up a cigarette and was sucking on it intently and blowing smoke through his nose. On the seat between us was a small duffel bag containing Rodney's things.

Hal drove slowly down one street and then turned on another and peered at every street sign at the intersections. It was an older part of town with three-storey rambling houses that had been turned into offices for accountants and chiropractors and so on. Cars were parked on the street, shiny Buicks with big bumpers, Fords. We cruised through an intersection. Rodney said, "What's the big rush, bro?"

Hal tapped his watch with his index finger. "Past twelve," he said.

"Yeah," Rodney said. "Like they'd leave without me."

"They might. Then what? They throw you in the can?"

"Go to hell," Rodney said. He banged one hand against the seat in front of him.

"All right," Hal said. He glanced over at Marvin. The top of his head was just visible to me, a rooster tail of hair.

Rodney sniffed. "And don't *all right* me." He dug around in the bag between us. "Look," he said. He pulled out a pistol and held it up to the back of Hal's head.

Hal said, "Oh Lord. Oh, good Lord." He shot another glance toward Marvin.

"I'm gonna use this on you," Rodney said. The barrel was right up against Hal's skin, making an indent in his flesh. Light from the passing streetlamps glinted on the metal. Rodney was breathing hard. "I oughta shoot you dead, bro, for all you done to me."

"Good Lord," Hal said. He had slowed the car but it was still moving. "Good Lord, now, Rod."

Rodney grinned at me. He had totally lost it then and he might have done anything. He pushed the barrel against Hal's neck, pressing hard against the flesh. "I oughta," he said. "One shot, over." He had his finger on the trigger guard, not the trigger itself, and his hand shook slightly.

"Good Lord," Hal breathed. His eyes were fixed to the road.

Marvin was looking into the back seat, eyes wide and mouth open. "What is it?" he asked. "What's going on, Uncle Rod?"

"It's nothing," Hal breathed. "Uncle Rodney's having a joke."

"Looks like a gun," Marvin said, his voice shaky.

"It's just a joke," Hal said, exhaling. "Tell the boy it's just a joke, Rod."

"Yeah," he said. "Me and your dad like to kid around sometimes."

I was wishing I was not part of what was happening. My guts were rolling and the streets going by outside were a blur of shadows and streaming light. It was like a movie I was watching or a nightmare I was hoping to wake up out of. Only I couldn't shake it off and had no idea what was going to happen next. I just wanted to be far away from there and in a quiet place, asleep or about to sleep, my life flattened out, like, without all this pushing and pulling.

"I don't like it," Marvin said. "It's not a funny joke, Uncle Rod."

"You're scaring the kid," I said. "Look at him."

He studied Marvin's face. The boy's lower lip was trembling and his eyes were blinking fast and shifting from one place to another.

"This is not good," I said.

"You," Rodney said. "Now you're on my case." Since he'd stepped into the river the slur had gone out of his voice. The words had an iron edge. He glared at me.

"Be a man," I said. I regretted it as soon as the words were out of my mouth. There was a moment then when I thought he might turn the gun on me and I was half hoping he would. Then something would happen. I was tired of all the posturing and shouting and just wanted the whole business to be over. Maybe this is the way soldiers feel when they finally go into a battle they've been preparing for and have nerved themselves up for. Let it be over, one way or the other.

Instead of turning it on me, Rodney pulled the gun away from Hal's neck and pointed the barrel at the floor. "I oughta blow my own brains out," he said. "End it all."

Hal said, "I'm not pulling over. We're going through with this."
Now that the gun was gone, he was twisting his neck about from side
to side, stretching out the stiffness.

Rodney breathed once hard through his nose. I could smell beer
on his breath.

"You hear? Rod?"

"No one's gonna get shot," Rodney said wearily.

"That's right," I said.

"I'm not gonna shoot nobody," Rodney said. His voice was thin
and it was clear he was tired of it all. He too was probably wondering how he happened to be where he was, heading to a bus stop that
would take him to boot camp and then Vietnam, life in the jungle,
possibly death by an enemy he would not see and did not care about.
He might have been wondering too how he ended up shouting at his
brother and pointing a gun at him in front of his wide-eyed kid. It
was all out of kilter.

Hal cleared his throat. "You all right, Johnny?"

"I'm okay," I said. "We're all right back here."

"We're all right, big bro. Steady as she goes." Rodney laughed
but it was a weak sound, a man appealing for others to see he wasn't
as bad as he'd seemed to be a moment ago.

"We're okay," I repeated.

Rodney sighed. "It's a damn shame, is all."

Shame is not what I thought it was all about but I held my tongue.

The pistol was dangling from Rodney's hand. He was backing
down and he would not shoot Hal or himself or anyone else. That
was the kind of man he was, a man who wanted to make a point
and didn't know quite how to go about doing it, but once he'd had
his moment and been forced to back down was chastened and had
had enough of that sort of thing. Now he was just tired and wanting
things to end and looking for a way out.

He threw the pistol onto the floor between my feet. "There," he
said. "Finished."

I pushed at it with my foot, shoving it under the seat in front of me. My mind was reeling from drink and my guts were rolling but that was not really the issue, the issue was I was sick at heart for Marvin, a kid subjected to cursing and ugly words between brothers, guns and wild talk about suicide.

Hal must have been having the same thoughts because he reached across to Marvin and squeezed the boy's leg. "We're almost there," he said.

I was glad to hear that. It was time for Rodney to be out of the car and out of our lives. I could hear that in Hal's voice too. He wanted his life to go back to something he could handle easier , a life less cluttered. He probably was thinking of his scrub farm and how he wished he was there now, grooming a horse or throwing hay down from the loft in the barn. It was small and run-down but at night the sun setting over the river was nice and the quiet in the middle of the night was so soothing to the soul you wanted to get up from bed and just sit outside on the stoop and breathe it in. The thought of doing that appealed to me. The thought of Carrie warm in her bed went through my mind.

We turned again and crossed railroad tracks and were suddenly in a run-down part of the town. Rusty pickup trucks, sagging houses, kids' bikes on the sidewalk. At the end of the street there was a squat building from which lights were shining. Two men in uniforms stood outside smoking at a kiosk in front of the building and another sat behind a sliding window talking to them. A little farther down the street sat a big grey bus.

Hal pulled the car to the curb and shut off the engine. Rodney sat and did not move. No one in the car moved. Rodney stared out the window at the men smoking and I looked at the bus and wondered where it would be taking him. No one had mentioned a destination. Hal got out of the car and walked around to Rodney's door and opened it. Cool air wafted into the car, I felt it on my neck, which was sweaty. A car engine started behind the bus and then headlights came on, throwing the shadows from nearby trees along the street.

"What now?" Rodney said.

"You know what," Hal said.

"I don't even know you," Rodney said. But he got out of the car. He did not look back.

One of the men in uniform started toward the car. He chucked his cigarette onto the road and ground it out with the heel of his boot.

Rodney stood on the curb but he did not look at the man. He hugged his arms around his chest. He was shivering and I felt sorry for him but I also wanted him to be gone, I wanted him out of my life so I could go back to being the way I was at the start of the day before we'd got in Hal's car to drive across the border. I suddenly missed Carrie and wished I was with her under the covers right then.

Rodney looked around wildly, his eyes alight , and I thought he might make a run for it, but instead of running he suddenly turned to Hal and shouted, "Fuck you, Hal, just fuck you." The words came out in a snarl but we could hear them in the car because the night was still and the air heavy with sound. I heard Marvin take in a sharp breath.

Hal stepped toward Rodney, his whole body tense, and it looked like he was going to shove him backwards or punch him in the face, I know I would have right then, but instead he grabbed him in a hug and held him close, breathing into his ear and shaking and whispering things we could not hear. They stood like that until the man in the uniform came up beside them and took Rodney's arm and bent down to pick up his bag.

When they were inside the building, Hal came back to the car and we drove away. No one said anything. Marvin was slumped against the window, I could hear his snuffling, regular and deep, a child heading toward the land of dreams. I wished I could go there but my heart was big in my chest and I knew it would be hours now before the relief of sleep came to me.

As we approached the border crossing, Hal said to me, "Where'd that gun get to?"

I reached under the seat and passed it up to him. He pulled over onto the wrong side of the street, rolled down his window and threw it down an alley where it clattered against a trash can. "America," he said. "Everyone's got a gun."

"It's a crazy place," I said, and I let out a long breath.

Hal glanced into the back seat. "A bit of the wild west. I'll be glad to cross that border."

"Yeah."

"Seems to have got into Rod. The violence."

"He was wild. He was."

"I don't know. Maybe it's not so much America, but just him, who he is."

"Could be." I thought about Rodney for a moment, how desperate he'd seemed all day, what I'd taken to be his weakness, what he'd said about shame, and I thought it was too bad that sometimes life just got away from some people. But the truth was I didn't know what to think, only that Hal was free for the moment from being tangled up in Rodney's life, and that felt good to me, a relief.

We sat there, the car engine throbbing, Marvin's snuffles the only sounds on the deserted street. Hal looked at his watch. It was past 12:30. "He's scared," Hal said.

"I know," I said.

"You can't blame him."

"No. You can't blame him for that."

"Not for that." Hal sighed. He looked down the street, which was deserted, except for a cat sniffing some garbage on the sidewalk. "You want to stop for coffee?"

"No. Just lay my head down somewheres as soon as possible."

Hal pulled away from the curb and crossed the white line back onto the right side of the street. "I'm not that unhappy he's gone," he said.

"No."

"It's a lot to take, is the thing of it. He was always that way. I'd forgot how much he was to take and it all came back and now I'm glad he's out of my life. It sounds awful to say, your own brother, but that's how I feel."

"You feel what you feel. You're entitled. Everyone is."

Hal grunted.

"Anyway, you're out of it now."

Hal shook his head, a man who was done in but relieved to have something behind him.

The words sounded cold in my ears, but I was not sure what else to say. Hal was on the outside now. I was too. It was not a bad place to be. I had my own worries about bosses and women and so on, and they were enough for me, I didn't need anyone else's. I saw that was how things would be with me now, I would have my own problems to deal with and not concern myself much with those of others, and it was a good feeling overall, a bit sad in the way it would separate me from others, but overall a good feeling.

"I feel guilty," Hal said, "but it will pass. It always does. But the thing of it is, our parents were killed, see, and Rod—oh, there's no point in going into all that, all that ancient history, it's just depressing. You know?" He sniffed and ran the back of his wrist under his nose.

I was thinking about Rodney being led into the building by the uniformed man and then being put on the bus with other recruits and driven across the state to wherever the boot camp was. It was not a pleasant thought. For some reason the sight of him and Hal clasped in that strange embrace brought a lump to my throat.

"Tell me something," Hal said. "You ever think you might like to join the army and let someone else do all your thinking for you, tell you where to go and what to do, feed you, clothe you, take the burden of responsibility off your shoulders?"

"No."

"It might be okay. No worries."

"My father was in the last war. It sounded like hell."

"Yeah," Hal said. "But it's tempting sometimes." He glanced across the seat at Marvin and tapped his hands on the wheel as he drove.

"You won't hold that against me," he said after a while, "will you?"

"A lot of things go through a person's head," I said. "What you think today you may not think tomorrow, what you believe tomorrow you might have dismissed yesterday."

Hal glanced at me in the rear-view mirror, holding my eyes a moment. "You're a bit of a philosopher," he said in the tones of a man much older than either of us. "I like that."

In truth I'd never had that thought before but now that it was out, I saw how clear it made a lot of things. Morals and principles and whatnot were good things, but you didn't have to be tied down to them as if they were a ball and chain. When circumstances changed, you could come to see things in a new light, you could change your mind and go in a different direction. You didn't have to answer to an inner voice that was your father's or mother's telling you how you should behave and what you should think, you could make it up as you went along and in the end things would work out. In the end everything would work out for the best. They hadn't for Rodney that day, but they would soon enough. Hal too. I knew that then, or was coming to. What I really knew was that I was young and adaptable and could make my life happy, or at least work to my satisfaction, and that would do for the time being.

We turned a corner and there were the spotlights at the border crossing and behind them the bridge that ran over the Rainy River to Canada on the other side. I was twenty minutes from home and my bed and that felt good and I closed my eyes and let Hal roll the car up to where the border guard was waiting for us.

BARMAIDS

Iris and Libby shared an interest in horses and riding, though that was not all they had in common. They both liked *Dallas*, too . And they were waitresses at the Shoonee Grill in Dufferin, where they had come to know each other, Iris working there summers to make money for college, while Libby had been at the Grill since she'd moved back from the city.

Libby was a smoker, which Iris didn't much like. She was sitting across the table from Libby, drinking a rum and Coke. Libby had a bottle of beer in front of her. She'd been smoking since we came in, blowing clouds at the ceiling, while Rory swigged back draft beer. They had been at the bar a while and Iris and me had joined them from the Finger Lake Hotel, where we'd eaten supper and had a glass of wine.

Iris was halfway through her drink when she stood up and tipped her head toward the back of the bar. She smiled at me and tossed her head of dark hair, running one hand across her brow to push back the lock that was in her eyes. I needed to hit the can myself but was feeling the beer a little in my head and decided to stay put. I studied the sign over the bar where the price list was posted and took in the bartender pouring draft and pulling bottles out of the fridge. It was a quiet night, only a few tables were occupied in the Crossroads. The bar was down the highway out of town. At one time it had been a supper club kind of thing, with an attached restaurant and dance floor. Times had changed and now that part of the enterprise was closed. There was a tiny dancing area up front and a place where musicians could set up, though there were no musicians, only country music over the speaker system.

Rory had been silent since we'd come in, letting Libby and Iris do the talking, which I was content to let them, too. He was clean-shaven and wearing a red-checked lumberjack shirt. I'd heard something about him from somebody years ago though I couldn't remember what, only that it was not good, but it was gnawing away at me. He turned in his chair and watched Iris make her way between the tables toward the washrooms. "Pretty little lady." He nodded, studying her all the way to the door and tapped the fingers of both hands on the tabletop.

My eyes were on the couple at the next table, who were eating fries and chicken out of a basket with their fingers, which were covered in grease. They were laughing and talking and pushing fries into their mouths between drinks of beer. The place smelled of frying oil and stale beer and cigarette smoke.

Rory turned in his chair and said to me, "Nice ass."

I studied him over the rim of my beer glass.

Libby said, "What's with you?"

Rory leaned back and smiled. "Just giving the little lady a compliment."

Libby jabbed out her cigarette in the ashtray. Her hands were red and there were fine scars across the back of her wrist. Iris had told me that Libby was the oldest of seven children who grew up on a scrub farm where their parents raised a few head of cattle and kept pigs and chickens. Her mother had died young and she'd been a kind of mother to the three youngest kids. When I looked at her face the word *worn* came to mind.

Rory leaned in toward me. "You share that around some nights?" He grinned at me.

Libby said, "You disgust me."

Rory chuckled. "Just let me know. I could use a little." He was a short muscular man. One of his eyes was cloudy and partly closed. It had been that way a long time. As a result, he looked at people in an odd way, studying them as if he was unsure of what was coming next. He drove a gravel truck and lived with Libby in a rundown house on the less desirable side of the tracks. He liked dogs, Iris had told me, and had boxers and huskies, which he kept in his backyard where he'd built a chain-link fence to keep them in.

Libby stood up and went to the bar to buy more cigarettes. Rory looked around the bar and then said, "Libby there's getting a little fat in the ass. Know what I mean?"

I'd banged my wrist on the sharp metal edge of a machine at work a few days earlier and I examined the red spot that remained after the swelling had gone down and flexed my fist. It was almost a hundred per cent.

Rory was laughing to himself. "Not much jump in the old sack anymore," he added. "That little lady, now ..."

Libby had come back from the bar and was settling into her seat. "Jesus," she said. "You still on about that?" She blew smoke towards his face.

"You lookin' for a smack, now, you gonna get it," Rory said. He leaned farther forward and his smile went hard, mouth turned down at the corners. "I had about enough off of you tonight."

Something had been going on between them before we arrived, that much was clear. But it was their business so I sat back and tried not to look concerned. There were a number of empty glasses on the table and the ashtray was filled. Rory sat back and lifted a draft to his mouth and drank it down in one swallow. His Adam's apple bobbed and when he put the glass down he smacked his lips with satisfaction. He had big, thick, wet lips.

Libby looked at the table, watching the cigarette burning down between her fingers. Iris had told me that she was a hard worker but sometimes forgot items on an order, like there was a part of her brain that shut off, or didn't work any longer. Iris remembered every detail of every order, including glasses of water. Most people, she told me, don't drink water but those who do are particular to have it on time. Waitresses, she said, tended to forget water in the hurly-burly of placing and taking out orders. It wasn't just remembering water that Libby had a difficulty with, Iris gave me to understand.

Rory leaned in toward me. "Hey, buster, you ever shoot a badger? Murray, is it?"

"No," I said. The question took me by surprise. I'd been thinking about other things and his voice jolted me out of the reverie. "I haven't had much to do with guns in a long time." That was the truth. I'd shot grouse and rabbits as a kid in Red Rock and then geese and ducks and even a deer in my teens. I didn't like killing things, and I didn't much like guns, they seemed to change men when they had them in their hands.

"Shot me one yesterday," Rory said. "Bastard was down in his hole but I waited him out and when he popped his head up, blam, I shot him right between the eyes. You shoulda seen the look in that badger's eyes. Blam." He smacked his hand on his knee.

"Yeah," Libby said suddenly, "that was something all right."

Rory stared at her.

"What?" She ran one hand back through her hair and took a swig of beer.

"I'm talkin' here," Rory said. "I'm telling this."

Libby said, "Jesus, but."

"Just so's he understands," Rory said. "So's youse both understand."

The things I'd heard about Rory had started to come back to me. He and other men gambled on dog fights out in the country at an abandoned barn where someone had set up a ring and bleachers. Rory had been in a scrap with an American who had come over the border to check out the action. Car headlights had been smashed, somebody knifed. Someone did time.

"So you never shot a badger, eh?" Rory sat back appraising me. "Well," he said, "how about that, then." He tapped his fingers on the edge of the table. "I hear you play rugby."

"That was a long time ago." I patted my gut.

"Now that there's a man's game. A little wham-bam action. Baseball. Piss on that."

"No speed any more," I said, "and it's a game of speed. I'm kind of a tennis guy now."

Rory grunted. He fiddled with his draft and gawked about the room. There was a time when I'd liked sitting around in bars but that time was passing. The music was loud and unpleasant and the smoke overpowering. I felt trapped between Libby and Rory, who were not my friends and not people I wanted to be friends with. I looked toward the washrooms, wishing Iris would hurry back.

Libby was toying with her bottle of beer, scraping at the label with a chipped nail.

The music had changed to a dance tune that everyone was singing and as Iris came back to the table she was snapping her fingers and twitching her shoulders. She sat down fast and took a sip of her drink. Her eyes were flashing about. She tossed her dark hair. Watching her I thought that someone who saw her for the first time at that moment couldn't help thinking how pretty she was—and full of life—and they would have been right, she was both those things and others too.

"Havin' a good time?" Rory asked. "Pretty lady?"

"I'm getting into the music," Iris said.

"That's a nice top," Rory said, staring at her breasts.

"Thank you," Iris said, ignoring his stare. "Murray bought it for me."

"Did he now?"

"That's right." Iris touched her throat. Her cheeks were flushed. Around her neck was a gold chain with a cross that I had given her for her birthday. She was Catholic and she liked it so much she wore it every day. When she turned her head, the chain glinted little knives of light from the overhead fixtures. She had big brown eyes and a happy look about her. She was a happy girl, filled with positive spirit and a cheery smile. She'd had little trouble in her life and she took life as it came, always an optimist, always telling me things would work out. I was less positive about life's prospects and more prone to moods and pessimism. I had seen things go bad for my folks and their families and was on my guard, waiting for the other shoe to fall, as my father was fond of saying.

"Let's boogie," Iris said to me. "C'mon, Murray."

"You like that," Rory said. "Dancing?"

"I like dancing," Iris said. "Boogie 'til dawn." She laughed and took a drink of her rum and Coke. A drop glistened on her lower lip.

I leaned over. "We should be going," I said quietly. I raised my eyebrows and tilted my eyes toward Rory and Libby, trying to communicate misgivings in that direction.

"One dance," Iris said, "come on already."

"It's getting late," I said.

Rory was looking at her and smiling to himself and tapping his free hand on the edge of the table. He glanced once at me and there was a curl to his lip that I'd run into before when I'd seen a miner bang a car door shut on another guy's arm.

"Little lady wants to dance," Rory said quietly to himself.

Iris had another sip of her drink. She was bobbing her head to the music.

Libby said, "That's a nice tune. You know the name of that band? I'd like to—"

"C'mon, then," Rory said, cutting her off. He gripped Iris's elbow in his hand.

"We should get going," I said more firmly. I laid my hand on her other wrist.

"Murray," Iris said. "One dance." She shook off my hand.

"Now."

"Oh, Murray," Iris said. "Can't a girl have a little fun?" She flipped her hair and smiled.

"Maybe he's right," Libby said. "It's getting late." She blew out smoke and gave Rory a look and then she reached out and laid her hand on Iris's forearm. The gold chain swung in the light as Libby tugged gently with her hand.

Iris shook it off.

"C'mon, then, little lady," Rory said. He stood.

I looked away at the bar. Two guys carrying construction hats had come in and were standing talking to the bartender.

Iris stood suddenly, the glasses on the table teetering. I heard her say as they made their way toward the little square of dance floor up front, "Murray can be an old poop sometimes." Her laughter tinkled. Rory had his hand on her back, guiding her between the tables, fingers splayed like a star fish. At the dance floor he gave her bum a pat.

I took a swallow of beer. We had been together almost a year and things had been going good, I thought, though sometimes I had the impression Iris was not keen on settling down. She talked about moving to the west coast, of travelling to Europe. She wanted to see Buckingham Palace and the Leaning Tower of Pisa. She imagined she'd work for the health department some day and have kids, but that was for later. It was her time of life to dance and sing, she said.

She was swinging her arms on the dance floor and her hair flew from one side of her face to the other. Rory moved towards her and she backed away and twirled, and when they were face-to-face, he grabbed her elbows and pulled her close so their faces almost touched. The first time she laughed and spun away, but the second time she pulled back suddenly. Rory swung her back and pulled her against his chest and tried to hold her there. She ducked her head under his other arm, but he still had her by the wrist and it was clear he was not letting go and that she wanted him to.

I took a deep breath and looked at the bar. The construction guys were shooting back shots of whiskey chased by draft beer. They too were keeping their eyes on Iris and Rory, maybe thinking they could horn in on the action. I turned my gaze to the dance floor. Rory was laughing but Iris did not look happy. They were caught up in a contest that was not pretty to watch, but I was feeling sore about what she'd said about me and I thought she deserved the little struggle she had brought upon herself. I recognized it was stupid to think that way but the drinks I'd had had made me sour and belligerent and I thought, Well, let's just see how you handle this, Iris girl, if you're such a free spirit and I'm an old poop.

Libby was watching them and she turned to me, her eyes narrowed and her jaw jutting out. "She's a nice girl, Iris," she said finally. "But that's a bad idea, what's happening there. Your girlfriend doesn't know what she's getting into."

"She likes to dance."

Libby grunted and ground her cigarette in the ashtray.

"She wanted to get up. Now she's up." There was an edge to my voice I didn't much like.

"You should get up. Go up there. She's your girl."

I grunted and took a swig of beer and glanced their way.

"A man like Rory." Libby looked like she was going to say more, but she took a drag on her cigarette instead and sighed and had another pull from her beer bottle.

I shrugged. "She's a fool to dance."

"You got that right." Libby took another drag on her cigarette. There were creases at the corners of her mouth and crow's feet walked out of her eyes as far as her temples. She was older than I had thought at first, and tougher. I recalled that Iris had said that in the city she'd worked in a factory where they turned cowhide into coats and belts and whatnot, the kind of work that sent you home with a backache and red, swollen hands.

There was a headache building in the back of my skull and causing me to squint. I was trying to blink it away. The smoke in the room was thick and the faces I tried focusing on were blurred like when an eye doctor puts drops in your eyes. I rubbed them with the back of my wrist and my vision cleared but it was obvious I had better stop drinking.

On the dance floor Iris was trying to keep Rory's hands from roving all over her. It was a losing battle and I felt sorry for her then and listened closely to the music, trying to gauge how close the song was to finishing. Part of me wanted to jump up and go onto the floor and steer her away from Rory, but part also wanted to see her have to fight him off. If I was being a shit, then it was a lesson for her to learn that I was at least not the kind of man who scared women. Truth was, I was mixed up about how I felt and I did not get up because the music stopped just then and Iris broke free from Rory and headed straight toward the table, arms pumping at her sides, dark hair swinging. Rory was following behind, a big grin on his face.

Iris did not sit down but she reached for her drink and took a quick sip before saying, "Let's get out of here." She looked at me as if that command should be enough to have me scrambling.

I stared at her but didn't say anything.

She tilted her head. "Come on, Murray. Now."

"Sit down, little lady," Rory said, "you and me's hardly got started." He placed the palm of one hand on Iris's shoulder and shoved her down into her seat. She made an odd sound, a kind of *chuffing* as she hit the bottom of the chair. I was starting to stand up. "You stay right where you are," Rory said, "you know what's good for you."

"For Christ sake," Libby said.

"Murray," Iris said to me.

Rory was sitting but still had one hand on Iris's shoulder, her small bones lost in his big paw. "Them's a nice set of tits you got there." He laughed and raised his beer bottle and took a long swallow.

"For Christ sake, Rory."

"Murray," Iris said again.

"We're gonna shake them tits around one more time, you and me." He looked me straight in the eye, waiting for me to respond, and when I didn't, he grinned again. Two of his teeth were chipped and the ones farther back blackened and unhealthy looking.

The anger I'd felt toward Iris before had been lodged at the back of my skull like a headache, but it had moved into my jaw, I could feel my teeth grinding. It was all directed at Rory. I stood and he rose suddenly and shoved me in the chest with a closed fist that took away my breath. I staggered backward into the table behind us. It was not occupied but a guy at the next table over said, "What the fuck?"

Libby stood up too. Only Iris was sitting, looking straight at me with her mouth open. Her eyes jumped quickly from one of us to the other. I righted myself. My fists were clenched and I knew something bad was about to happen but I knew too that it was unavoidable. I'd read somewhere that taking a punch was not as bad as most people feared and I hoped that was true. In school I'd belonged to the box-ing club and the coach had told me always throw a punch from the shoulder as hard as you can, and don't stand watching it land, be throwing the second as soon after as possible. He'd said, too, not to close your eyes because that was when you were likely to get hit back. I was trying to remember all that. Rory was grinning at me like he'd been waiting to show me up as a man. I took a step forward, thinking I'd at least get in one shot.

Rory was grinning. It struck me this was what he'd wanted all along. Me. Not Iris.

Her voice came out of the smoke and confusion of the room. "Murray, don't now."

Just then Libby picked one of the empty bottles up off the table and swung it at Rory's head. There was a crack when it hit his skull and he went down like a cow that's been hit with a mallet, knees buckling. The sound of him hitting the floor was like no sound I had ever heard before. His lips blew out and he made a kind of *umph*. He reached one hand out toward the edge of the table but missed it and in a moment he was pawing at the floor, a spot of dark blood showing through his hair.

"Get out," Libby said to me. "Get the hell out of here." Her eyes flicked from me to Iris. She'd dropped the bottle to the floor. Her hands hung loose at her sides. There was resignation in her shoulders but determination in her eyes. I wondered later if she had struck Rory before, if it wasn't a common occurrence for them to be in scraps in bars, and I wondered what kept a nice ordinary woman with a man like Rory. Was it just bad luck that she was with him, or do some women have trouble figuring out who they want to be with and make bad choices they regret but can't get out of easily? Maybe there was a sort of inertia that followed along behind those bad choices, like there was an energy that went along with good ones. You were stuck in a place and just kept sliding downwards.

The bartender had stepped out from behind the bar and was moving toward us, wiping his hands on a towel.

"Get," Libby said, "now. Before he comes back to his senses."

She was red in the face and she had one hand on Rory's shoulder. It was not obvious if it was there to steady him or strike him again if he tried to stand. A sound like a dog makes when it's dreaming came out of Rory. His head was still down and the blood trickled down to his ear and into his shirt collar and then one drop after the other dripped to the floor. The thought that another man would have kicked him at that moment crossed my mind and I realized I was not that kind of man and never would be. I was sorry for him, though I hated everything about him and was also glad he was down on his knees and not pawing at Iris any longer.

I said to Libby, "What about you?"

"Forget that," she said. "Just move. The hell out of here."

"He'll kill you," I said. I believed it. He was the kind of man who killed innocent animals with guns and set dogs to fight each other in a pen and I believed he would kill anyone who got in his way, including Libby. He was unpredictable, likely to do anything, and it was a frightening thing. I had never seen that before but I have since and it sends a cold chill through me.

"I'll take care of this," Libby said. I wasn't sure I believed her but I wanted to.

By then the bartender was up beside her. "Leave," he said, "the lot of you. Get out." He was wringing his hands in the towel and hoping the tone of his voice would send us on our way. I don't know what he would have done if we'd turned on him.

Libby ignored him. "Get her out of here," she said to me.

All this time Iris had been silent, eyes bugged out, rising from her chair slowly when Rory went down and looking puzzled rather than frightened. Now she came back to life and what she said surprised me. "Don't stop that bleeding," she said, pointing one finger at Rory's head. "If the blood clots he'll die of brain damage."

Libby gave her an odd look and the bartender, who was about to say something, stopped with his mouth open.

"Get her out of here," Libby said to me. "She's out of her mind."

I reached for Iris but she turned away from me. I reached again and felt her bony arm as she tried to wrench free of my grip. "Don't!" she said. But I would not let go. I felt her anger in the way she held herself off from me as I pushed her toward the door. It seemed farther away than when we came in, the EXIT sign a little red rectangle at the end of a tunnel. My heart was in my throat and I could see the blood surging in Iris's face. She stumbled as we dodged between two tables and my hand shot out to steady her and I felt her trembling and felt terrible about what I'd thought earlier, how she deserved a little mistreatment for being mean to me. There was nothing right about it, and it made me sick inside to realize I could be that way, judgmental and vindictive. But she was angry now, too, and my head and guts were all turned around. I thought she was getting ready to tell me it was over between us.

"You watch out girl," Libby called after us. Her voice was loud and brittle. Everyone else in the place had gone silent.

I turned back to her, surprised at her tone. It was the voice of a butcher's wife and it took away some of the sympathy I'd been feeling toward her. She was blaming Iris and that was unfair and cruel. I yelled back, "Hey!"

"You keep her in line now," she shouted. For a moment I thought she was putting on a show for the bartender and my emotions swung that way, but she was truly angry, it was clear in her red face and the way her eyes had narrowed into a hateful grimace. She was not someone I felt very good about right then.

"Fuck off," Iris called out over her shoulder, just loud enough to be heard.

"Hey," Libby shouted. "Hey, you little bitch." She took a step forward, but we turned and made our way out the door.

"What the fuck," Iris muttered. She was not trying to break my grip any longer.

"Leave it," I said and blew out a big breath.

"What the fuck!" Iris yelled.

Outside the air was fresh and cool and when I breathed it in it stung my lungs. I looked down the street at the pickup trucks parked one behind the other. Mine was the only car in sight, an older model Ford Falcon in two-tone red and white. An owl hooted in the trees and then flew out noisily and flapped over the street and landed on the flat roof of a MACLEOD's store. The moon overhead was a cold white disc and I shivered as I guided Iris to the car door and shut it behind her.

When I had the motor running I said, "What the hell."

"What the fuck," Iris said. She punched the dash.

It was silent in the car for a moment and then I said, "You want to go for coffee?"

"No," she said. "I've had too much to drink. I'll be up half the night as it is." Her voice cracked and she shifted suddenly on the seat and slumped against my shoulder. She was crying softly and shaking and I put my arm around her and then she cried more and shook more intently.

"That was stupid," she whispered. "Stupid and ugly."

"Yes," I said. "It was. The whole thing."

I was wondering about Libby and how she was dealing with Rory. The dripping of blood came back to me and the wet circle on Rory's head, like a silver dollar. The blood and so on was one thing, but not the most important. Would he beat her when they got home? She was used to that, probably, but being used to brutality doesn't make it any easier to take. I was wondering too what Iris and Libby would say to each other at the Grill on Monday. Maybe they would never speak another word. That was a cheerless thought, but it was what Libby had got herself into, being with a man like Rory. It was the price she paid not to be alone. And Iris would know how to deal with it. She had not seen any scraps in bars before that night but she'd grown up among women and knew her way around slights and silences.

After a while Iris cleared her throat. "What's wrong with me?" she said.

"Nothing," I said. "You're a fine girl. Lovely."

"I caused that. Libby thinks so. You too. Right?"

"I don't."

"How stupid. I'm stupid and totally fucked up."

"It's not you. The world is a crappy place."

"I don't want to hear that," she said. "It's too damn sad. To think that a person can't even have a little fun without ."

"It's the shits. And you're too good for it." I believed that and I said it with conviction.

"No," she cried. She punched me in the chest, a weak blow that hit my sternum and made me gulp for a second. "Don't say that."

She was right. It was a shitty world where a nice-looking woman couldn't follow the lead of her feelings and dance with a certain abandon at a bar and not have men ogling her and pawing her and letting her know they were prepared to rape her. I was thinking of how light her step had been when she'd come back from the washroom, snapping her fingers and twitching her hair, and how furiously she'd had to struggle to escape Rory's grasp. She might never let herself go like that again and it was terrible to think that a part of her life might have ended that night and that there was nothing much anyone could do about it. I tightened my grip around her shoulder. It was all I had to offer, it was all anyone had to offer, and that was sad too.

"Take me home," she said. "I want to snuggle under the covers like a little girl."

I pulled the car onto the highway and we drove in silence. The headlights picked out a high chain-link fence behind which sat bulldozers and front-end loaders and other heavy equipment, painted yellow and orange. A German shepherd was running along the fence, barking at the car. At the curve in the highway sat the Husky station where one of my friends had worked pumping gas on weekends when we were in school.

"Tell me something," Iris said after a while. "Tell me the truth. When I was out on the dance floor were you mad at me because of what I said about you?"

"What did you say?"

"No, Murray, no," she wailed, her voice going small suddenly. "You can't do that."

"No," I said. "You wanted to dance and that was your right. I wanted to sit and drink and that was my right. Two people just doing what they wanted." These seemed like sensible thoughts and I marvelled at how quickly they came out of my mouth and at how reasonable they sounded. They shocked me, actually. Was I becoming one of those men who had a ready response for probing questions, glib and untrustworthy? I hoped not. I didn't want to be known as slippery and devious.

"You're lying," she said. "You were angry and you wanted to teach me a lesson." She tugged my elbow with her hand. "You left me out there. Alone."

"No. No."

"That's the truth, isn't it? Murray?"

I looked down the highway. The white markings in the centre of the road came toward the car and disappeared under the wheels, replaced by more white lines. I blinked to bring them and the road and the ditch back into focus. In the distance a yellow sign indicated a curve ahead. The pines loomed at the verge of the highway. I knew that Iris and I had come to a crossroads of sorts. It might be the last time we were together. I leaned closer to her and smelled her hair and felt her trembling against me. I did not want to be alone but I knew I had to do the right thing.

"Yes," I said, "I was angry and that was stupid. There was nothing attractive in it and not a lick of dignity. I'm a cad." I felt I owed her that, whatever it might cost in the long run.

She snorted. "A cad is a man who doesn't return a girl's love letters after they've broken up."

I laughed. "Is that the dictionary definition?"

"That's the only definition that counts," Iris said, tugging my arm and laughing very softly. "Mine."

"All right," I said, laughing softly myself. "We'll go by that."

I knew then it would be okay between us and I was glad. We had a lot to learn about life, about men like Rory and women like Libby and how they came to be that way. We were not like them and did not want to be like them, lost somehow, as if they'd made a wrong turning a long way back and couldn't find the road home again. It could happen to anyone. A little bad luck, a few wrong-headed decisions that were impossible to reverse and one day you woke up and found yourself in the position you'd sworn you'd never want to find yourself in. Desperate and angry, everything out of your control so you didn't know what was important any more, and then you took another wrong turn and were running downhill too fast for you to do anything about it. I did not want that to happen to me and I knew Iris didn't either, and I knew it wouldn't but that we would have to love each other hard and look after each other to keep it from happening. You could not do that alone. I knew that and I said that to her, not in so many words but in the way I held her close to me on that drive home and she said it back to me in the way she clutched my shirt in her trembling fist.

COLLEGE BOY

My father thought Earl was a loudmouth and a bullshitter. When he overheard me agree to go for beers with them he waited until Jed went upstairs, then pulled me aside and said, "You watch out now, that Earl is a trouble maker." He'd seen plenty of those in his days in the army. He'd told me about men who'd been knifed over dice games, and guys at a dance jumping someone in a parking lot who'd looked at them the wrong way. "You gotta be ready," he'd warned me more than once. "Just because you haven't done anything doesn't mean nothing to a certain kind of creep. And once a guy like Earl is into it with someone, you're into it too, whether you want to be or not."

I was in my first year of college. Jed was married to my cousin Lori, a telephone op in Brandon. They were older than me by a few years. Jed worked for the railroad as a switcher but his real love was breaking horses and riding around on his acreage, and Lori liked that too. She was pretty and full of life, a favourite of my mother, who treated her like a daughter. I'd attended their wedding, a modest affair, and I remembered how happy Lori looked that day and how much promise life seemed to hold for the two of them.

When Earl came over my father opened beers. He may not have liked the man, but he was sociable, my father, and he did the right thing. Earl bragged about the new car he'd just bought, a 1965 Thunderbird. "Goes like a goose that can't shit," he claimed. He had a fleshy face and beady eyes that looked out from folds of flesh. My father studied me over his bottle of beer, his eyes narrowed. He'd put Earl down as a guy who bought things on time and then had them repossessed. "Anyone can drive a flashy car that way," he told me. At the door my father put his hand on my arm. "Watch yourself now. Have a beer, sure, have a good time, but keep your eyes open. You never know what might happen."

The inside of the car smelled of Brut aftershave. We drove to the first bar down Pembina Highway and Earl pulled into the parking lot. "Sandy McLaughlin hangs out here," he said. "Bastard owes me fifty bucks." He pounded his fist into his open palm. He was not a tall man but he had a barrel chest and a mean way of swivelling his head about.

He swaggered into the Cambridge and pulled out three chairs at an empty table, knocking a chair at the next table over. He said to the guys sitting there, *sorry*, but he was waiting to see if one of them reacted, he knew it and so did they. When the waiter came around he ordered six draft. "We got a thirst on," he told the waiter, "so make it snappy." While we were waiting he looked around the bar, then stood suddenly and strode to the back where half a dozen guys were drinking, two of them with their backs to us. He came back in a minute.

"Bastard's not here," he said. He looked around. "Where's them beers?"

Before anyone said anything the waiter appeared and Earl said, "About time." The waiter was a war vet who had a hole in his forehead where a bullet had lodged. I knew him because me and my friends went to the Cambridge after classes. The draft was cheaper than at the bars near the university. Earl waited until Frank walked away before calling out, "Oh, hey buddy, three whiskeys too. Pronto like."

Jed and I had been talking about Lori while Earl was gone. He'd been telling me that she wanted to start a family and that was alright with him, he fancied being a father. I was about to ask him how they'd met, but Earl said, "So, you boys fancy a little pussy tonight?"

Jed said, "Earl, for Christ's sake."

"What," Earl said. "He don't like pussy? You don't like pussy?" he said to me.

"For Christ's sake, Earl," Jed said, "the kid's Lori's cousin."

"But Jesus," Earl said. "You a queer or something?" He fixed his eyes on me.

"No," I said. My voice rose. I lifted my glass to my lips and drank.

Jed stuck his chin out and looked around the bar. He was a short man, muscularly built, with blond hair and bow legs. I wondered about him. Once when he and Lori were visiting they went for a walk near our house and when they came back Jed had scraped knuckles on one hand. He'd been in a scrap in the back lane, Lori said. A guy had said something Jed didn't like and they'd punched at each other. I thought it unusual, violence right in our backyard, but everyone was talking about what was said and who'd done what, so I kept silent. But I noticed that Jed swaggered about the house after that in a way that reminded me of mean guys I'd played sports with.

Earl was leaning back in his chair and taking in the bar. "This whole place is filled with college kids and queers," he said. "Makes me sick." By then the whiskeys had arrived. Earl tossed his down and poured half a glass of beer after it. Jed took his down in one swig too. When Earl saw I didn't down mine right away, he said, "Christ, college kids and queers." He reached across the table and grabbed the whiskey in front of me and shot it back. I'd been intending to have it. He looked at me as if challenging me to say something.

We drank in silence for a minute. I heard the clinking of glasses as the bartender filled them and placed them on trays. Earl shifted on his seat. He picked up an empty glass, then smashed it on the edge of the table. Shards scattered over its surface and into our laps. I jumped back. Earl laughed. He scooped up a handful and put them in his mouth. Glass crunched under his teeth. He swallowed. He looked at me. "You like that?" he asked, "you impressed, college boy? Maybe later I'll make a stupid cunt from the North End *eat* glass." He laughed and fixed his beady eyes on me. "Maybe if I get bored, it'll be you."

"Let's blow this dump," Jed said.

"Fucking right," Earl said. He was on his feet before I had the chance to finish my beer.

He squealed the tires of the car on the way out of the parking lot. He'd bought a six-pack at the Cambridge and he fished it out from between his feet and pulled off a tin, then tossed it to Jed. I'd drunk in the car before but always out on the highway. Jed snapped one open and passed it to Earl, then took one for himself and tossed the others back to me. I pulled one off and opened it.

"What you think of them seats?" Earl asked. "Genuine leather, these."

"Nice," Jed said.

I ran my hand over the material to my side. A good vinyl imitation.

"Hey," Earl said, "I tell you about that cop I busted up?"

Jed was drinking and he waved his hand as if to say, Bring it on. The car was whizzing along Pembina, Earl driving with one hand, weaving from one lane to another.

Earl shouted, "That Terry March, eh? Plays for the cops' hockey team. The cunt thinks that he's a smart guy, that 'cause he's a cop he can give you the stick and get away with it. Not with me, boyo. I waited for him outside and gave him a shot to the head he didn't see. Bastard."

"You blind-sided him?" Jed said, "That wasn't a bad idea?"

"Had it coming," Earl said. "Put the cunt in the hospital. What you saying?"

"I mean cops have a way of evening things out, eh?"

"Fuck that." Earl banged the dashboard with his beer can. Foam and beer splashed down the radio knobs. He took a swig and said, "Anytime is what I say. Anytime any fuckin' where."

He finished his beer before we came to Portage Avenue and called back to me, "Hey, college, toss me another, eh?"

I passed it up to him and he said, "What's this shit then? You never teach this college boy nothing?"

Jed glanced into the back seat. "Driver gets an open beer," he said. He took the can from Earl, snapped the tab and passed it back to him.

"Jesus," Earl was saying, "what the fuck is with this kid?"

"He's just a kid."

"But fuck."

"He didn't mean nothing."

I'd always thought of Jed as his own man. But he followed Earl's lead, drinking whiskey, passing beers, laughing at jokes, like the kid on the playground sucking up to the bully. He was apologizing for me where I wouldn't have apologized for myself. There was a pecking order and Earl fancied himself the alpha male. I looked out the window at the neon lights of downtown. A bus pulled out in front of us, belching diesel, and Earl leaned on the horn and zoomed past.

North of Portage we went west and then north again. Earl slugged at his beer. Foam stuck to the corners of his mouth. He wiped it away with the back of his hand. He said, "I tell you about the broad I finger-fucked at the Plaza?"

Jed was sipping his beer. I held mine in my lap.

"Picked her up in the Plaza, eh. Last Tuesday. Big tits, you know. I thought she had a room there but no we had to go out to my car where I finger-fucked her and then told her she had to suck me off. She's trying to tell me she doesn't do that, fuck. I was born yesterday? I had to push her head down and hold it there, you know? But Jesus."

"Easy," Jed said, "the kid. You were saying about the White brothers?"

"Reminds me of the time," Earl said, "when I took that divorcee out in my boat on the lake and told her come across or swim. Karen something or other. Jesus. She put up a bit of a fight you know. What a fuck, though. They like it rough, eh, broads like that Karen."

Jed glanced back at me. "You like that Extra Old Stock?"

I held up the can in a kind of salute.

"All right. Good man."

In grade school there were guys who bullied other kids. They called one boy "Pansy" and pushed and elbowed in the halls, looking for fights. They hung around in twos and threes, as bullies do. They picked on me a few times. It was run or be beaten up, so I ran. They never subjected me to the worst of their bullying but the running was humiliation enough. After high school I thought I was done with all that, but watching Earl drive and listening to his talk I saw that the bullies had not grown up, they just hung around in different places than me. There were still bullies around and they would pop up some day. I would have to face them.

"Yeah, fuckin' Lenny White," Earl was saying. "That's who I'm looking for at the Conti." He drank from his can and said, "We find him, you back me?"

"Sure," Jed said. "Whatever."

"Fuckin' Lenny White. Bastard needs to lose a few teeth. See how easy he finds it to yap about me behind my back then."

Ed White had played for a couple of teams in the NHL. He didn't score many goals but he got into a lot of fights. In one of them somebody had cracked him over the head with a stick. The doctors had to put a metal plate in his skull. He and his brother were North End toughs, and so was Earl, who lived on a nice street near Polo Park and was always in a shouting match with one neighbour or another, I gathered from Jed.

We wheeled up to a bar in the North End. Earl chucked his empty can under the car as we got out and spat on the concrete. "Maybe there's a little pussy here," he said. "Or Lenny White. Cunt."

Inside there was a haze of smoke and country music blaring. We stood near the bar, then Earl spotted an empty table and we made for it. The place was crowded with men. There wasn't one woman in sight. Voices competed with the music and other voices. Waiters scrambled between tables with trays of beer. We sat down and Earl said, "All right then. This is more like it." At the table next to us were four biker types with long hair and jackboots. At the one behind them sat two big Indians wearing buckskin jackets and baseball caps.

Earl stuck up his fingers at a waiter. Ten. He said, "Yup, no college boys and fags here."

Before our beers came there was a ruckus at a table near the front. Shouting and scuffling. Two beefy waiters went back there and escorted a guy out the door. Jed grinned at me and I saw that he was beginning to enjoy himself. He started drumming his fingers on the tabletop. The waiter came over and plunked ten beer onto our table. "Keep 'em comin'," Earl said. He drained back one glass of beer and smacked his lips and stood up. "You girls carry on about horses or whatever. Earl's gonna have a little gander about."

"Got ya," Jed said.

"Don't lose sight of me, now."

When he'd melted into the crowd Jed shook his head. "Quite a guy," he said, "a real character."

I drank halfway through a glass of draft and looked around. The room smelled of spilt beer and urine. It was hazy with smoke. Guys stood beside tables joshing and looking around, as if expecting something to happen. Earl's squat figure disappeared among them and reappeared as guys stepped aside to let him pass.

"He can be a bit much," Jed said. "I'll grant you that."

"I guess," I said.

"But he's an all right guy really."

I don't know who Jed thought he was fooling. "I guess," I said. The beer was making me groggy. I was used to beer but I wasn't used to drinking so fast. I looked at Jed's drumming fingers and thought that for the past few years I'd been believing that I could be a tough enough guy to take care of myself but still be a good man, a father type with integrity who treated women and kids decently. But I saw that I had been wrong about that and that I was going to have to choose between meanness and ordinary decency, and that the choice was coming soon. I thought about Lori then, about how much she knew about this side of Jed and what kind of a man he really was. She was not a fool but love does strange things, it blinds us to the deeper faults and provides us with explanations for bad behaviour and cruelty to others.

Earl popped through a throng of guys and plunked himself down with us. "Them cunts ain't here." He punched his fist into his open palm again, then picked up a glass and drained it. "This shit's warm," he said. "Warm beer, for shit's sake."

Just then a guy wearing a baseball cap came up to our table. He had a cigarette dangling from one lip and he took it out of his mouth. "Hey," he said, putting his hand on Earl's shoulder, "hey, Earl old buddy, ain't you gonna offer an old buddy a beer?" His fingers trembled and ash danced off the end of the cigarette.

"Shakey," Earl said, pointing at the table, "grab one. College here is slow on the uptake."

"College, eh," Shakey said, "he queer?"

"Leave the kid be," Jed said. He'd stuck his chin out and slid his chair back a little.

"Huh," Shakey said. One of his front teeth was missing and the others were yellow from cigarette smoke. He looked fifty but he was probably thirty. "You got that hundred?" he said. "Buddy?"

"For Christ sake," Earl said. "I ain't had time to sit my ass and drink a beer but you're all over me pissing and moaning for a couple bucks."

"I been waitin'." Shakey took a drag on his cigarette, then a swig of beer. His fingers trembled, an affliction rather than nerves.

"Maybe you're just gonna have to keep waitin'," Earl said. He smiled up at the other man, the same look he gave me when he'd grabbed my shot of whiskey. A kind of snarl.

"Huh," Shakey said.

"Or you wanna settle it right now? *Mano a mano?*"

Shakey looked at Jed. "It's a hundred bucks," he said. "It's not like twenty or whatever."

"You talkin' to me," Earl said, "you talk to me." He'd shifted in his chair so Shakey's hand fell off his shoulder.

Shakey put the empty beer glass down on the table, being careful not to tip it over. "Well," he said. "Anyways."

Earl tipped his glass at me. "You called this boy here a queer. I don't take kindly to that."

Shakey looked at Jed and then back at Earl. He put one hand on his hip.

"See that?" Earl said. "Got a knife, does Shakey. Thinks that makes him a big man."

"Maybe—" Jed began.

"Thinks he can take me," Earl said. "Get his hundred bucks in satisfaction." He leaned in toward Jed and said, "You want my opinion? I don't think he's got the guts, does Shakey, knife or no. That's my opinion." He looked at Shakey. He drank his glass down to empty and then banged it hard on the table. "What do you think, college boy?"

Whatever I said was going to be wrong, so I kept quiet, though that was wrong too. I felt sweat running down from both armpits.

"I'm talkin' to you, college." Earl's voice was hard as iron.

"Leave him out of it, now," Jed said. He'd placed both palms on the edge of the table.

"We haven't heard a lot out of you, college boy," Earl said. "Pussy got your tongue?"

"Leave it," Jed said.

"You shut the fuck up," Earl said, pointing his glass at Jed. The bit of beer in the bottom sloshed onto the table. I slid my chair back to avoid the run of foam and suds.

Jed said, "All right, all right now."

"And don't fuckin' *all right* me." Earl banged his glass down on the table." It cracked and a shard of glass flew past my hand. "I heard enough of that pussy talk tonight. Queers and pussy talk. The both of youse."

Jed stood up suddenly, tipping his chair back. One of the biker guys said, "What the fuck."

Earl snorted and said to Jed, "Oh, you're a big man, are you?" He had his hands at his sides but his chin was out and his fists were clenched. Jed's were too. I'd stood up too. I was groggy from beer and everything in the room was like underwater and I was trying to blink it away.

All this time Shakey hadn't moved but he suddenly slashed his elbow into Earl's mid section. Earl must have been expecting it. He grabbed Shakey's wrist and twisted it hard and fast. A bone cracked. "The fuck," Shakey said between gritted teeth. But Earl hadn't let go of his wrist. He twisted it farther. Shakey slowly sank to his knees. Sweat stood out on his brow.

"You see," Earl said, "you see what happens?" He released the pressure on Shakey's wrist but pushed him so Shakey rolled away holding his arm and came to rest at the feet of a burly guy at a nearby table.

Earl hitched his shoulders up and rotated his bull neck. "You see what happens, college? A man comes in for a quiet drink and some cunt tries to get the jump on him. Jesus." He placed one hand on his rib cage.

Jed said, "Let's blow this here dump."

Earl squealed the tires leaving the parking lot and the Thunderbird roared down McPhillips and then onto Notre Dame. Traffic was light near the hospital and he sped up to make the turn toward the south end of the city. On a nearby street a fire engine was wailing. Neon signs and car headlights came at me in a blur. I closed my eyes and opened them, and then put one hand on the seat to steady myself. Earl said, "Toss me one of them beers, college."

There were two left and I opened them and passed them forward.

"Fuck that," Earl said.

"Fuck that," Jed said. They drank their beers.

I was still bleary and I missed what they said to each other over the next few blocks as we made our way back to my parents' place. Blustery talk, curses and the like. I wondered if Earl really had meant to go after Jed. It seemed possible, as likely as anything that had happened. Jed had not seemed surprised when Earl turned on him. He almost seemed to expect it. I understood how the scrap in the back lane at home had occurred. Jed and Lori had claimed he was the injured party, but he had brought it on somehow. He had been itching for a scrap the same way Earl had been itching for a scrap that whole night. Swaggering, chins out. I'd thought that when guys said they were in a punch-up in a bar that someone had forced them to defend themselves, but it was clear that was not the case. Earl and Jed had gone out looking for a fight. To them it was part of the evening's entertainment, they wanted it to happen and had provoked it.

After we went through the underpass at Jubilee, Earl said, "You don't see that every day at college, do you, boy?" He laughed. But it was cut short when he put his hand to his rib cage for a sharp intake of air.

"That there was a different kind of education, that was," Jed said laughing.

"No books here, eh?"

"No more pencils, no more books," Jed sang.

"Don't take it serious now," Earl said, glancing into the back at me. "Don't get hurt feelings, college boy. Don't be coming after old Earl." He laughed again and thumped his open palm on the dashboard. "That's a good one," he said. "College here coming after me."

"That is a good one," Jed said. "I'll drink to that."

When we drove up in front of my parents' place they didn't make a move to get out and it was clear they were going to sit in the car and finish their beers. I opened the door and got out. "That's right, college," Earl said, laughing, "you trot up to bed and jack off now." I turned at the bottom of the steps going into the house. They were both looking at me and laughing. I went inside and closed the door behind me.

My parents were in bed but my father got up when he heard the door close and came out of the bedroom. "How'd it go, then?"

"All right."

"You're okay, then?"

"I'm okay."

"Well, go to bed and sleep it off." He was wearing boxer shorts and a tank-top undershirt. He was a wiry man and he seemed smaller than when he had his regular clothes on. But I was glad he'd taken the trouble to get up. "And forget that Earl," he added, "he's a bullshitter and a bad influence on Jed. He's just trouble looking for a place to happen."

I sat on the edge of the sofa and took off my shoes. I lay back and looked at the ceiling. The room whirled about and when I closed my eyes it was worse, so I opened them again and breathed deeply while I thought about what had happened. It had been sickening in one way and thrilling in another. I saw the attraction of it but mostly I was sickened.

Jed was right. The evening had been an education. Maybe that's why my father let me go. He must have known what I came to understand that night: that some people are trouble, plain and simple. Wherever they go, whatever they do, trouble just seems to follow them around. Some of it comes to them and they have no choice. Shit happens. But some of it they go looking for. It's like they can't be who they are without getting into some kind of scrape and then scrapping their way out of it. That's how they want their life to be. The worst part was not that. Everyone has their own life to lead, and who is anyone else to judge? Troublemakers will go looking for other troublemakers and they'll find whatever satisfaction they need to at each other's hands. The bad part is they drag others into their crap with them. They don't seem happy unless they're knee deep in it but they're also not happy unless you're in it with them. The trick is to stay well out of it. That's what my father had been trying to tell me.

Jed and Lori lasted together two more years. She came into the city on the bus one day with a black eye and said that he'd had her down on the kitchen floor choking her and calling her a bitch and threatening to kill her. My mother took her in her arms and patted her back and said, "There, there." My father said he was jumping in the car, by God, and driving out there to settle matters with him, what kind of a man was that? But Lori stopped him. "He's crazy," she said, "off his head. He's as likely to kill you as anything. And what would that prove?"

Lori had made the mistake a lot of women make, of thinking she could reform the man she loved. Some think, He just needs a good haircut. Others think, Once I get him out of those army surplus pants he'll be respectable and even Mother will like him. For certain women, men are projects. But it's not easy to change men like Earl and Jed. They've got a streak of meanness in them that goes too deep. And they're not looking to improve, they don't want to change, they're happy the way they are. Happy being unhappy but looking to make other people as unhappy as they are.

Lori moved in with us and in a couple weeks had a job working for the phone company and her own place. She hired a lawyer and began divorce proceedings. For a few years after that we referred to Jed as "The Psycho" and everyone agreed that Lori was well out of it. She met a guy who worked for the city in the planning department and they seemed happy together, going on camping expeditions and motoring trips to Minneapolis and Chicago.

About a decade later in a bar downtown I spotted Earl sitting at a table with a frumpy woman. He'd gone to fat and his face was red and lined with broken capillaries, the face of the habitual drunk. At one point he laughed the way I remembered him laughing at me, but it was a frail sound with no strength in it. His hair was thin. He finished a couple of draft beers. His head dropped to the table and he had to rouse himself to keep on drinking. He'd been a braggart and a bully but now he was just a bum. But that drew no sympathy from me. I'd filled out and stood over six feet and was hardened from playing hockey and was a bit cocky myself. I studied him over my drink. Nasty thoughts crossed my mind.

He looked at me once but didn't recognize me. That was a good thing. You never know what might have happened.

RINGERS

At the dip just before Edgeley I glanced at the gas gauge again. I'd been looking at it with a sinking feeling in my gut for the past twenty minutes, the orange arrow pointing its accusing finger at the red E. There was a service station on the far side of town, I knew that from having driven through before. I geared down at the main intersection and heard the exhaust growl back at me. A hole had developed in the muffler and at gear changes it was becoming noticeable. I turned the dial on the radio to lower the volume and thought about the last twenty-dollar bill in my back pocket. The Indian Head Chiefs paid me fifty bucks a game plus travel expenses but I wouldn't be paid until the game was over.

The town was quiet. Supper hour. Lights were on in the MacLeod's store but it looked deserted. The Cut and Clip had its CLOSESD sign out. Dust swirled from one side of the main drag to the other but otherwise all was shadowy, inert, and silent. Not a soul in sight. Whenever I drove through one of these villages on the prairies

I recalled "The Lottery," a story about a small town where the yearly ritual was to stone one of its own members to death. I thought, I wouldn't want the Falcon to break down in one of these places. God knows what might happen. I glanced down the side streets. Pickup trucks, tarps over snowmobiles, derelict sheds.

A brown mutt was sniffing at garbage near the turn into the Husky. When I braked, it looked up and trotted a few paces off. The chip bag it had been nosing fluttered up as the Falcon passed and the mutt bounded off after it, tail wagging. I pulled up to the pump. A red pickup pulled in right behind me and parked at the side of the station, big rust spots in the wheel wells, a wooden ladder sticking out over the tailgate. Two people were inside but I couldn't make out anything else. It was cold outside, the wind whipping down from the north. Late October and the prairies already in winter mode. I pulled the collar of my jacket up and looked out across the prairie. Dull grey sky, a double row of firs acting as a wind block for the half dozen bungalows that were scattered in a line out to the grain elevator, a long, flat, and mute vista. Outside the door of the service station stood a dozen yellow plastic containers of anti-freeze.

The place seemed deserted. It smelled of deep-fried food and motor oil. The plastic radio on the counter was turned up loud: "Corina, Corina" done by two cowboys with scratchy voices, "I been worried about you baby." The clock on the wall behind the counter indicated 6:30. An hour and a half to game time in Fort Qu'Appelle. I had to keep moving. A man in his forties wearing a blue-and-red-striped welder's cap and dressed in soiled jeans and a blue work shirt with a name sewn over the breast pocket emerged from the service bay. A dead cigarette stub dangled from his lip. "Fill 'er up?"

"Ten bucks," I said. I headed for the toilet in the back corner.

"Right, chief," he said. I heard the door bang shut behind him. EARL, the tag had read.

When I came out Earl changed the twenty and handed me back

a soiled ten. He had lit up the butt and was puffing at it like his life depended on it. "Right," I said.

"You guys take 'er easy out there," he said around the butt. "Road's likely to ice up tonight."

I folded the ten into my back pocket, wondering what was snagged in my brain. Earl disappeared into the service bay. The pickup was still parked near the station but no one was in it. The dog was standing near the car and I put my hand down and scratched it behind the ear and then opened the door of the car and slid in. I hadn't noticed but a man was sitting in the passenger seat. "What's this?"

"Shut the fuck up," he said. "Drive out."

There was a guy in the back too. He'd been hunkered down so as not to be seen. He was sitting behind me. I smelled cigarette smoke on his clothes.

"Look," I said.

"Shut the fuck up," the guy in front said. He had a baseball cap in his lap. The light from the station shone into the car and fell onto his legs. I could see the butt of a revolver in his hand, but the barrel was hidden by the cap. It was pointing at me.

"Jesus," I said. "You got the wrong man."

The guy in back had a knife. I felt its point in the hair on the nape of my neck. "You're driving," he said. "We're talking." He pressed the blade into my skin, so the point dug into bone. The metal was cold. It was a big blade, a hunting knife.

"That's right," the gunman said. "We're talking, you're listening." His voice cracked, shaking.

I turned the key in the ignition and eased the car into first and then out of the lot. I put on the headlights. They splashed across the street for a moment, lighting up a rundown building with boarded-up windows. HARDWARE was faintly visible stencilled above the door. We were back on the highway headed toward Fort Qu'Appelle. The headlights picked out the white line in the centre of the highway. The ditches to the side were just visible. I thought about turning the wheel sharply toward the ditch and crashing the car, jumping out and running back down the highway, my hockey gear in the trunk, the two guys bleeding and banged up scrabbling to get out of the car. The town was still close. I could find a hiding place.

I must have given my thoughts away. "Don't do nothing stupid," the guy in back said.

"You got the wrong man," I said again. My tongue made a noise at the back of my throat.

"We know who you are," the guy in back said.

"I'm nobody. Not to you."

"Shut the fuck up," the gunman said, "or I'll blow your fucking head off." He had the gun away from the ball cap now and was waving it in my face. He had a scarf around his neck, I saw, so his jaw and mouth were partly hidden.

"Easy with that thing," the guy in back said.

"We should kill this fucker."

"Yeah," the guy in back said. "Look at them hands."

"Shit," the gunman said. "What you say this fuckhead does in the city?"

"Teacher. The big man teaches at the college."

"Shit. Fucker deserves to die for that alone."

"Kill him, you think? Gut shoot him and leave him to bleed to death slow?"

"Blow his fucking head off. Chuck him in the ditch."

The sky was growing darker by the minute. The moon was just visible over the treetops, a bright half-crescent.

The guy in back coughed, a smoker's rattle. "What you think this crap-can car is worth?"

"Fuck," the gunman said. "Piece of shit like this. Who would want it?"

"Teacher's car," the guy in back said. "Not a real man's auto-mo-bile."

"Automobile," the gunman said. "Fuck. Auto-mo-bile." He laughed, a kind of snort.

I geared down and the exhaust growled. My tongue clicked when I said, "Take the car. If that's what you're after. Just take the damn thing and I walk away. It's yours." I eased my foot off the accelerator. "No questions asked."

"Huh," the guy in back said. I felt a thin spray of spit hit the back of my head. "The big man wants to give us the shitbox now. Now Sammy wants to deal."

So they did know who I was. "Jesus," I groaned. I stared down the highway, the centre white line bending off in the distance at a curve. Each of the white marks on the asphalt came at me slow and separate, like a beam from space that was about to strike the car and blow it to nothing. In this moment of silence I felt a vast world was opening inside me and it scared me, and I found myself staring at the odometer, which read 84,521. Something bad was about to happen.

"Sammy," the gunman said. "What kinda name is that, anyways?"

"Sounds like a Jew name," the guy in back said. He pressed the point of the knife harder into my skin and twisted the point left and right. It felt like skin broke. "You a Jew boy?"

"Samuel Buechler," I said. "German."

"Fuckin' Nazi," the guy in back said. "You hear that? Got us a fuckin' Nazi here."

"We should cut each of his fingers off like the Nazis did in them camps to the Jews."

"Put 'em in a box and mail 'em to Frau Buechler." The guy in back laughed. It was an ugly sound. The knife was twisting and digging. "On behalf of Mister Adolf Hitler."

"Ah, Hitler wasn't so bad," the gunman said. "He was good for the German people."

The knife point eased off and I felt the guy in back breathing heavy on my neck. There was whiskey on his breath. "What the fuck do you know about it?" His voice rose, unsteady with petulance. "Hitler, Christ!"

"Plenty, I know plenty." The gunman moved the gun away from my face and turned to look into the back seat. He was short. He was wearing a denim jacket with ragged cuffs. "You know the Volkswagen?"

"Everyone knows the bug," the guy in back said. "Shitbox of a car if there ever was one."

"Biggest selling car in the world."

"Christ Almighty."

"Hitler invented the Volkswagen."

"What's with you?" The guy in back let out a long breath with a kind of irritation. "First it's this Armenian what-you-call-it, and now it's the fuckin' Volkswagen fucking bug. You're always shooting your mouth off about such crap. Christ almighty."

"Holocaust," the gunman said. "Armenian holocaust. I saw it on TV. The Turks did it."

The guy in back jabbed the knife into my neck. "You ever hear of that? Teach?"

There was a long pause. The Falcon bumped over a railroad crossing.

"Well?"

"I've heard of it. But I'm no expert."

"Christ."

"See?" The gunman snorted. "Most popular car in the world, the Volkswagen." He was waving the gun into the back seat. I saw myself hitting the brake and everyone being thrown forward, the gun flying out of his hand. I could outrun them, I knew that. But where would I run to? Edgeley was a long way back now.

"Crap can," the guy in back said. "Volkswagen's nothing but a krauthead crap can. Piss on that. And keep that gun on Nazi boy, eh. No fuck-ups this time."

We came to a Y in the road and passed a sign saying FORT

QU'APPELLE 10. I geared down for a rise and then back up for a long, flat stretch. I heard the throaty growl from the muffler. I wondered what it would cost to replace it, and realized what a stupid thought that was.

"You so much as flinch," the gunman said, prodding my shoulder with the end of the gun, "I'll blow your fucking head off."

I didn't doubt he'd take pleasure in killing me. It would be easy to pull the trigger and splatter blood on the window and windshield. I saw my death from outside and it had a clarity and precision that didn't seem so bad viewed that way, as if it were happening to someone else.

We came to an intersection with another paved road. There was a car parked facing us, its emergency flashers on. I lifted my foot off the accelerator.

"Keep moving," the guy in back said. The gunman slid the gun into his lap again.

We rolled past the car. There seemed to be no one around. When we were past I glanced into the rear-view mirror and saw the red tail lights blinking. I caught a glimpse of wispy blond hair on the guy in back.

"We should kill you, Sammy fucking Buechler," he said. "But we ain't."

I cleared my throat. "Is this about Liza?"

"Liza?" the gunman said.

The guy in back had eased off the knife. It felt like a tiny stream of blood was trickling down my shirt collar and onto my back. "Liza's the little broad that Nazi-boy here's bonking on the side. While her old man's doing an honest day's work at Stelco."

"Jesus," the gunman said. "These college types, screwing someone else's wife."

"Right, Nazi boy? She's hot to trot, eh? Nice little set of tits on that Liza."

"Fuck. We should cut off his nuts. Then blow off his head."

"You gonna die bad," the guy in back said. "One of these days. Liza's old man, eh, he's a mean fuck. He's gonna come down on you."

The gunman leaned toward me. "We tell Liza's old man, see, he'll cut your nuts off."

"We *have* told Liza's old man," the guy in back said.

"Yeah, that's right. We already told him."

"Christ," the guy in back said. He sighed. I could tell he was shaking his head.

There was silence in the car. We were coming into the Qu'Appelle Valley, rolling hills, a relief from the flat and endless fields. A river, a long lake that ran west to east for several miles, with Fort Qu'Appelle nestled about halfway along, a fur-trading post back when and a railway town in the nineteenth century, still a prosperous-looking place with red brick buildings and trees lining the streets, schools, the hockey rink. There was a sign for the Rotary Club at the side of the road and another reading POPULATION 1919. Out the side window I saw the empty night and the moon chased by the clouds and the lights of a farmhouse winking in the distance.

"Okay," the guy in back said. "Here's the deal." He'd put the knife back against my neck, but on the other side, pressure on the vertebrae. "You're not the goal scorer, right? Sammy? That's Melly."

"Right." According to league rules, the Chiefs were allowed to sign two players not from the immediate area. Ringers. Melly Dawson was a shifty centreman. I usually rode out to the games with him to save the team travel expenses but he was down with a cold. "I'm defence."

"We know that, Sammy. We know. A defenceman who never scores."

"Rarely. Like nine, ten goals a year. Maybe ten for the season."

"None this year," the guy in back said. He dug the knife in and I felt the skin break again. "Not tonight, not never again."

"Hell," I said. "That's—"

"You hear? None." The guy in back had leaned forward. He

jabbed the knife point into my neck and this time blood spurted out. A flash-like head rush went through my skull.

"Or we blow your head off," the gunman said.

"Right," I said. I swallowed hard. "Never."

"Now you got it," the guy in back said.

"Now you're talking," the gunman said. He waved the gun in my face. "And don't forget. We're not the only ones in this."

"He won't forget. He knows what's good for him." The guy in back had his mouth close to my ear. I felt the hair on my neck stand up. "Pull over here," he said.

We were on the edge of town, where there was a John Deere dealership. A gravel access road ran beside the highway and a pickup was parked on it. I eased off the accelerator and pulled over. When the car came to a stop I felt the knife lift off my neck. "This is serious," the guy in back said. "We know where you live."

I nodded.

"We're watching you," the gunman said. "Melly too."

Farther down the highway there was a motel with a sign saying VALLEY in red neon. A woman and a little girl were walking across its parking lot, holding hands. This didn't happen, I thought, I won't have to deal with this again. My throat was dry and my heart thumping but this was one of those things that occurred in a life that way, passing suddenly and then over, a truck flashing through an intersection a half-second before your car, your life that close to over, but then it wasn't and it didn't need thinking about, as if it hadn't actually happened, or happened to someone else, you just needed to outlive it for your life to go on, steady and unaffected. I wanted to put this into that place, filed away from further concern, leaving me to go on as before.

The knife point suddenly dug into my neck again. "We know where you live. We know where you crap. We're not messing around. Right, Teach?"

"Right." My knees were shaking and I put my hands down to steady them.

"Hands on the wheel."

I put them up and thought, They're not going to kill me, they said they wouldn't.

"All right," the guy in back said. "We got an understanding."

There was a silence and then the sound of doors being opened.

"Have a good game," the gunman said as he jumped out of the car. He and the other guy were both laughing, deep guttural sounds that made the hair on my neck stand up. They slammed the car doors shut and walked away. The lights of the town illuminated the sky a bit. After a few moments passed I put one hand up and felt along my neck. The hair was sticky with drying blood. I put my hands back on the wheel and gripped down on it but they shook anyway. My watch indicated 7:15. As the two guys walked across the gravel toward the pickup I thought, What the hell? I banged both hands on the steering wheel hard, so hard an electric jolt shot into one elbow and headache flashed into my eyeballs. But then I rolled the window down and the cold air struck my hot face like a blow. It was so quiet outside I could hear the wind in the dead grass of the ditch.

PICKET LINE

I was stirring the sugar into my first cup of coffee of the day when Roberts came in from the cells. He had been back there checking on Butch Russell, who he'd brought in an hour or two earlier. I'd gone back and had a look at Butch myself before I put the coffee machine on. He was sitting on the bench with his hands on his knees. There was a lump on one of his wrists and a good-sized bruise under his right eye that was swelling and affecting his vision. Roberts had had to go into the alley behind the Rockland Hotel to bring him out, and he had told me he went in there with a baseball bat and that it had not been easy or pretty. He had a welt on his forehead to prove it, and the palm of one hand was scraped badly. Ann Hobbes was coming over from the hospital to check them both out, he told me.

It was a Saturday morning, which was never quiet, because Friday was payday in Red Rock and all hell broke loose in the bars and at the lodges around town and sometimes spread into the streets and down the alleys. And there had been talk of another wildcat strike on

the road to the pits. I'd got up earlier than usual, leaving Janey snuffling in the pillows and asking me what time it was and telling me I
didn't have to go in for another hour, which was true, but I didn't
want Roberts to be in the station house on his own on that day for
any longer than was necessary. So Janey was sore at me, but just a
little sore and I knew she'd be okay when I got home later. She didn't
hold grudges.

"How was it back there?" I asked.

Roberts said, "He's quiet now." A lot of emphasis fell on the last
word.

"Quiet," I said, "but not calm."

"Right." Roberts sucked his teeth and glanced about, as if looking for a place to spit.

"Waiting."

"But not to get right."

"No. To get even."

"That's the Russells." Roberts stepped over to the coffee machine.

The idea of going into the alley with a baseball bat was his. It's
dark down alleys and in the fall darker, but you can't be seen going
down one with your pistol drawn, or Sam Stein at the paper or the
mayor or someone else who's never had to go into an alley in the
middle of the night will be all over you. I don't know why it is but
miners like to carry knives. Some have hunting knives on their belts
in a sheath and others carry switchblades in their pockets. They can
cut you bad. I learned that the hard way. So the Chief takes a chunk
of bicycle chain with him in one hand and the ball bat in the other,
ready to wrap the chain around the wrist with the knife and disable
his man before cracking him with the bat. Though you'd like to take
the bat to the guy's skull, it's better to hit him at the shoulder. So
Roberts says. That numbs the muscles and renders the arm useless.
Then, if you feel like it, you can have a go at the head. That's the
one advantage of the dark alley, no one can see what's going on back
there.

"He give you a hard time?" I asked.

"Just at the first." Roberts grinned. "He was slugging but I had the Louisville."

We both laughed. I liked him. He was a stand-up guy who had good advice about the job and stood up for us when it was time for negotiations with the mayor. He was short and wiry, with thinning brown hair, and he'd done well at boxing in training school. Fast hands. Bright blue eyes. Roberts was not excitable but he was tightly wound and seemed always ready to spring. He was not a joker himself but still chuckled over the times I had filled his boots with shaving cream on his birthday and had nailed young Dave's shoes to the floor the first night he'd had a date with Penny Showalter.

He said, "They're going out on wildcat." He'd poured himself a coffee and was blowing steam off it. "There's scabs coming."

A legal strike is one sanctioned by the union, but when the men go out on their own without the say-so from the union bosses, that's a wildcat, unscheduled picketing and blocking of roads that the scabs have been hired to cross on the way into the mines. It's always an ugly scene. I don't know why the mine execs hire scabs, it seems to be a reflex of theirs when negotiations stall, but it always inflames the situation and leads to violence. Like the Chief, I prefer that the men and the company keep their battles to the boardroom, but that's pie-in-the-sky thinking. Sometimes you feel both sides are just itching for a showdown and we cops end up in between on a dusty road trying to keep the peace and getting whacked on the head for our troubles.

I took a swallow of coffee, which was hot. "Well, at least Butch Russell won't be there."

"No," Roberts said, "but that leaves Kenny and Norm."

"I don't know why Judy Russell had to have all those boys. Brutes."

"To keep us in paycheques." Roberts winked. "Otherwise there'd be—what?—no street scraps to take care of every Friday night."

"Don't count on it," I said.

"Larry boy, there's only two things you can count on in this town."

"Yeah. Trouble and more trouble." I sipped coffee and checked my watch. It was just before 8:00 and Roberts was due to go off and young Dave to take his place. I didn't like the idea of Dave being on with me on a strike day. I'd have preferred Roberts, who had been through them before, but the schedule had to be followed, so Dave it was. I hoped he hadn't burnt himself out with Penny the night before. We'd need our wits about us on the mine road.

He came through the doors just then, hurrying, his face red. "They're out there already," he said. "On the mine road."

"Jesus." I put my coffee cup down fast, sloshing some onto the desk.

"They don't usually get going until noon," Roberts said. "What the hay is this?"

I turned to Dave. "You sure?"

He was a big man, a boy really. He stood over six feet and weighed in at two hundred. His mother was Swedish and his father from Finland so he had that pasty complexion and hair that was so blond it was almost white. In school he'd been called Moose, but no one called him that after the time Reg Silver yelled it at him it outside of the Rainy Lake Hotel, where he'd taken Penny to Sunday supper. He had hazel eyes and he looked at you intently, even when you were chewing the fat about what was in the paper or on the radio. When he first came to the job , I wasn't sure I liked him, but he'd grown on me. I'd come to understand that his staring was a vision issue and not belligerence. He was very serious about the job but he laughed at the pranks I played on him, and he laughed at himself, which is unusual among cops.

"We'd best get out there," I said. I looked at Roberts, who was due to go off shift.

"Ah, Jaysus," he said. But he was already pulling on his jacket.

The sky overhead was grey, but breaks in the cloud promised a good day. There was a thin skin of frost on the windshield of the squad car and ghosts of breath puffed out of our mouths even when we were seated inside. Winter was on its way. When we turned off River Street and onto the road that went to the mines, everything was as usual. Quiet. No vehicles, no pedestrians. The miners like to set up picket lines there, just across from the Husky and Elmer's Foods. It's maximum exposure. That's to their benefit when it's a legal strike, but wildcats disrupt road traffic and upset the women and are a hazard to kids on their way to school, so they piss people off, though very few have the gumption to say so. Red Rock is a mining town, so everyone's dependent on what happens out there, even preachers and cops.

"Humph," Roberts muttered. "Not here."

"At the Caland turnoff," Dave said from the back seat.

"Right." I cleared my throat. "My favourite spot." I'd been conked on the head with a picket there the last time there'd been a wildcat. It had taken the Chief some weeks to talk me out of putting in for a transfer.

I wheeled the squad car along the road. It had been recently surfaced with asphalt and shone with dew where the sun struck it in open spots. Thin mist from evaporation billowed up around the sides of the squad car as the wheels cut through it. "Now remember," Roberts said, repeating what he'd said a dozen times on previous occasions, "go in slow, boys."

"Right," I said, "we're not here to start something, we're here to end it."

"Enforce the law," Dave said, "not impose it."

Roberts looked across at me and raised his eyebrows. He was probably thinking the same as me, that Dave was so green he repeated the exact words the Chief had used to him only a week earlier. He said, "You've got the pistol, but—"

"But keep it holstered."

"Back-up," Roberts said decisively and sharply, "only back-up."

His voice told me that he was working himself up. He adjusted the cap on his head, lowering the peak and checking that it fit snugly. He tapped his open palms on his knees. I felt in my temples the surge of adrenaline, a potent rush combined with the coffee. I could manage that, I believed, I'd been through stand-offs before. And I trusted Roberts.

It was almost a kilometre to the Caland turnoff, and the houses that dotted the roadside, crumbling bungalows built twenty and thirty years earlier, where the poorer miners lived, thinned suddenly and the road on the left opened up onto a swampy lake. Mist was rising off its surface. A moose stood on the far edge, knee-deep in water, eating rushes. The sun sparkled on the flat lake surface, giving a glow to the swamp spruce, and I thought of how Janey and I liked getting up early on mornings in the spring to drive out to Crystal Lake and watch the sun come up over the water. She wanted to build a cottage out there and had already brought a piece of property on the lakeshore. Pickerel and pike were still abundant in the lake and Janey never tired of sketching the shoreline and the shadows thrown by the pines on the water.

"There," Dave said. His voice rose and he leaned forward and pointed between Roberts and me at the cars up ahead, parked along the roadside. Men were milling about, smoking, waving pickets. A few were sitting on the hoods of cars drinking from mickey bottles and when they spotted the squad car, busied themselves concealing them under jackets. They were waiting for the scabs to arrive and had no bone to pick with us.

I pulled the squad car to the side of the road some distance back. I studied Roberts who was saying to me but actually talking to Dave: "Stay calm." His jaw was set tight and a vein in his throat throbbed with each heartbeat.

We got out of the car. Roberts banged his door shut, and the miners who hadn't noticed our arrival before, did then. I saw Sven Hansen and that surprised me. He was a blasting foreman in the pits and usually stayed out of wildcats. I wondered if he was there to calm things down with the more hot-headed types. The Russell boys stood in a circle of men wearing red leather jackets with the union logo emblazoned on the back. Someone shouted, "Man the line!" and bodies leapt off of car hoods. Cigarette butts cartwheeled through the air, tips aglow. The voice was that of Pete Hearn, an angular man with glasses, who was intent on rising up the union ranks and was an officer of some sort at the local. He attended the same church as Janey, and I knew he was not an unreasonable man in other circumstances, but union squabbles bring out the worst in everyone. When he saw Roberts, his picket dipped. He stepped out of the crowd towards us.

"We've done nothing illegal," he shouted across the space between us. He was wrong but he was putting up a show for the other men. Standing up to the law.

Roberts had singled him out right away and had shifted position to walk straight at him.

"We haven't blocked the road," Hearn went on.

"Not yet," I muttered. The Chief was moving forward at a steady pace. He was on my right and a little ahead, Dave on my left. They were breathing heavy. I felt my hands tense but my heartbeat was steady. I kept pace with the Chief.

Hearn stopped in the road. "Look." He glanced over his shoulder. There was just space enough between the men for one car to go down the road.

I was tempted to rest my hand on the butt of my pistol but I followed Roberts' lead: eyes straight ahead, back squared. He'd told us often enough, Try not to touch anyone. Stay calm.

"Nothing illegal," Hearn shouted again. The sun glinted off his glasses and for a moment it was as if he did not have eyes.

Roberts had told me he'd learned not to engage miners on a picket line verbally until it was necessary. Silence gave you the upper hand, as it did in any dispute, and shouting back and forth showed a kind of weakness, like a man who comes at you on the street with his fists up but then at the last moment does that thing where he raises one leg as if he means to kick you. Stay within yourself, he'd told us, which was easier to say than do. This was Dave's first wildcat and I hoped he'd have the nerve not to overreact.

The men by the cars had been silent since our arrival but suddenly someone called out, "We got no grudge with the cops."

A louder voice yelled, "Butch Russell does."

Roberts had slowed but not stopped. The distance between him and Hearn had diminished down to a few metres. "You know me," Hearn said. He'd let the picket fall to the side and was holding it with both hands, like a bat.

"Larry Murty," a voice called out, "you Irish bastard." There was suppressed laughter. I did not recognize the voice. The Chief paused for a moment, waiting to hear more, but that was it, apparently.

I felt a surge of blood in my face and heat in the middle of my back. These were men I'd gone to school with, and their fathers who had coached our teams and taken us fishing on summer afternoons at the floodwaters. My own father owned a small hardware business, so I'd grown up with miners but not as a miner. It made me uneasy to hear my name shouted out on the street and at times like that I felt it would have been better for me to have transferred to a town where I was not known, but Roberts disagreed. "The men trust you, Larry," he told me, "you're one of them and they know you're trying to do the right thing." He was from Regina and had done a stint in the Korean War before taking the Chief's job in Red Rock. He knew all about hand-to-hand combat and not cracking under pressure, and the knowledge of this gave me great confidence in him.

Roberts and Hearn were almost face to face. Hearn said, "We don't want trouble."

Roberts stared past him at the men, cocking his head for a better look at the crowd. He raised his voice so they could hear him too. "You're going to let the cars through?"

"Don't just start something," a voice from the crowd shouted.

"You neither," Roberts shot back.

"We have the right," Hearn said.

The Chief coughed phlegm into his throat and spat deliberately past Hearn's boots where the gob hit the red dust and then rolled into a ball. He was a bit shorter than the miner and stared up at him, squaring his shoulders. "That was not an answer to my question."

"Butch Russell," a voice called out, "he's got your number, mister."

Roberts moved one step sideways, quicker than you would have thought possible, a fighter ducking a punch, and stared into the crowd of men milling behind Hearn.

"You a man," he barked back, "you going to come out and show your face or hide behind your buddies and your paper pickets?" His hands hung down at his sides, twitching slightly, the stance of the boxer waiting to go into the ring. Roberts had told me once that the mass of men are cowards and once you confront them they back down. Looking into the faces in the front line it was clear he was right. No one was stepping forward. No one looked into his eyes.

The men were silent. Dave was breathing hard and I felt heat coming off his big body. I wanted to tell him everything would be okay but I daren't speak and could not with confidence make the claim anyway.

Hearn said, "We got no grief with you."

Roberts spat again. "Or us with you. If you let the cars through."

"We got the right," Hearn said.

"And if I say you don't?" Roberts was back staring into Hearn's face. I'd seen dogs do this and half expected fur to rise on the back of the Chief's neck.

I breathed out long and slow, tensing my hands for what was coming. Then a horn honked behind us and we all jumped and glanced back. It was a pickup carrying scabs in the truck bed and behind it were three or four more. "Good Christ," I heard Roberts say. My heart had leapt at the horn and I swallowed a couple of times. My mouth was dry. When I looked back Hearn had melted into the crowd of miners.

It took only seconds for the pickups to move into the space where the miners were massed with their pickets and then only moments for the men in the trucks to jump out or be hauled out by the miners, so the road was surging with men shouting and cursing before we had conferred over what line to take. Roberts had glanced back at us and yelled, "Calm!" but then the crowd swallowed him up and all I could see of him was his hat, bobbing between other heads. I thought Dave was still right beside me but he was gone too. I saw him off to the right near the roadside, his head above the crowd. I put my hands out front, trying to make my way between the press of bodies toward him. Men were shoving and grunting. I felt a hand on my shoulder. It yanked me sideways and I threw out one arm to catch my balance. It was Garth Owen, who was the captain of the hockey team when we were in high school. He shouted, "Stay out of it, you know what's good for you." The odour of onions and beer came out of his mouth. He was gone in a second.

Pickets were swinging all over the road and the crack of wood on wood was everywhere. The scabs had brought sawed-off baseball bats and they were giving as good as they got. I felt a crack on my ankle and a sharp poke in the ribs and forced my way past bent backs and men with their hands on each other's shoulders, lunging about. Curses. With a great effort I shoved aside a fat miner in a leather jacket and stood on the side of the road but I could not see Dave, so I leapt onto the hood of a car.

In the distance I saw Roberts standing with his hands on his hips surveying the melee from another roadside position. He'd put his back against a car door so no one could come at him from the rear. His face was crinkled with worry. Then he spotted me. He tipped his chin up to let me know he'd seen me, but did not move his hands. Just in front of him the mass of men was surging forward and backward but not with the energy of only a few minutes earlier. The men were playing out. In a few more minutes they would tire completely, like guys fighting in a hockey game. That's what Roberts was waiting for. It was the only way to deal with these confrontations. Three cops were no match for eighty or a hundred angry men, even if they were cowards. Clashes like this had their own life cycle and when the energy went out of the men, there would be calm and we would escort the pickups of scabs through the picketers and the event would be over, and in an hour we'd be back in the station house drinking coffee while the miners gathered at the union hall and plotted further strategy over beer.

If we were lucky their union bosses would show up in their black Cadillacs and talk the miners into letting them sort things out with the company. These were men from Montreal who wore leather coats with fur collars and diamond rings on their fingers, men who smelled better than women and who appeared in Red Rock every couple of years to make sure the locals voted them back into office. They hung around as briefly as possible and then were gone until the next episode, or when voting time came around again.

Off to the side of the road in front of me one burly man was throwing haymakers at another who appeared to be down on his knees. On a slight rise off the roadside two dogs had appeared, one sitting scratching itself, the other barking.

There was a surge in the crowd further away and I spotted Dave. He seemed to have his hands in the air, like a man surrendering in a war movie. Roberts had told us it was best not to touch anyone and he was taking him literally. I saw two men in red leather jackets circle behind him and my heart leapt into my throat. I wanted to call out to Dave and I actually opened my mouth to do so. Then I saw his head go down in the crowd. A brief sigh came out of the crowd *ahhnnhh*, like at a football game. I leapt off the car hood. The crowd in front of me was thin and I pushed my way roughly through. I smelled whiskey and the odour of rank flesh. The end of a picket jabbed into the back of my leg. A voice said, "Who the fuck?" The men were standing in a circle near the side of the road, miners and scabs alike. Garth Owen was there. When our eyes met he turned his away. The red leather jackets had disappeared but I thought I saw them farther along in the crowd, moving away fast.

Dave was down on his knees in the middle of the circle. I ran up to him. He had one hand over his chest and when he saw me he reached the other out. I grabbed it but did not try to pull him up, which I thought maybe he was expecting. I dropped to one knee. There was a jagged hole in his jacket. Blood was seeping through his fingers. When I eased his hand to the side I saw that the wound was below the rib cage. He said, "I didn't touch no one."

A flush went through my body, a hot wave that started in the gut and came to rest in my throat. He's apologizing, I thought, the big galoot thinks he's messed up. "You're okay," I said.

"I was calm," he said. He coughed and blood flew out of his mouth and onto my chin and arm. I shoved my hand down the front of his shirt. His flesh was hot. The wound was small. The knife had not easily penetrated the leather jacket he wore, that we had all been wearing since Roberts came on as Chief, and I was thankful for that. Leather was not easy to puncture. I looked around to see if Roberts had made his way through the men yet.

"You'll be all right," I said. I looked Dave straight in the eye. It was important he believe that. I wanted to be able to do more but that was all I had.

"I know." He blinked once and managed a crinkled grin and I felt my gut give way.

"Cops," someone behind me said, "fuckin' cops."

I could not see who and thought again about how Roberts had

called them all cowards. If I could have, I would have leapt up at that moment and pistol-whipped whoever it was.

"I didn't go for the gun," Dave said to me. He was trying to look up but the pain was too much and he winced and put his chin down onto his chest.

"You did good," I said. I felt a constriction in my chest, which made breathing difficult, and I sensed a great heat in my guts and wondered if this was the beginning of something that I would have to live with from that moment onward.

"Get this man an ambulance," a voice shouted. It was Roberts. He threw a man aside as he came into the circle. His hat was askew and his face red. He pointed at Hearn, who had come to the roadside and was standing looking down at Dave. His mouth was twisted. This would not look good on the union report. "I hold you responsible," Roberts shouted at him. Hearn took a step backwards as if he was expecting Roberts to come at him. But Roberts knelt beside Dave too. "Bastards," he said, "cowardly sons-a-bitches."

"It's not a big wound," I said. Roberts stared at me. His gaze was hard and his lips were set tight. He brought a glove out of his pocket and pressed it firm against Dave's chest. Blood seeped past it and dropped onto Dave's thigh.

"I didn't go for the gun," Dave repeated.

"Right," Roberts said. "You did good, kid."

"You did good," I said. I was watching the blood make a bigger and bigger pool on his leg and I was hoping the ambulance was on its way. The hospital was just off the mine road, only a minute or two away.

"Lay him down," a miner standing nearby said.

"No," Roberts shouted. "Just as he is. The blood will pool." He was pressing the glove hard against Dave's chest and had hold of his shoulder to increase leverage. His face was red and he'd lost his cap. A breeze had come up and it lifted the hair on the crown of his head. His gaze met mine. I'd seen him angry and seen his jaw locked tight when he'd stepped between two men but I'd never seen the look on his face I saw then. Powerless terror. He'd been to Korea and had seen men die so he was used to that. Maybe it was that Dave was so young, maybe he felt like a father to him, maybe he felt he'd failed him. I know I felt wild myself. I could have killed the next man who said a stupid thing and I wondered about that for a moment. That's how little it takes, I thought, to turn a man crazy. Your friend goes down and your blood goes up, and you don't know what you're liable to do next. Killing was not out of the question. I saw how that could happen in a war, how a man could go crazy seeing a buddy cut down beside him and then charge a machine gun nest that there was no chance of overpowering and get cut down himself. In the line of duty I'd struggled with men in bars and punched them in alleys but that was not the same thing, that was reasoned, it involved the training you'd taken and the exercise of judgment as well as force. This other was a savage instinct and it did not please me that I felt it well up in me. It was a dangerous thing.

Dave moaned and tried to stand. "No," Roberts said. "Stay put."

"I hear the ambulance," I said. It was a lie but a necessary one and in a moment it was no longer a lie. "See," I said.

"Okay, now, Dave," Roberts said. "One quick hoist and you're on your feet, boy."

The drive to the hospital was short. The young doctor who sat with us in the back had an oxygen tank and a mask to go over Dave's mouth. With scissors he cut away the bloody shirt and exposed the wound and wiped away blood with a thin towel treated with antiseptic. The smell it gave off made my nose itch. Dave was on a stretcher, his torso and head elevated. His eyes rolled and mucus ran out of his nose and down his chin. He seemed puzzled by what was happening to him. At one point he put up a hand as if he wanted to say something but the doctor took his wrist and laid it back down at his side, which was heaving. I had never seen a man die. I was not the praying type but I said a few silent words in the back of that ambulance and saw by the grim look on Roberts' face that he was doing the same. We looked at each other only once, when we were coming to the driveway into the hospital, and the grimness I read in his eyes fit the hollow I felt in my gut, and they were both something I hope never to experience again.

BLACK COAT

When Uncle Stanley died I didn't have a coat to wear to the funeral. He was my mother's brother, a merchant seaman who shipped out of Montreal to ports all over the globe, but mainly up and down the St Lawrence Seaway between Thunder Bay and Quebec City. As a child I remember coming across pictures of sailors in adventure books and imagining Uncle Stanley on decks of frigates bound for Tahiti or breaking through ice near the North Pole, a knit stevedore's cap on his head, arms blazoned in tattoos. I imagined him mouthing the words *mate* and *fo'c'sle* around a stogie clamped between his teeth. Though he was something of a hero of mine when I was a boy, Uncle Stanley never lived up to these images when he appeared every year or so on our front step with a bottle of rye whiskey in one hand. Like all the men in Mother's family, he was overweight. He was drunk much of the time, too, and with the loud stories of the barfly he kept us up into the early hours during his brief stays.

It always made Mother tearful to think of how things had turned out for him. He hadn't intended to ply his trade on the Great Lakes. He was a farmer at heart but had fallen out with his stepfather and had run away from the family place at sixteen. His life was one of those minor tragedies, sad but not heartbreaking. He'd started out with one idea about his life in mind but had had to settle for something else entirely.

Mother broke the news of his death to me over the phone and added something which made my insides turn: "They want you to be a pallbearer."

Mother's family is Ukrainian Catholic. When one of them dies they say prayers in the chapel the night before the funeral. On the day of the funeral itself the priest's prayers echo in the cramped chapel while the women weep into handkerchiefs and the men sit stiff-backed in dark suits and shift their meaty hands from one knee to the other, accompanied by nervous coughing and the constant, eerie clearing of throats. Then comes the public viewing, which involves shuffling past the open casket. Invariably I become upset at that point, once so badly that I vomited in the bushes behind the church and had to be taken home in a cab while the rest of the family ate sandwiches and drank punch in the basement. I suffer from an acute dread of death, which started at the funeral of my cousin Daniel.

I communicated my misgivings to my mother in sighs and silences over the telephone. "Besides," I added, "I don't have a coat to wear."

I was a student at the time. I had no money and regularly ate Kraft Dinner and day-old bread, which I bought at the wholesale bakeshop around the corner from my walk-up apartment in a crumbling neighbourhood. Mother arranged to meet me downtown the next morning.

At Eaton's we found a rack of coats and I was fingering a charcoal herringbone with a black leather collar when Mother came up behind me and said, "No, that won't do."

I gave her a quizzical look. My hand still rested on the herringbone coat. It was sporty, I decided, formal but sporty. I would look sharp. "It's only a funeral," I said.

"Not to me," she said.

"It's just one day," I said. "One afternoon, really. And this coat, this herringbone—"

"It's Stanley's funeral. I want the other. It's more formal, more—more dignified."

"Of course, Mother, but—"

She shook her head. "You've never quite understood," she whispered, "have you, Arnold? About the family, I mean."

I continued fingering the collar of the herringbone coat.

She jerked my hand away from it. "Listen," she whispered, "you think yourself a little bit better, don't you? You look down your nose at your uncles and aunts and cousins. Don't deny it." She sighed. I heard the exhaustion in her voice and thought of the hours she'd spent on the phone the night previous, talking to her brothers and sisters about the funeral arrangements and so on. "I don't know where you got that from," she added. "That superiority. Probably from your father's family." She sighed again and looked away from me, as if trying to make up her mind about continuing. Finally she said, "Just because they're German and my lot is Ukrainian, his sisters thought he was too good for me. You know that, don't you, those aunts you're so fond of?" Tears had formed in the corners of her eyes and she brushed them away with her fingers.

"No," I said. "I did not know it." I thought about Aunt Idress and Aunt Sophie. I had heard Mother telling Father they wouldn't be coming to the funeral.

"Well," she sniffed. She produced a tissue from her handbag and blew her nose in it loudly. "Now you do."

I was studying the black oxfords I was wearing. The leather was cracked. Soon I'd have to buy new ones.

"You don't need to behave that way," she said. "Just because you're going to university and all that, just because—"

"That's not it," I said.

She waved one hand in the air and whispered harshly, "Look down your nose at your cousins, I mean. They're people too, you know. They've got good hearts."

"Mom," I said. I put my hand on her arm. "I never realized."

"Your uncle Stanley had nothing but heart. You remember when he bought you that bell for your bicycle?"

"Mother."

"It's okay," she said. "It's just when I think of poor Stan, what he went through as a boy. All those years he spent travelling up and down the Great Lakes. He didn't even like the water. He couldn't swim. He was afraid he'd drown." She pointed at a plain black coat on the rack. "I just want this to be right for him. This one thing, see?"

"Okay," I said. "The herringbone was just a passing fancy."

"That's right."

"And I like that one." I pulled the black coat off the rack.

Mother took it from the hanger and held it up in front of us. It was black as night, the kind you might expect a gangster to wear—or an undertaker. "It's just that I want this to be right," she said. "For Stan."

"I know."

"I know you do," she whispered. "You're a good boy, Arnold. Underneath."

I don't know how much the black coat cost but it was probably more than the herringbone but that didn't matter to Mother, not that day. The lining had a silky sheen to it and the fabric was thick and deep and looked like it would wear forever. I posed for Mother and the clerk in front of the mirror, squaring my shoulders and swaggering a bit. Mother clucked her tongue and when the clerk wasn't looking whispered to me, "Handsome." It was the first time she'd said anything like that. But it was true. The black coat made me look older than my twenty years: elegant, prosperous, serious. I would look good in it in a sombre way, but it was not sporty like the other.

At the funeral Mother wept and Father patted her hand. He'd been fond of Uncle Stanley in the way of men of their generation—that is to say, respectful but distant. In fact they always got into arguments when Uncle Stanley showed up with his rye and the drinking went on into the early hours. They argued about unions, and the New Democratic Party, and medicare—all of which Uncle Stanley was in favour of and Father thought the beginning of the end. Father believed in the free enterprise system and fancied himself an entrepreneur. After he'd come back from the war, he'd owned a hardware business before moving on to commercial laundries and had joined the Chamber of Commerce in 1955. Uncle Stanley was a steward in the stevedores' union and had picketed in front of the Parliament Buildings during the Seaway strike. So they stood on opposite sides of the capitalist fence.

Their arguments had a rhythm. Father railed against unions, claiming depressions resulted from inflated wage demands. Uncle Stanley blamed multi-national corporations for everything from the Diefendollar to the price of beer. When they tired of economics they moved to other subjects, wrangling about abortion, about capital punishment, about Tommy Douglas. They agreed about some things, like bankers and politicians, groups they both swore were doing the country in. But it was their disagreements that were memorable. They argued long after I'd turned off the light in my room and stopped playing WLS in Chicago. While their voices rumbled through the house I tossed in bed and listened to Mother's slippered feet padding along the hallway between the bathroom and the bedroom, hoping to calm them with her brooding presence. At some point far into the night and far into the rye, Father would grow maudlin about the Salvation Army, which had treated the boys embarking for Europe to sandwiches and hot coffee at the train stations, and Uncle Stanley matched this by swearing that Father was the kind of man who'd give you the shirt off his back.

That wasn't literally true, but Father had always been something of a rock in the family. He alone of seven children paid his mother's hospital bills when she fought with and then died of cancer, long before medicare. To his credit, it was not a sore point with him, the money he had put into hospitals and into drugs while his brothers and sisters had done nothing. In addition to what he had done for his mother, he'd bailed one of his brothers out of a gambling debt and backed another who started a turkey farm after the war, a turkey farm that went bad, Father claimed because of his brother's ineptitude. He kept a wad of twenty-dollar bills in the pocket of a housecoat in the closet in case someone got into trouble.

When we stood at the graveside during Uncle Stanley's funeral I noticed that Father's coat was getting old and worn. It was a raw spring day, and as we listened to the priest intone *ashes to ashes*, he pulled his collar up and clutched the throat closed with one hand to keep out the wind. He held my mother's arm when the casket was lowered into the ground. He had a white handkerchief ready when she started to cry. Aunt May, who was closest in age to Uncle Stanley, cried until her nose dripped. Father had a handkerchief for her too. On the way back to the cars Aunt May said to Mother, "Now there's more of us *in* the ground than *above* it." She was right about that. In the past decade we had buried four of their brothers and sisters and two of my cousins who had committed suicide. As they left the cemetery Mother and Aunt May paused for a moment at the headstones marking the graves of Grandmother and Grandfather and wept a little.

I stood behind, watching the wind tug the hairs at the back of Father's head. They'd grown thin over the years and had turned waxy yellow near the crown. Father was looking at the plots he and Mother had purchased for their own graves, tucked into a corner of the cemetery and bounded on one side by the caragana hedge, where I'd vomited after my cousin Daniel's suicide. Father's shoulders were slumped forward and he seemed to be listening for something, the way he listened suspiciously to the motor of my car whenever I visited. He had his head cocked to one side like a bird. He had been wearing a cloth cap at the graveside, which he held in one hand and tapped nervously against his thigh.

Suddenly he turned on me, his brown eyes wide. "You scared the daylights out of me," he said, "standing there in that black coat." When I stepped up to him he put his free hand on my arm and added with a grin, "Like the devil his own self come to fetch *me*, too." He laughed at that, an unexpected brief sound in the cemetery, perhaps the first time anyone had laughed there among the tombstones and soughing trees. "It's that coat," he added. "Nothing personal." I laughed, too, in a tight-lipped way. And I remembered how we had enjoyed laughing together over Father's stories when I still lived at home. He was a good storyteller, and his reminiscences of growing up on a prairie farm and basic training had bound us together while I was growing up, despite our differences. We hadn't laughed that way in years. I nodded and grinned.

Father said, "I liked Stan."

"Me too."

"He was a kind man, a gentle man. He shouldn't have died so young."

I pictured the two of them setting the world to rights over their glasses of rye. They had both been disappointed in life. They'd started out thinking they were heading to one place and ended up in another. My own experience was not a lot different. I'd begun college at the school of architecture—drawing, graphics, design—but was completing a degree in literature. We live with the illusion that we're in control of our lives, that we set our eyes on a goal and then go about achieving it. The truth is that we're buffeted about—by diseases, bad decisions, needs of children, personal betrayals, a whole string of unpredictables. Chance controls our lives, not our wishes or our determination. We're froth on the surface of life's waters, whipped this way and that by winds and currents of Fate.

Father broke in on my thoughts: "He died fast."

"Thank God," I said.

He studied me. "You think?"

"Yes," I said confidently. "No pain."

"Well," he said, "you're young. When I go, I want to be spared nothing. I want to feel the pains of death as I've felt the joys of life." His voice was intense, and though whispered, he emphasized each word.

It was unusual, the way he said it, like a rehearsed speech.

"The way you put it, it sounds like an article of faith," I said. "Are you sure you mean—"

"I mean," he insisted, "that when my time comes I want to live as long as possible. As long as possible, you understand. Every minute, God has given to me. Every second. Whatever the pain."

I raised my eyebrows. "Maybe you'll change your mind."

He looked at me. "People change their minds about the colours of wallpaper they like and whether to buy a Chevy or Ford. Not about how they want to die."

I said, "I'd never really thought about it."

"You understand?" he went on. He was suddenly determined to make his point, and he squeezed my forearm in his hand and said firmly, "Even if I beg you to put an end to it, even if I beg, I want you to let me live, to suffer but to live. You see?"

"Well," I said, "no need to worry right now."

"I mean it," he said. "It's important that you see what I mean."

"I do see," I said, though I didn't understand what he meant at the time and still don't. I wanted to say so right then, to argue with him about willfulness and about the peace that passes understanding, but Father tugged his cap on, a gesture I had grown to recognize as the end of conversation. I left him looking for Mother, and I sat in the funeral director's limousine waiting for the traffic to disperse from the cemetery. I got warm inside the black coat. I felt as if I needed to wake up from something but I wasn't sure what or how to do it. It was a strange feeling, one I'd never had before, and I shook my head as if that might accomplish the feat. Then I thought about what he'd said and how he'd said it and I was sorry I hadn't argued more strenuously about accepting the end with grace and so on. He was a fighter, my father, and he said these things.

I pictured him in the lane in back of our house yelling at another man, who was halfway up the winding staircase of a two-storey apartment block. That had happened many years before. His face was red. The other man had yelled *fuck*, the first time I'd heard the word, and my father had called back to him to come down and say that again. The other man was bigger but he didn't come down to face Father. I pictured him at the kitchen table in Red Rock going through figures written on a pad of paper, trying to figure out a way to save his dying business. A cowlick stood up on the back of his head, and he scratched at it as he did calculations. He didn't back down on that one either.

After the funeral I hung the black coat in the closet with my anorak and ski jacket, intending to wear it on certain smart occasions. None ever materialized. Season after season passed. Wherever I was invited, the black coat was not quite appropriate—too formal sometimes, too heavy and hot others. I couldn't help thinking of all the money Mother had spent—and which I wasn't putting to any use. The black coat hung among my other overwear like a dark and silent reproach, and after a while I bought a plastic cover for it so it wouldn't collect dust. Finally I moved it to the back of the closet where it was not in the way and ceased to remind me of how little I wore it.

One day a year or so later I was visiting my parents. It was a frosty November. We'd spent the afternoon reminiscing about the days when my parents were young marrieds and I was a child in knee pants with a fondness for Cheezies and breaking basement windows with errant rubber balls. Father had brought out a bottle of his homemade wine. Mother had produced an old photo album and we'd sat on the sofa looking at black-and-white snapshots of my sisters and me in school and so forth. We had a few drinks and became sentimental in our way, and later Father stood up to go for Chinese take-away and pulled on his coat. It had become threadbare since I last saw it. The collar was worn through in several places. He had bought it, I recalled, shortly before the laundry in Red Rock went under. "You need a new coat," I remarked casually.

"I've told him a thousand times," Mother said, her voice betraying long-standing petulance. "But do you think he'll listen?"

Father said, "I keep meaning to buy a new one." Retired and suffering from emphysema, his voice was muffled in the scarf he was arranging around his neck.

Suddenly I remembered the black coat hanging at the back of my closet, and I offered, "Take mine."

Father looked surprised. "Yours?"

"Yes," I said eagerly. "The black coat."

"That," Father said. He paused while pulling on his gloves, then said, "Thanks, for the offer, but that coat, it seems so ..." He trailed off, though he clearly wanted to add something, but as he was making up his mind, Mother cut in.

"It's a wonderful coat. Wonderful."

"And I want you to have it," I said. Over the years he had given me many hand-me-downs, but nothing had ever gone the other way.

"I like it," he said, "the rich colour, the way it hangs, and all, but it makes me think of ..."

Father's hesitation encouraged me, so I protested, "I don't wear the darn thing." That was more than true. It had only seen the light of day once. Besides, I wanted to give him something in return for all he'd given me over the years: Little League baseball, the carpenter's tools his father had given him, homilies I couldn't recall but which had become the benchmarks of my adult life. I added, "That coat hangs in my closet reminding me of how much Mother spent for it. Like a ghost or something."

Father laughed. Then he shook his head and stared into his cap. He stamped out of the door without anything being resolved, but the next time I visited them I brought the coat with me.

"I couldn't," Father said as I removed it from the wardrobe bag. Mother and I badgered him and eventually he tried it on. We were the same size. The coat hung beautifully and after the many years that had passed still looked very stylish. Mother had been right about that, as she was about a lot of things. She brushed the coat with her palms and flicked away lint with her wetted fingertips. She nodded approval. She touched my elbow with one hand and we both looked admiringly at Father as he settled into the coat.

Father looked at himself in the mirror. He tried the deep pockets. I remembered how the satin lining seemed to swallow your hands. At first he was unsure, biting his lower lip miserably and trying to think of a graceful way out. Mother fetched his best hat. He stood in front of the mirror. Seeing him preening there, I recalled the photos of him in his army uniform and the wide-brimmed hats he'd worn when we lived in Red Rock. I remembered, too, Mother saying he'd once been something of a dandy: he'd won a dancing competition at Grand Beach one summer and had given lessons at Arthur Murray's for a few years. He opened the lapels of the black coat and tested the inside pockets. He was still hesitating, but he turned and asked me, "What do you want for it?"

"Want?" I looked from him to Mother. "This is not a matter of money."

Father repeated, "I couldn't," and shook his head. "It was a gift." He said this as if it were the end of the conversation, and I glanced at Mother who mouthed something that indicated it certainly was not the end of the matter in her opinion.

"Look," I said, "it's precisely because it is a gift that I can't take money."

He said, "I won't take it otherwise."

"You gave it to me," I said, my voice rising. "Now I'm returning the favour."

Mother nodded approval but Father stuck his chin out and refused to say more. He slipped out of the coat, replaced it carefully in the wardrobe bag and hung it in the closet. No more was said about money but when I got home I found five crisp twenties stuffed in a pocket of my anorak.

I saw the black coat on Father a couple of times after that. He looked good in it. Not so much elegant as earnest. That coat squared his shoulders and gave him an air of authority, just as it had on me. I recalled how the one time I'd worn it I had stopped before several mirrors, ostensibly to adjust my tie. Actually I was admiring how fine I looked in the black coat: dashing somehow, adventurous in the way of hard-boiled detectives in the movies—and other men who put their lives on the line. A coat reminiscent of an earlier time when life was simpler. Father bought a hat to go with it, a dove-grey Stetson with a feather and a narrow brim, and Mother gave him a pair of black leather gloves for Christmas one year. It made a smart outfit.

Last week he died. It happened suddenly in the night, heart attack. Mother phoned my apartment and I drove over in time to talk with the doctor who signed the death certificate.

"How did he—?" I asked. "What were his last minutes like?"

"Died within seconds. Nothing anyone could have done."

"No pain?"

"No pain."

There was one odd thing. Father died on my birthday, something that occurs fairly often I gather from what the undertaker let slip at the funeral; family members seem to vibrate on the same wavelength when it comes to these momentous occasions. The whole business seemed strange. I was turning forty and felt peculiar enough on that

account alone. At the funeral Aunt May wept, and my remaining uncles and cousins stood about stiffly in their dark suits. Mother hooked
her hand through my arm and looked dazed after the priest's prayers
and the touching eulogy by one of father's old war pals. Someone
played "Taps." My sisters threw flowers onto the burnished casket as
it was lowered into eternal darkness. Everything seemed out of joint:
the fact we were burying Father, the unseasonably cold weather,
which hastened the priest's words at the graveside and made us turn
up our collars against the wind, even my queasy stomach.

My mother squeezed my arm and we sighed in unison.

Once again I was wearing the black coat.

ACKNOWLEDGEMENTS

Thanks to the folks at Turnstone, Sharon Caseburg in particular, to my wife, Kristen, and especially Ralph Smith, for his sharp eye, good sense of humour, and readiness to bash things about.

"Red Rock and After" appeared in *Border Crossings*, and in *The Journey Anthology*; "Meteor Shower" in *The Antigonish Review*, and "Borderline" in *Prairie Fire*. "The Black Coat" was a finalist in CBC's literary competition.

BE WOLF
by Wayne Tefs
winner of the McNally Robinson Book of the Year Award

In *Be Wolf: A True Account of the Survival of Reinhold Kaletsch*, Wayne Tefs delivers a thrilling novel based on a real-life experience.

Whenever possible, Reinhold Kaletsch, a German doctor and inventor with a passion for the Canadian Shield, escapes to his farm in northern Manitoba, relishing its severe beauty. Kaletsch has a taste for adventure, fulfilling his creed: a life without risks is one not worth living.

One spring, Kaletsch sets out on a month-long camping trip accompanied solely by his two dogs, Blondie and Simba. But a moment of carelessness leads to a serious accident that thrusts the trio into a deadly situation. With debilitating injuries, including a fractured spine, Kaletsch must rely on his intelligence, his knowledge of bushcraft, his medical training, and his devoted canine companions, in a desperate struggle for survival.

Be Wolf is "docu-fiction"—a gripping and heart-wrenching tale of courage, endurance, perseverance, loyalty, and love set in the wilderness of northern Manitoba.

"Be Wolf is one heck of an adventure story, a gripping tale of how tragedy is only a mistake away."

—*Owen Sound Sun Times*

Fiction, ISBN: 978-0-88801-321-7
$22.95 CDN/$19.95 U.S.
Quality paperback, 5.5" X 8.5", 452 pages

4 X 4
by Wayne Tefs
winner of the Manuela Dias Book Design Award

The Dokic family, like any other, has its problems. Brothers Clint and Darryl are constantly at odds and just similar enough not to cut each other any slack or let past feuds slide. Darryl sees real-estate salesman Clint as a slick boor, overly fond of himself and his achievements. Clint sees Darryl as an over-educated under-achiever who flaunts his smarts to belittle others. Their mother, Meg, referees their sniping with more knowledge than either of them imagines.

When a snowstorm cancels Clint's flight from Winnipeg to Thompson, where his pregnant wife Kaly waits, Clint forces Darryl and Meg into an ill-advised road trip.

As the three leave for Thompson, they think the worst they'll have to face is low visibility and icy roads. What rests between them in Darryl's 4x4, however, is much harsher than the weather, and it will force them to face what they know and what they think they know about each other and themselves.

"As (they) make their way through Northern Manitoba, Darryl reflects on the fact that even today there are still a few places on Earth that have not been formally surveyed. Cartographers call these places 'sleeping beauties.' They are not unexplored places, just places that are not thoroughly understood; they are places where surprise is still possible if you look hard enough. It's a comforting thought that applies not only to geography, but to the most intimate relationships. It is a beautiful metaphor that perfectly sums up the novel."

—*Quill & Quire*

Fiction, ISBN: 978-0-88801-300-2
$19.95 CDN/$15.95 U.S.
Quality paperback, 5.5" X 8.5", 404 pages

MOON LAKE
by Wayne Tefs
winner of the Margaret Lawrence Award for Fiction

At Moon Lake the moose come to drink and the waves lap on the rocky shores of the Canadian Shield. The serenity of the land and lake are disturbed by the relentless violence that follows the LaFlamme family through several decades.

LaFlamme is an abusive and explosive man who hurts everyone around him. When he meets a violent end, everyone is suspect: his wife and children, whom he tormented, the farm hands he mistreated, and the Native trappers he cheated.

Death sends the family away from Moon Lake and a new death brings them back, re-opening old wounds and mystery surrounding old man LaFlamme's unlamented death.

Rugged yet fragile, like the weatherworn pines of the Canadian Shield, Tefs' crystalline precision in language is matched by his sensitivity to compelling characters and picturesque landscape.

"Moon Lake has appeal for anyone who loves the beauty of the wilderness and for those who wonder about the unsolved mysteries hidden in its depths."

—*Winnipeg Free Press*

Fiction, ISBN: 978-0-88801-251-7
$18.95 CDN/$16.95 U.S.
Quality paperback, 5.5" X 8.5", 362 pages